Debbie,

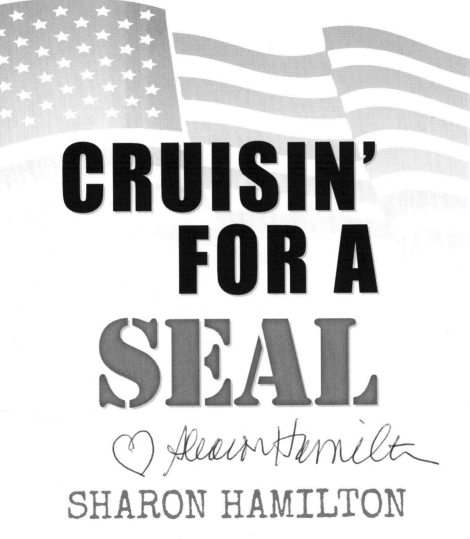

CRUISIN' FOR A SEAL

♡ *Sharon Hamilton*

SHARON HAMILTON

AUTHOR'S NOTE

I always dedicate my SEAL Brotherhood books to the brave men and women who defend our shores and keep us safe. Without their sacrifice, and that of their families—because a warrior's fight always includes his or her family—I wouldn't have the freedom and opportunity to make a living writing these stories. They sometimes pay the ultimate price so we can debate, argue, go have coffee with friends, raise our children and see them have children of their own.

One of my favorite homages to warriors resides on many memorials, including one I saw honoring the fallen of WWII on an island in the Pacific:

"When you go home Tell them of us,
and say,
For your tomorrow,
We gave our today."

These are my stories created out of my own imagination. Anything that is inaccurately portrayed is either my mistake, or done intentionally to disguise something I might have overheard over a beer or in the corner of one of the hangouts along the Coronado Strand.

Wounded Warriors is the one charity I give to on a regular basis. I encourage you to get involved and tell them thank you: https://support.woundedwarriorproject.org.

CHAPTER 1

Navy SEAL Mark Beale searched the buildings and shops along a quaint Italian street barely wide enough for one very small car. Hitching up his jacket against the cold wind only accentuated the chill in his bones. He knew what it was. Grief.

He would not find her face anywhere in the restaurant and shop windows, or hear her voice up above in the shuttered apartments.

The rest of his band of brothers were having drinks by the inlet, admiring sailboats and catching conversation with some of the colorful seafaring population of Savona. The team guys had brought their wives and girlfriends because they would be deploying within a month, and not coming back was always a possibility. It gave the ladies some quality one-on-one time with their mates, memories to last a lifetime if it came to that.

He liked the melodic ebb and flow of the Italian language, grateful he couldn't understand a word. It somehow reassured him that life went on, that his life would go on, even though they'd laid Sophie to rest four months ago.

He hadn't known her well. When his former roommate and fellow SEAL, Nick Dunn, introduced them, Nick's sister Sophie was in the last stages of cancer, but he instantly recognized that she would have been perfect for him. And he could have rocked her world, given half a chance.

After she died, Mark went into a self-imposed exile. Just seemed hard to be in the company of men and their life partners. Life partners who were getting married. Having babies. Not that he wanted the whole world to grieve with him, but the constant interruption of happier things only added to his dark mood.

He'd also tried to hook up with girls he'd previously enjoyed, but even that hot sweaty sex had lost its appeal. He just wasn't into it, and the girl usually felt terrible afterwards, just like he did.

He was a shell of his former self.

His LPO, Kyle Lansdowne, was concerned about him. He kept an eye out for all his men on SEAL Team 3. Kyle had a keen eye for when something wasn't right. If a guy didn't go out drinking, spend time with the ladies, or had an especially sensitive streak with the smacktalk among Team members, it was cause for concern.

In this case, Kyle had reason to be concerned. Mark had seriously considered just checking out completely.

He decided to sit, have a cappuccino, and watch the passersby. A pretty brunette with long, long, well-toned legs and wearing high-heeled camo boots, got his attention. An older woman who could have been her mother joined her. The two took a table next to him and the Italian flowed all over his body like a gentle rain.

The coffee was delivered to him and he nodded his thanks without speaking, not wanting the ladies to identify him as American. Not that it would make any difference, of course, because he had no intention of talking to them.

The heart-shaped design in the foam on top of his cappuccino rammed a fishhook to his chest. He stared down at it for a moment with a pang, but welcomed the creamy taste, and the shot of caffeine gave him the jolt he needed.

His eyes drifted from the cluster of pigeons dodging scooters and pedestrians to the table next door. The younger woman slipped off her black raincoat, revealing an ample chest delicately restrained by a stretchy black dress that came down low in a dangerous V. She held her water glass in long, elegant fingers with short, red nails. A colorful charm bracelet danced on her small wrist.

Mark followed as she lifted a glass until it mated with her full, red lips. Her large brown eyes darted in his direction, and then she looked back at the woman who shared her table. But then she smiled. He knew that smile was intended for him, just as he understood his dick was interested for the first time in three months.

The Italian language was luxurious. No other way to describe it. An Italian love ballad was playing somewhere down the arched tunnel between the piazza and the homes of the locals above. He didn't know the words, but loved the feeling it imparted to him. He understood some of the words, like *amore*. He wouldn't have tolerated this sappy show or sensual drifting before tonight, but he was caught in a fantasy that the lady was rubbing the glass against her bottom lip for him, as she sucked the ice cube she held in her left hand, popping it inside and out of her lips, wrapping it in her pink tongue.

She smiled at her companion, and he wanted to lick the dimple that dared to peek at him from her left cheek. He knew she'd taste good. He knew just a drop of her juices on his tongue would send him places he'd missed. His little head had the pompoms and the little cheering section going. Was already nekked with the young lady with the big tits and the beautiful, full, red lips. His fingers had already found how her silky inner thighs quivered under his touch.

What the hell are you doing?

She was a pleasant fantasy, and if he was completely honest and thought she might understand him, he'd thank her for the brief respite, since it was becoming a burden to remember Sophie in past tense. Sophie dead and buried in the ground.

This beautiful, seemingly full-of-life woman with the flashing eyes and healthy smile had, for the first time in months, distracted him from the heaviness in his chest.

He wanted to meet her, to actually do some of the things playing in living color inside his head. And, yeah, he was a dog. He was a dog about to embark on a cruise from Italy to Brazil with some of his best buds. He'd never come back here to Savona, and would never see her again. Perhaps that's what piqued his interest in her after all. In less than twenty-four hours he'd be gone, leaving her behind.

The older woman left amidst a flurry of kissing the way the Italians do it. He recognized the "Ciao, Mama," as confirmation this was indeed her mother. She took her place back at the little table and finished her cappuccino.

He got up and left some coins on the table, then made the mistake of looking over at her. He gave her a crooked little smile. She'd have to be completely insane not to pick up on the fact that he found her attractive. She arched one eyebrow as he admired her rack. Okay, to be perfectly honest, he was actually imagining what they'd look like released to his hands.

He was normally the gentleman with these types of hot women, when he didn't know anything about them. It wasn't proper to admire another man's lady, and this one was too fine not to be attached. So he closed his eyes by way of an apology and then looked back at her with a small shrug, as if to say *Sorry. I couldn't help myself.*

She did the wrong thing. She rose slowly, tilted her head and blew him a kiss with those red lips. The flirtation was delicious. She slung a yellow Gucci bag over her shoulder, stepped up next to him, slipped her soft arm around his and snuggled against his ribs.

She said something in Italian. Mark was stunned. His legs felt like lead, unable to move as she unexpectedly squeezed her body next to his. He could feel her full breasts pressing his willpower to the breaking point. His arm suddenly became the second most sensitive of his body parts.

She was holding him close, but leading him, as if he was reluctant. "Si, si, si..." and then something he couldn't understand. Well, hell, he was kinda reluctant, because he really didn't know where she was taking him, but for some reason he followed along anyway.

She looked over her shoulder, checking out the deserted piazza, maybe looking to see if her mother noticed her leaving with him. Why would that be a problem? On second thought, if he were her father, he'd definitely not want his daughter going off with some stranger.

But, shit, he didn't care. Whatever she had in mind, unless it involved something dangerous—well, hell even dangerous would be fine, since he did dangerous all the time. If it involved some dark, underground cellar and beefy guys with lots of dark chest hair, okay, then he'd get out. But he kind of liked how her tits bounced as she walked in those amazing boots with the highest heels he'd ever seen. She had a fresh lime-spice scent and something else wafting up from her hair, too.

She kept babbling on as they rounded the corner. She gestured towards the apartments above shops lining the cobblestoned street he'd just walked down to the cafe.

"Honey, this is all real fun, but I'm don't understand a word you're saying," he blurted.

"Ah, Americano! English? No, Americano?" Then she added some other comments he didn't follow.

You promised you'd learn Italian before the cruise, and hibernated instead. Now look at where it's gotten you.

"You speak English?" he stopped and asked.

Her laughter fell like warm water all over him, bathing him in a golden glow. He wanted more. In between her gestures and her giggles, her brown eyes danced. She'd checked out his chest, the size of his shoes and the tent in his pants. Those were things professionals did all the time, or so he'd been told.

He began to worry he'd made a mistake in being too compliant. It suddenly hit him that he was not behaving with his usual conscious self-control. He dropped his arm and hers slipped out of his grip. He pushed his hands into his jeans pockets and shrugged.

"I'm sorry. Perhaps you got the impression I wanted—"

She cut him off before he could finish. His English was obviously not going to be an impediment to her communication, but it sure was to him.

"Scusi, scusi, signore," she said, laughing. Then she said something that sounded like *tey ammo,* and there was all that fluttering around of her hands. Her breasts were bouncing and the little bracelet was damned distracting as it jangled on that wrist of hers. Her brown curls flew in all directions. She could have been Brazilian, Italian, Spanish, or anything, but whoever she was, she was alive and full of fun and, hell, he decided he didn't care if she robbed him. It might even be worth it.

He pulled his pockets inside out, as if to say he didn't have any money. Her reaction was immediate. She slapped him. Hard. She slammed her hands on her hips and scolded him. God, how he loved seeing her angry. She must have called him every name for a dog and no-good boyfriend and dirty American male, because he heard "Americano" several times. He hung his head, nodded as if he agreed, yes, he was a dog. He just shoved his hands back in his front pockets and shrugged a lot.

He started to walk away, worried about attracting even more attention than they already had. A shopkeeper leaned on a broom nearby, watching them. A wizened older woman with no teeth leaned out of a lace-curtained window overhead and shouted something in agreement.

"Scuuuusiiii," the beautiful lady called out, stopping him. She crooked her forefinger and gave him the signal to come back. Well, it was more than a signal, it was delivered with all the punch of a full-throated command.

She continued with the finger action, unwilling to be deterred. He brought his palms out to the sides of his pants and didn't shrug, but knew it was useless to speak. He shuffled back in her direction. She pointed to the ground at her feet emphatically. That brought him almost close enough to touch. She made little growling noises with her throat he took to mean approval. The voice got soft, more melodic. He'd have to say chestier.

She'd dropped her hands but then she raised one again and begged his face to come down to her level. He obeyed. His lips ached to kiss her, did she see it? He saw the soft hairs on her upper lip and the way her nostrils flared as she took in a deep breath, assessing him. He'd stay there as long as she wanted. He never did this, but it became more important than breathing to stay right in the vicinity of her aura.

Mark was rewarded when she pulled his face to hers, locking her lips on him and sucking his tongue deep. He had never been so scared and excited at the same time. He hesitated with his hands.

Oh, fuck it.

He grabbed her waist and pulled her tight against him, holding her butt cheeks, pressing her into his groin and daring to rub against her, squeezing her fine ass. She made little cooing sounds that drove him mad, giving his little head the come-on of a lifetime.

She arched back and stared into his eyes, whispering something he desperately wanted to understand, hoping it was very naughty. Whatever it was she said, he understood clearly that she wanted him, and it wasn't about money. It was about pure lust.

She ran ahead and then ran back to his arms, leading him down and around the nearly deserted alleyway. He was going to say something about the safety of the area, until she stopped at a door and took out a plastic door key.

"Come, come, come," she said in clipped English.

He had no choice but to follow.

CHAPTER 2

She slipped into the dark foyer, closing the door behind them, then scampered up a narrow stairway to the apartment over the shop. The first thing he smelled was fresh lemon. She had a big bowl of them on the kitchen table of her tiny apartment. Posters from the United States adorned the walls, which were plaster and easily nine feet high. She had one sunny window that overlooked the tiled roofs, with a view that stretched to the blue Mediterranean in the distance.

He felt a little shy at having been invited to her one-room studio, her inner sanctum. He never brought women to his, but that was for different reasons. There was nothing adorning the walls that said anything about him or what he did for a living. Up until recently he'd roomed with Nick. But Nick was not cycling with the Team this time, even though he had traveled with them to Italy. After their cruise, Nick would stay in the states on limited duty, till he fully recovered from death of his sister, Sophie.

My Sophie.

He had his back to the pretty Italian lady who smelled so nice and seemed so willing, because he was embarrassed to be thinking about Sophie when he was about to have sex with another woman. Mark feared if she looked hard enough, she might see Sophie's face in his eyes. Nick's sister had been a chance encounter as well.

His courage restored, he turned and—*whoa!*—there she was, in black panties and bra, and nothing else. The universal language of sex and lust hit him right in the groin. He took it as a sign from God that, if he were willing, somehow Sophie would be okay with this dalliance, since they both knew nothing would replace her.

The lady slipped off one strap but stopped there. Just as he'd thought, those breasts of hers plumped out over the top of her bra, and were duly restrained. They looked even bigger than she'd allowed to show.

Her full lips beckoned him as she threw back her head and studied him with half-lidded eyes. She regarded him cautiously, perhaps realizing something about him wasn't right. Maybe trying to figure out if he was safe enough?

He made a point to soften his stare at her chest. She probably saw the need there, so he smiled just a bit, roamed his eyes over her luscious body, and let her know he loved the view. Apparently that worked.

She slid her palms up under his shirt, and then pulled it off over his head. His body was a canvas of Celtic crosses, death skulls, and Latin sayings. He held up his forearm so she could see the frog footprints tattooed from inside his elbow to his wrist, like he was saying, *see my tattoos, and see my soul.*

It didn't get any more basic or simpler than that. He turned so she could see the ancient Roman helmet tattoo that took up almost half of his back it.

That was where she started. No one had ever kissed that helmet on the lips, so to speak, or on the gap where the lips would have been, if the warrior were inside it. He could feel her little pointed, pink tongue looking for penetration and stopping at his flesh. She rubbed her mound up and down the back of his thigh, then pressed and doing figure eights into his butt cheek through his jeans.

She reached around and undid his button fly, finding him inside and kissing up his spine as her fingers fondled him, squeezing, pulling on his hardness. He reached around to find that fine little ass and shuddered when he felt her velvety cheeks. Digging his fingers and squeezing her, he felt her moan, her whole chest vibrating against his insides until his ears buzzed.

She was the softest, sweetest little thing he'd ever touched. Delicate, but perfect as a naughty wet dream. He was used to stumbling a bit with women, because most the time he wanted them more than the other way around, but she was just....

Perfect.

He could feel her nipple drag over his back and upper arm as she slipped around to stand in front of him. He stepped out of his pants after they dropped to the floor and remembered he'd gone commando today, wondering what she'd think about it. Then he remembered the foil packet he carried so bent down and retrieved it and sheathed himself, which made her smile as she watched him stroke himself in front of her.

He kind of liked the way she looked, one strap down, her amazing breasts spilling over the lacy, flowered pattern of the bra. When she inhaled, the cleavage got breathlessly deep. Licking his lips in anticipation, he bent down and tasted that cavern between her tits, inhaling a mixture of perfume and the musky scent of her arousal. One-fingered, he snagged her panties, and they slid down her thighs effortlessly.

He preferred his women's sex nude, so it was a total turn-on to see her naked, pink folds. His fingers massaged her soft, hairless lips, dipping into the cream of her sex and spreading it up over her nub. She was sensitive there, jolting with each little touch, so he continued pressing it until he heard that satisfying moan he'd known was just there under the surface of her good judgment.

He wanted to take his time with her, so he moved slow against her, pushing his index finger into her opening a tiny bit at a time, snaking his way up and inside her and feeling the shudder of her thighs. He changed the angle and plunged in again. But she was impatient and jumped up, encircling his waist with her legs, smashing his palm between her belly and his. With her strong thighs she held him tight around the hips, arching back slightly, giving him just enough room to get himself properly positioned for entry.

She sighed as she slid down on his rigid member and then gently rode him up and down with slow finesse, seeming to savor every inch, each time forcing him deeper into her core. Her perfumed hair fell all about him. She began whispering things to the side of his face, her tongue tracing the arch of his ear. The Italian was mind-blowing. Part of him wanted to know what she was saying, part of him didn't care, as long as she didn't stop.

He stepped back toward the bed littered in colorful pillows, and sat on the edge. She continued to ride him, using her knees against the mattress, lifting herself up enough so he could taste her nipples. He buried himself between her breasts, tasting her sweat.

Her fingers were sifting through his hair, massaging his scalp, and she urgently brought his lips to hers and spoke to him again in long luxurious words he licked and sucked and inhaled between kisses.

She pushed him back on the bed. His hands smoothed over her creamy thighs, reaching around to her butt cheeks, then onto her hips as he pumped her hard on his shaft. She held her hair on top of her head, letting ringlets drop over her shoulders and onto her chest as she undulated on top of him like a dancer, moving her hips from side to side, grinding down and turning to angle his penetration, coaxing him deep. He was mesmerized by the way her tanned stomach muscles contracted, the creases at her sides above her hips where his fingers dug in as he held her. Everything about her was tiny and ample at the same time, and he lost himself in her body that seemed to be made for the sole purpose of pleasuring him.

He could feel her nipples gently touching his chest as she bent over and covered his mouth, again speaking to him, holding his face in her palms, speaking things he was grateful to hear, even if he wasn't sure what they meant.

She pressed her fingers over his mouth and said something like asking his name. He heard "no-may" or something like that. She kept asking it over and over again as her agile body rode his shaft.

"M…Mark," he gasped as she wrapped her feet under his knees, her hips hugging his thighs tight and sending him deep.

"Marko, Marko, Marko," she whispered between kisses. She sucked his lips, "Marko…"

He was lost. He rammed his hips up with his cock fully embedded until it swelled against her insides and he began to explode. He couldn't stop the satisfying, deep, guttural groan that overtook him as he spilled. She continued the whispering of his name in his ear, speaking something of love, surely, as it prolonged his release.

He'd crossed a threshold, shattering the hesitation and regret, the memories of a love not fully satisfied. He felt the tears he'd been shedding melt off him like ice crystals. Color and life flew back inside him, heating him, filling him with expectation, and, more importantly…

Hope.

As he felt the muscles of her insides milk him, his last satisfying thrusts came as sweet dessert when he heard her squeal, and then felt her pulse around him.

"Come for me, baby. I need to feel it, baby."

As if she understood him, she placed her lips to his ears and whispered, "Marko," again in a long, deep, aching plea.

He'd hadn't realized how much he needed this kind of an encounter. This beautiful muse, this stranger on his journey back to wholeness, had given him his life back. Whatever else happened, it would be an afternoon he would remember for the rest of his life.

And he didn't even know her name.

CHAPTER 3

Mark woke in the late afternoon to the distinct high-pitched siren of an Italian police or ambulance, the seesaw of two notes back and forth reminding him he wasn't in the States. For a brief moment, he thought he was back in Afghanistan.

She was draped warmly across his chest. He opened his eyes to see if she still was as beautiful as he'd thought, and found she was watching him already.

"Wish we could talk, honey. I'd tell you how beautiful you are."

She smiled as if she understood him. He fingered a curl, placing it behind her velvety soft ears. "I'd tell you that you make me hot all over again just looking at you, and because you don't understand, I'd tell you that the way you make me feel…well," he watched his thumb caress her lower lip, "I'd be embarrassed to tell you this, but I—I haven't felt this good in months."

She smiled and covered his lips with her palm, softly silencing him. He ached to be able to talk to her, and knew, from the position of her eyes that demurely looked down to his chest, that she did too. He saw more than a little sadness there when she focused on him again and he saw her eyes watered. It was reflex, he decided, but his did, too.

He glanced away quickly and covered his eyes with his forearm. She began to trace the frog prints, then the scar on his left side where he'd taken a glancing round. Her delicate fingers found the line under his left chin where the Afghani rebel had tried to garrote him and ended up paying for it with his life.

She kissed all those places, lifting his forearm to kiss every frog print one by one. When she was finished, he knew he'd never forget her strong face illuminated by afternoon sunlight. The stucco walls of her little place almost seemed to glow. She was his mystery woman, the one who'd turned his life around, and who didn't even know what an important gift she'd bestowed.

He watched her well-toned and tanned body cross the room to open the refrigerator. She pulled out a large bottle of water, put it to her lips and threw her head back, taking a long gulp. Her profile, with her pert nipples on ample breasts rising above a flat tummy, her powerful thighs that had hugged him just as surely as her arms had when he'd made love to her...she was such a stunning picture he nearly gasped.

She held the bottle up. Yes, he nodded, he did want some. He didn't care if she poured the ice water all over his body, he'd stay the course if it meant she'd love him again. She motioned to his mouth and tilted her head back to tell him she wanted to pour the water there. God, yes, he would. He opened his lips and she straddled him, pouring the liquid carefully on his tongue, diverting some of it to her mouth as well. Tiny trickles of water fell down his neck and cheek onto her pillow. The dampness accentuated the perfume that rose from her bedding.

Her mouth was chilled but still sent a hot shudder through him as she tongued her way inside him. Sharing a water bottle had never been sexier. She drank some and then poured it inside from her mouth to his.

He sat up and forced the water bottle from her hand, setting it firmly on the floor. He threw her back against the mattress on her back and pinned her beneath him.

"No-may?" he asked.

She giggled and shook her head.

"No-may," he insisted.

She pointed to her temple and rolled her eyes, as if she'd forgotten.

"Nah, nah you're not going to play that game with me. You have a name and I want to know what it is before I fuck you again."

"Fuck?" she said, her Italian eyes widening. "Ah, Inglese." She pointed to her temple again.

"Yea, you understand the word fuck, but not name? No-may, dammit."

She laughed, arching those impossibly beautiful breasts into him, her fingers playing with the long strands of her hair. He was getting annoyed that she wouldn't tell him what he obviously wanted to know. Her eyes flashed as she danced with his heart. As she wrapped his waist with her legs, daring him.

He knew it was best to keep the woman happy. But it irritated him that she was messing with him so obviously. As he plunged in, perhaps too needily, he banged her bed against the wall loudly with his thrusts. The windows shook and something fell to the floor, like a picture, and shattered.

She laughed and he kept pumping her into oblivion. Until she stopped laughing and slowly inhaled as she ran her palms over his shoulders and upper arms. When she traveled back up to his face, tracing his lips, he drew her fingers into his mouth and sucked them.

He kept up the desperate action of his hips as if he could make them both fly away somewhere, somewhere they could talk and understand each other. Somewhere he could tell her what she was making him feel, so he could hear what she felt from her mouth. It became important, urgent.

He could already tell when she was about to orgasm. She sucked in air and gave that long, wonderful, rolling cry, punctuated by the sounds of their flesh slapping together, and filled his heart with music.

I can take you places, baby. Places you've never seen. Give me half a chance and I will worship the ground you walk on, even if it's only for this glorious afternoon. I want you to smell me on your sheets and call to me and I'll come to you. Again and again. I'm coming to you, baby.

They'd dressed after a long shower and more play. A tiny bit of grief crept back in. Separation was a problem for him. The cappuccino helped. Their affair ended the same way it began, on the piazza, overlooking the boats, emergency vehicle sirens still screaming in the early evening air. He smelled like her lemon shower gel, but his insides wore her aura like a warm, permanent blanket.

As he watched her walk away, noticing she didn't turn around to say goodbye, he thought he saw her hand go up to her face, perhaps pulling the wayward strands of her curly hair away, but wasn't sure.

He knew, since the cruise left in the morning, that her refusal to give him her name meant there was no future for them. He did have her address, though. He'd written it in his little notebook. Maybe he'd send flowers, maybe a letter. Perhaps they could write, have someone translate for them. Perhaps the long distance would help them become friends first, though God knew they were well suited in bed.

As she drifted further away from him, he couldn't help but feel cold, like the coldness that had shrouded him every day since Sophie's death. For this glorious afternoon, this mystery woman had healed him, taken his mind off the fact that he was alive and alone. Now he didn't feel so alone any longer. Even though he would never see her again.

Just as she turned the corner and was out of sight, he got his notebook out to find the page where he'd written her address. What he also found was something she'd written in Italian.

And underneath her words, she'd written her name,

Sophia.

A large hand slapped him on the shoulder. Cooper's giant body blocked the sun from the whole table, plus the one next to Mark.

"Where the hell you been? We've doubled back here like ten times, and you've been a no-show."

Mark smiled, licked his lips and tasted her. "Been a little busy." He quickly tucked the little book inside his vest pocket.

"I'll bet. The local girls are all over Jones."

"Fredo too, I hope."

"Not a fuckin' chance," Coop said grinning. "Poor dumb fuck. Although I do have to say that Mia has softened a bit toward him."

Everyone should be in love.

"Soooo...who is she?" Coop demanded.

"Who?"

"The girl. Has to be a girl. You're, like, MIA. We took a tour of the fort and came back. Christy and the girls went shopping, and we doubled back again."

Mark shrugged and looked down the street where she'd disappeared.

"I wasn't far away."

"Halfway to Heaven, I'd bet."

"Roger that," Mark said as he put on his shades and stood. "Where's everyone now?"

"Right around the corner at the Ferrari place."

"Who's buying a Ferrari?" he asked while they walked.

"Damned if I know. Kyle's thinking if we all pitched in about thirty grand, we could own it together."

"Like that would be a smart thing."

"You can rent them for fifteen minutes for about a hundred Euros."

"No shit?" Mark said as he glanced over his shoulder…just in case she'd changed her mind and had come back. But the street was empty. He had a fun fantasy of a very fast drive through the countryside with afternoon delight. The girl he now knew was named Sophia. Was God playing a trick on him?

No, not a trick. There were no accidents, he'd been told. Everything was part of some big plan. And for some reason Mark's plan was to find her again. Even if it took the rest of his young life. He knew he would. Somehow.

They rounded a cluster of colorful yellow, salmon and light green buildings to another courtyard with several shops downstairs and residences on top. A red and yellow Ferrari sign hung above the glass windows of the shop on the corner across the yard. Kyle's wife, Christy, was leaning over the red "California" convertible while Kyle took pictures.

Nick came out of the shop with Devon, laughing. She was modeling a red Ferrari jacket with matching red cap. He winked over Mark's way and left Devon to join Christy and the girls posing in front of the Ferrari.

Standing next to Mark, the two appraised the crowd of beautiful women throwing themselves at the handsome Italian proprietor.

"He must be in heaven," Nick said, grinning as he everyone else and took a picture, too.

"I'm guessing he hasn't had that much attention all week. Nice looking guy, though. Kinda reminds me of Armani," Mark said. "By the way, where the hell is he?"

"Scouting for dinner," Armani said behind them. "You're gonna love it."

They meandered along the cobblestone streets until they crossed the inlet bridge and were on the other side, in the old town. Row upon row of narrow alleyways barely big enough for a subcompact car revealed their twisted and mysteriously dark innards. The smells emanating from the cozy neighborhood were a mixture of tomatoes, basil and eastern spices. There were kebab houses and pizza parlors. Some of the little dives played American jazz, and others Italian opera or pop Italian.

Mark watched the couples in his group holding hands. Even Mia walked with Fredo. He noticed young couples along the street, not afraid to show their affection. He'd seen more public kissing in Italy than anywhere else, and that surprised him. It also left a little lonely hole in his heart.

Malcolm Jones fell back to walk beside him. "You were like a ghost this afternoon."

"On a private mission," Mark said. "I'd tell you, but then I'd have to kill you."

"Roger that. I found me a little lady I'm going to meet up with later. She's got a best friend...hell, it could be her sister or her mother, and the way I speak Italian, if you're interested. No promises. But the lady I'm meeting is fine. Just fine."

Oh yeah, the language thing. "Tell me about it."

"Kind of fun, though. I think I managed to get my intentions across," Jones smiled confidently. Mark felt more than the usual kinship with the young officer and knew he'd make a good career on the Teams. And he'd be popular, leading his own platoon someday, just like Kyle was.

"It's kind of fun that she speaks Italian to me, and I only speak English. We let our bodies do the talking, know what I'm sayin'?" Mark agreed.

"I know exactly what you're saying. Sometimes American girls talk too much."

"On that we agree, my friend," Mark said as he thumped Jones on the back.

"So, what about tonight?" Jones asked again.

"I'm going to try to find my lady again. If the lady wants to be found, that is."

"Ah, one of those stories. I know it too well." Jones was pensive as they continued down the narrow street.

Mark would have been game on any other night. He knew he'd be knocking on her door, and he doubted she'd answer. Just something about how she rushed off told him that.

At dinner, they drank red new wine that was light as punch in color but big in alcohol. The girls showed off what they bought as the men laughed and soaked up the family bond of their brotherhood they would be depending on strongly very soon. No one discussed the fact that they were going overseas in three short weeks. This little trip was partly to bond the Team, but also to complete something Gunny had sparked in all of them.

The old Marine had gotten to know his son Sanouk before he passed away the week of Thanksgiving. Sanouk's mother even came over from Thailand to tend to Gunny during the last month of his life. Though the former Marine complained, she bathed his shriveled body and changed his bed sheets, and did it as lovingly as if she were tending to a newborn, which in fact Gunny had become.

In the end, they'd all cried when news of his death came to them, just like they did when one of their Team or another branch member fell. In many cases, Gunny was the father some of the guys never really had. He'd driven them home when they were too drunk, and his crusty old gym was a place for former Team guys to rub shoulders with those who carried on in their place. They'd had a party for Sanouk when he arrived, the only one of Gunny's off-spring that littered the world that he actually got to meet. But when Amopep arrived, her quiet beauty and dedication to the wizened old man took their breath away, and they allowed the two of them a reunion beyond anything Gunny had ever expected.

There was no party.

Mark knew it was exactly what Gunny needed, to be reunited with one of the several women he'd married. He'd marry the next one without divorcing any of his previous wives, because he said he believed in marriage, just didn't believe in divorce. And he wouldn't have sex with them until the marriage was official. All of the women had been from Southeast Asia. Gunny called himself a serial husband, but everyone knew he was an honorable one. And underneath his tough exterior he had a romantic heart.

Mark watched the faces of his Teammates and their ladies. Even Mia and Fredo shared a laugh over what Fredo was served, thinking they'd ordered him something else.

"What's this green shit?" Fredo said as he examined his white fish on a bed of sautéed vegetables. Mia leaned over and planted a kiss on his cheek, which made Fredo's eyes bug out.

"I think you're in danger of becoming a healthy man," Coop laughed. "Next thing you know, you'll be ordering tofu and drinking protein shakes."

Mia was served big red tubes of delicious-smelling pasta ladled with a spicy marinara sauce and covered in cheese.

"That's more like it," Fredo announced to the crowd.

"You can have some of mine," Mia said, and the crowd hushed.

A group of young Russian girls caught Mark's eye. Rory and Tyler had already started a flirtation. The girls whipped around, looked at the two of them and then quickly turned back to their friends, giggling.

Mark liked that about girls. They could giggle, and it just seemed to lighten the room. He'd liked the way Sophia's breasts shook when she giggled, especially if she threw her head back. That beautiful, smooth neck, the way her hair went all over the place, all unruly and just-fucked looking. Carefree. Boy, was this an afternoon he'd needed. And here he wanted to make it all complicated by going back for seconds.

He still felt wrapped in the memory of their afternoon together like a warm blanket, and it soothed part of the heartache of knowing he'd never see her again.

But that didn't mean he'd ever stop trying. He was snagged already.

CHAPTER 4

The embarkation procedure was long and tiring. Mark had seen more orderly operations at a meat packing plant. Groups of people pushed their way through lines that were non-existent, ignoring the gentle urging of cruise ship staff who tried desperately to keep the traffic lanes roped off.

Mark listened to at least a dozen languages, and rarely English, which made this trip something special. That, and the fact that it was the only cruise to the Equator this time of year. The ship was being repositioned from the gentle waters of the Mediterranean to sail around South America, since it was always sunny and summer in some part of the world.

The Russian girls were there, too. Still giggling. Examining their leggings and odd clothes, he realized they were probably part of the on board entertainment.

What a life!

But then there were men who would trade places with him in the killing fields overseas in a heartbeat. Nice to know that people were still out cruising, enjoying themselves, flirting with foreign girls, and having a normal life while they were out there getting shot at and bombed to pieces. And he wouldn't trade it for anything. Not anything.

He'd go back there and face Dr. Death, and still wear some of the sparkle of their giggles like beads at Mardi Gras, the remembrances of Sophia's sighs and smooth skin, the pushier tourists trying to board ship first—all of it. He'd take it all in his toolkit, just like he'd take his H&K and his Kimber. He'd use whatever he needed to get through the next four to six months.

The immigration officer who scanned his passport and visa squinted. He was nearly a head shorter than Mark, with island features. Hard, dark eyes bored into him and, without a smile, sized up Mark's shoulders, glancing sideways at a couple of the other SEALs standing in the line next to him. Mark could tell the man knew who he was. Who *they* were.

With a curt bow, he presented his papers and passport back and said in unaccented English, "Have a nice day."

Another security officer grabbed Kyle from behind after he'd made it through the gauntlet of immigration.

"Moshe!" Kyle yelled as he embraced the tall, handsome Israeli. The big guy looked awkward in Kyle's huge arms for a second before he managed to pull himself away with a huge grin.

"Never thought I'd run into you here in Italy. You're going on vacation with your lovely wife?" Moshe asked. "You brought the children?"

"Nah, man. Just a little cozy one-on-one with Christy. And I've only got one rug rat. Brandon is almost two. But that doesn't mean I'm not going to start him a little brother or sister this trip," Kyle said and winked.

"Excellent. Lots of time at sea, rocking and rolling. Should make for some good playtime, my friend."

"Guys, this is Moshe," Kyle said to the group.

Cooper was next to embrace the Israeli. "You clean up real good, Mosh. I like you better in navy than that sand camo."

That made the big security officer blush.

"This is Fredo, you remember?"

"Ah, yes, the wrestler."

"Mark here, he's newer. Along with our young Lieutenant Jones, and Nick. Back there ogling the girls are Tyler and Rory."

Moshe shook their hands. Cooper threw his arm over Sanouk's shoulders. "And this here is our friend Sanouk, our bud Gunny's son. Came all the way from Thailand."

"Nice to meet you, son," the Israeli said.

They all left out the part about spreading Gunny's ashes at sea. That was a strictly need-to-know factoid. They had it mixed with the strongest potpourri they could find so they could get it through security. Kyle had told Mark he'd hoped Gunny would forgive him eventually.

People around them were impatiently trying to get by the bottleneck, so the group retired to the side and finished their introductions.

"So you're doing security on cruise ships now?"

"It's what I do." Moshe nodded.

"How's the family?"

"She took the kids and moved to New York, my friend, so I need to do a little bit of wandering at sea, if you know what I mean. This is a good job when you no longer have a family to come home to."

Mark was saddened by what the Israeli told them. It happened to Team guys all the time. Coming home to a pregnant wife in love with someone else. He could never understand why someone would give up on a guy when he was putting his life on the line somewhere in a shithole of a place, but it happened. If Kyle knew him, then they'd worked together, trained together. Been there for each other, and would always be brothers.

"Well, we'll try to distract you a bit, but not too much, okay?"

Someone from the line of tourists behind them started complaining, so Moshe stepped back, gesturing for them to go forward to embarkation.

Looking over the railing while waiting for their turn with the ridiculous photographers—someone with a whale costume and a clown-like sailor girl in pigtails and freckles—Mark watched the containers loading. Large white storage bins were loaded by forklift. Several pallets of water bottles wrapped together in plastic shrink-wrap were loaded. One of them leaked from underneath and, as it landed on the conveyor belt to the hull of the ship, gushed liquid all over the area.

Standing above the ant-like activity, Mark was glad to see that the actual cruise preparations were more organized than the boarding process.

Christy and the girls posed for pictures, but all the Team guys passed. They kept their shades on the whole time, and knew they would need to do it for most of the cruise.

It didn't matter how mopey the little clown sailor was, the answer was still no.

They had booked cabins adjacent each other, all with large balconies off the aft. They dodged bags left in hallways as porters delivered to rooms and passengers found their bearings. They found their cabins at the end of the hall. Fredo and Jones shared a cabin, Mark and Sanouk were in the one next door, which adjoined, and shared a balcony. Next to them rounded out the rest of the bachelor group, Tyler Gray and Rory Kennedy. Mia was with one of Christy's friends from San Francisco at the other end, with Kyle and Christy, Nick and Devon, Coop and Libby, and Armando and Gina between the two groups of singles.

Mark opened the cabin door and saw the baggage for all four of them had already arrived. Both he and Jones checked over contents. They'd each managed to bring along a sidearm, dismantled and tucked into several compartments. Though highly dangerous and illegal as hell, they'd all automatically travel packing for the rest of their lives.

"How'd your evening turn out last night, Jones?" Mark asked.

The big SEAL shrugged. "I'm glad I didn't convince you to go. She was a no-show. The area she had me meet her was none too pretty, either."

"Maybe I should have come." Mark thought about both of them on different missions. He' rang Sophia's little buzzer so many times his finger got sore. There wasn't a light on upstairs, so he figured she'd gone out for the night.

And that thought was okay. Really, it was the way it should be.

He'd heard Jones was unlucky, which was odd, because the guy was built like a sprinter, with powerful arms and shoulders, and thighs so huge he had to have his dress pants custom made. And he was a gentleman, too.

"You suppose they was setting you up for a robbery, took one look at you and decided wasting ten of their own for probably what little cash you had wasn't worth it?" Mark teased.

Jones chuckled. "Thought about that. Really did. 'Cause she knew I was leaving on the cruise today. But hey, who walks around with a wad of cash all the time these days?"

Then they both looked at each other and said simultaneously, "Christy," meaning the wife of their LPO. With an upper six-figure income, she was a clotheshorse, never saw a designer bag she didn't have to own and loved jewelry.

They'd plan to have drinks up top for castoff, and when Mark heard the sharp intercom system blurt out instructions in Italian that was nothing like what his body had heard yesterday, he knew the ship was about to leave port.

Checking outside their cabin door, they laughed to see the rest of the gang had the same thought. The guys followed each other up to Deck 12 to watch Savona sink out of sight.

Nursing draft beers, they stood side by side along the flat, white railing that ran alongside the deck overlooking the blue and white churning wake, while Kyle led them in some personal thoughts.

"Well, gents, we're all here, most of Gunny's boys. A few more couldn't come, but all the important people are here. Here's to Gunny," Kyle said and raised his glass.

"To Gunny," came the salute followed by thirsty gulps of the frothy amber liquid. Sanouk was included and had toasted his father as well, but he quickly turned away from them, but not before Mark saw his eyes tear up. He knew exactly how the kid felt. Meeting his dad so close to the time of his death, the kid hadn't been able to spend nearly as much time as he wanted getting to know his dad.

Mark stepped next to Sanouk and put his arm around the kid's bony shoulders. "Your dad is with us, son. He always will be."

Mark saw Sanouk's chin wrinkle, and then bravely stiffen as he nodded, but kept staring down at his shoes.

"I wished I'd known Sophie ten years ago. We'd have had some fun."

Sanouk was stoic, so Mark removed his arm, not wanting to intrude on the boy's private thoughts.

The boy spoke abruptly. "My mother, she told me to come. She had a kind of vision. She said my father was calling to me. Said he wanted to meet me."

"That's nice. I'm sure she must have loved him," Mark said softly.

The ship started to pull away from port. He felt the loss and the separation all over again. Sophie gone. Sophia lost forever in his dreams. He couldn't do anything about either one of them.

"She loves him still. She told me that. She's never loved any other. He was her first, and she gave her heart to him, and it never belonged to any other man. Even when she married my step-dad."

Mark wondered what kind of wonderful guy would marry her anyway, knowing he had stepped into the shoes of another man who couldn't carry out the mission. Gunny had the capacity to love, all right. He had just lacked the capacity to maintain.

"She ever tell him?" Mark asked.

"I'm not sure she had to. I think she showed him when she took care of him. She is that way. Right after my Thai father died, she started reading about America. Started taking English lessons, inquiring about positions, even thought about doing a cruise ship. We had little money, but somehow she needed to come back to him. And he never even wrote her one letter."

Sanouk's brown eyes searched Mark's.

"Not one."

Mark looked back at the town that was beginning to look like a scale model.

"That's the way of it, Sanouk."

"What?"

"Love. It's crazy. Makes no sense. It drives you. It comes back like a homing beacon and makes you right. Makes you do the right thing. In the end, Gunny got what he deserved, a woman who had given her heart to him, even though he couldn't reciprocate. She did the right thing by you...marrying and helping get you raised right so you could have a life she couldn't have. She did that because she loved you. But she also loved the part of Gunny that is inside you. That's partly why she did it, I think."

Sanouk nodded. He could see the kid was going to take that gym of Gunny's, and, if they could get the proper strings pulled, he and his mother would make it something totally different than the old, crusty place they'd liked to hang out in. But he knew they wouldn't touch the equipment, or the name. It would always be Gunny's.

And any SEAL or man or woman who served their country in uniform would always be welcome there too. One family. Many colors. Many countries.

But one pretty fuckin' awesome family.

CHAPTER 5

At dinner, Mark brought his little black book, hoping to find an Italian waiter who could translate what Sophia had written for him. He sat in the middle of the long table that had been provided for them. The maître d' came by, followed by a sommelier to announce the wine selections and the various meal packages available. Mark discovered the sommelier was Italian.

"Please, would you help me?" he asked the older gentleman.

"Si, si, si."

"A friend wrote this for me, and I wondered if you would translate it for me."

The heavyset sommelier put on his glasses and held Mark's black book up to his face and then snatched it away. "Pornographic!" He tried to hand it back to Mark.

"No, no. I really want to know what it says."

"This is not for polite company," the gentleman said, eyeing the ladies in the group.

"What the fuck have you done, Marky Mark?" Kyle demanded.

"I got this note and I just hoped him would translate it for me."

And now he really wanted to know what it said. Nearly everyone was looking expectantly at the sommelier, not wanting to be deprived of some juicy fun.

"Please, sir," Kyle began in his velvet tongue. "Don't worry about offending anyone. We are all very good friends."

"And I'm sure nothing you could say would be considered pornographic to this crowd," Nick chimed in. The only two people who weren't paying rapt attention were Armando and Gina. It was a sure bet they wouldn't be sticking around long enough to have dinner.

Kyle followed the sommelier's gaze and noticed some hot and heavy going on at that end of the table. "Armani!" he hissed.

Armando surfaced quickly, looking around, dazed, and noticed the LT's frown.

"Ixnay with the uckinfay in publicpay," Kyle warned.

Armani actually blushed, although Gina just giggled as he stood quickly, grabbed her hand, and hustled her out of the room.

The sommelier cleared his throat, examined the words carefully again and shook his head. "Scusi, but who wrote this, sir?"

Mark grinned, glad that the mystery would soon be solved. "Like it says, Sophia wrote it."

Sophia came the refrain from several voices.

"So this is Miss Mission to Mars yesterday?" Jones asked.

"More like Heaven, I'd say, right, Mark?" Christy flashed him one of those legendary smiles.

He was proud he could nod and get the catcalls as a result. "Moved her enough to write this poem here," he said.

"Is not a poem, sir," the sommelier huffed.

"Go ahead, you might as well tell us. We're all dying to know," said Cooper.

He cleared his voice again and began. The Sommelier read the passage in Italian. "Vorrei poter scoparti cinque volte a notte per il resto della mia vita. Mi mancherai, purtroppo. Amore, Sophia."

"Sounds nice," Mark said. He'd heard the "amore" at the end and was encouraged. "What does it mean then?

"I wish that I could fuck you five times a night for the rest of my life. I'll be missing you sadly. Love, Sophia"

"You sure she didn't say 'make love?' There's a difference, you know," said Devon.

"No madam. We are Italian. We know the difference."

He dropped the book in Mark's lap and departed quickly.

Mark thought he ought to feel happy. Now he *had* to find this mystery woman. She was probably hundreds of miles away by now, stuck onshore, and would be thousands by the end of the cruise, but somehow he'd find her again.

Next day was spent at sea, and it was unusually sunny. The cruise staff had arranged a dance party by the covered pool area. It was warm enough for bathing suits and flip-flops, the SEALs looked like a cadre of Roman gladiators with their tattooed crosses, symbols and bulging muscles. They hung out in the outside corner, very close to the bar. They'd made friends already with several of the Thai help staff, and Sanouk helped with the translation and became a sort of celebrity with the waiters. He was getting attention from the several ladies as well, which Mark could see was making him feel a bit uncomfortable.

"You have any questions, you let me know," Mark whispered.

"Mr. Mark, I've had sex. I know what to do."

"Not what I'm talking about, Sanouk. You want to be careful. These ladies have been around the world more than a few times. Customs and polite behavior are sort of out the window. I'm not sure your mom prepared you for this. I sure as hell know Gunny didn't."

"Oh, yes, he did. He told me not to do what he had done."

"Which part, the serial marriages or the dotting the world with offspring?"

"He told me to find something of value to do in life first. Then find the woman who will fit into that. Not the other way around. He told me I'd be miserable if I chased without knowing what I wanted."

"That's a fact." Mark couldn't agree more. Old Gunny had way more common sense than he'd ever given him credit.

See you upstairs someday, Mister. Not too soon, I hope.

A band had set up on deck and a heavy drumbeat began, making all conversation stop. A tall black dude with orange hair, reminding Mark of Dennis Rodman, walked out wearing a long purple robe, and carrying a staff of glittering streamers that fluttered down from a green satin skull with horns of Satan.

He was kind of a crazy scary guy, and in any other place they'd have been on guard for the women, but Devon and Christy lead the ladies in a line of dancing in their hopelessly tiny bikinis purchased in Savona. Armando's Gina had the dance moves down, along with some belly dance techniques aimed in the guys' direction. Wasn't more than two seconds before Armando swooped in, grabbed Gina's hand, and hustled her out of sight.

Mark was happy for them.

He was still chuckling about his black book incident when a flash of red caught his eye. He turned to see the back half of a beautifully proportioned—he'd have to say perfectly proportioned—woman in a tiny red crocheted bikini. When she stood, he saw the bikini bottom was made of little hearts, and hugged her perfect little ass.

Mark never considered himself an expert in ass recognition, not like his skills in the language and signals field, or some of the medic training he'd had, but he knew, just *knew* he recognized that ass. Her hips undulated as she held her long mahogany hair up on top of her head. She turned her head in profile just like she'd done to him in bed, and her expression was the same. And how dare she show it to a crowd of overweight, middle-aged guys who were drooling over the view.

Mark thumped his beer down and jumped up. While he was on his way over to her she turned, looking down. Two little red hearts covered her areolas, but just barely. Her tanned, toned body was practically naked. Her hips undulated in a figure eight and he could see those unbelievable abdominal muscles flex and curl beneath her satiny skin. If she was getting ready to do a lap dance for someone, that person would wind up in the deep, blue sea, Mark decided.

She rolled her eyes up to his and then stepped back in shock, dropping her hair and nearly falling on her perfect ass. Her look of ecstasy was replaced with a definite frown. Was she not happy to see him? Sure as hell, he was happy to see her.

With the ridiculous Brazilian music as a backdrop they stood motionless in front of the crowd and searched each other's faces.

She was every bit as beautiful as she'd been in her bed, in his arms. The sunlight showed all the golden highlights of her hair, even lighting up the delicate tips of her eyelashes. He was hungry and shocked at the same time. Thrilled to see her, but feeling betrayed. His anger and confusion began to wrap around him like a dark blanket.

"How is it you are here?" he asked, finally finding his voice.

"I work here," she said in perfect English.

"You speak English after all? You let me say all those things?" He had to look away but couldn't stay away for long. "Why did you pretend—why did you—"?

"It's complicated. And obviously I never thought I'd see you again."

One of the dancers, a tall tanned guy nearly Mark's size, came up to her. "Sophia, everything all right?" He put his hands around her waist, stood too close. Mark felt his hands fist.

"No problem, Roberto. He's an old friend." She gave her fellow dancer a sweet smile to send him away. Mark felt lucky he'd never seen that smile aimed at him before.

"I want you to put something on." It was the first thing that popped into Mark's head. He felt stupid and totally ill equipped to communicate with words at this moment. His tongue felt dry as leather.

He stepped close to her, so close he smelled her lovely scent again, felt her heat and, inside, felt the vibration of her need. She didn't retreat. He'd loved the Italian she'd spoken while he enjoyed her body with everything he had. But her English words were even more seductive.

And so dangerous. He was left stunned in the middle of a firefight without protection. Out of ammo, his mates too far away to help.

Why had she created this charade? Was his heart a plaything she'd picked up on a whim, only to discard later? How could he have been so wrong about what they'd shared?

But the evidence of her betrayal stood before him, lovely and just as deadly beautiful as it had been yesterday. How he desperately wanted her to say something.

And then his desperate wish was granted when she said, "And I want *you* to take something off."

CHAPTER 6

Sophia could hardly believe her eyes. She'd not been able to concentrate for the past twenty-four hours, ever since she'd parted ways with Mark, her Marko, the man who was destined to haunt her dreams forever. And now here he was.

The look on his face, the hunger and betrayal in his eyes, the croak in his voice when he spoke to her, made all the color and passion of their lovemaking come alive again. And she felt the strong presence of her fantasy man, suddenly there, real flesh and blood before her.

He stood completely still, and for a few desperate seconds she thought he might turn and walk away, which would have been smart on so many levels. But in matters of the heart people were rarely smart. Seeing his stunned hurt was the last thing she'd ever thought she'd have to do. And he was making it very clear that he wasn't going to go away until he got a complete explanation.

How can I do this when I don't even know myself what has happened to me?

She was on her way to meet the man she was supposed to marry. How could she explain to this wonderful man that she was already taken? That she'd dallied briefly in a life that could never be?

"We need to talk," she finally said.

"Damned straight we do," he said, grabbing her hand while using the other to throw the first towel he could find around her shoulder. As they walked through the automatic glass doors on the deck he gave the finger to catcalls coming from the far corner.

Away from the prying eyes of his teammates, he stopped and asked her again, "Sophia—is that even your real name? What's going on?"

"I'll do my best, Mark. Let's find some place private." She kept his hand in hers, desperate for the strength she felt in his touch, as if it would be the last certain thing in her life, a life of indecision and torment. Even if he was angry, and he had every right to be angry, the feel of his fingers threaded with hers gave her the courage to tell him, even though he'd probably hate her afterwards. But in the few minutes it would take to get him to a place they could talk, she let the wonderful feeling of his touch continue the fantasy of a happily ever after.

She led him to the disco lounge, which was empty this time of day. The brilliant colors almost mocked her heavy heart. Shiny blue tiles like the glistening seas outside wrapped large columns. The ceilings were amber mirrors, and the chairs a bright combination of blue, neon yellow and orange leather. There was a full bar and a small dais with a grand piano on it.

She pulled him to the corner hidden from the opened glass doors, and sat down on the bright fabric at a black marble cocktail table. Mark sat next to her on the upholstered bench seat that wrapped the seaward side of the room.

He had dropped her hand and sat back with his fingers drumming his thighs. She leaned on the obsidian tabletop, clasping her hands together, bracing herself to speak words she'd never expected she'd need to say. Her body still ached for the touch of the handsome giant next to her. He deserved more. So much more. But he also deserved the truth.

"Mark, I'm engaged."

She could feel the hitch in his breathing, and then the smoothing-out process he did to keep himself calm. She could sense the vibration inside him. God, she didn't want to hurt him, but she'd deserve anything that resulted.

"I am traveling on this cruise to Brazil, where I will meet my fiancé, his family, and we will be married. All the plans have been made."

Mark started to stand, but she stopped him with a hand on his forearm. He did sit back down, but he crossed his massive arms over his chest, leaning back into the couch and looking away from her.

"I know none of this makes sense. Not sure I do, either. I thought that—well I just thought a little night of anonymous sex with no strings would be something—and I admit it was totally selfish,—I thought I could just have..."

This was going to be much harder than she'd believed. Everything she wanted to say sounded wrong. "I just wanted one more night being single, being free to choose, being with someone without complications. And I'm sorry. I realize now that that was a huge mistake."

His passive, hulking frame and dispassionate stare into the distance broke her heart.

"Please Mark, look at me." He did, but his eyebrows were raised, his eyes clearly saying he thought she was full of crap. She mustered her courage and added, looking into his sky blue eyes, those eyes she'd gotten lost in, eyes she would remember forever, "I am truly sorry. I am not a good person at all. I did this without any regard for your feelings."

Their eyes did connect, and for a second she could see the hurt there, the little dream in his heart that was dying, too, just as hers was. Instinct told her to reach over and kiss him, hug him, tell him how sorry she was, but she knew that was the wrong way to handle it. As much as she wanted to touch him and let him know how awful she felt, she needed to keep her distance.

Just tell him the truth and get out.

Mark hadn't dropped his eyes. He was searching for something in her face she hoped didn't show. He was looking for evidence that she cared for him. Wouldn't it be wiser to show coldness? Let him fully understand there was no future for them?

But was that the truth? Really the truth? Did all this happen because of her niggling doubts about Matheus and the life she would have with him in Brazil? If she were certain of her decision to marry him, would the night with Mark have happened? She honestly didn't know the answer.

"It was the most beautiful afternoon I've spent in my entire life. I will never forget it. Never, Mark," she said.

His crooked smile…with a dimple just to the right of his full lips…was sexy as hell, and softened the mask of his face.

"It was a pretty incredible afternoon, but, hey, no worries, Sophia. I'm not looking to get hooked up with anyone. I'm getting ready to deploy. This is just a little R and R before we go. It kind of worked, in a sick sense of the word." He looked at his palms.

She hadn't expected that.

"You aren't angry?"

"For an afternoon of the best sex of my life? Fuck, no."

It was a nice thing to say, but she felt the blunt force of a verbal slap. "I think it was more than that, is what I'm trying to say," she said, her voice low and husky.

Mark shot up, shoved his hands into his cargo shorts. "I'm glad. While you're working your way through the cruise ship males, I'll be having beers with my buds and probably swearing off Italian girls for a while." He turned to walk out of the bar.

She had to do something. She ran up and stood in front of him, to stop him.

"Wait a minute. What I meant to say is that it wasn't just a hookup for me. I mean, it started that way, but it became more, I guess is what I'm saying."

"Well, that's fine, honey. And if you get that itch again, I'll scratch it. No worries. I'm not going to get pissed off and ruin another good time." His brilliant white teeth and blue eyes melted her bones.

"So it wasn't—"

"You don't have the right to that privileged information, honey. You're engaged to someone else. I don't gotta tell you anything about me or how I feel about anything, remember? But if you want another anonymous hookup, I'm not going anywhere for the next few weeks. We've got, like, twenty days together. We've already proven we can let our bodies do the talking, since the words seem to get in the way."

He left the bar. She felt her heart drop to her ankles.

It wasn't easy to put it out of her mind, the look on his face as he turned, bowed slightly and walked out of her life. She'd already cried for him once while she away from him in the piazza. She'd left a part of her with him that day, and now, today, he took away another piece as he stalked down the marble foyer, pushed the up button and left in the elevator.

For several seconds she just stood in the elevator lobby, completely stunned. Then reality set in. They'd be asking about her up on Deck 12 with the other entertainers. Besides, they weren't supposed to mingle with the passengers, she reminded herself. Being seen talking to him could cost her the job she'd waited two years to get.

As she took the chrome and glass elevator up to the party deck, she wondered what her mother would have said.

I was young, Sophia. The man I was supposed to marry was from a good family. Our mothers were friends.

Sophia thought it odd this could happen in Italy during the wild 1960's. Men immigrated out of the country for work, and were especially in short supply. Women and children were left alone, fending how they could, and usually trying to work full time as well as tend the family. Her mother was the youngest of five girls and she watched as every one of them made poor choices from the lack of a good gene pool. But just as in ancient times, her family needed the help and assistance of his wealthy family. He was older, but had lost his wife to cancer and had been crazy about her.

Much like Sophia, her upcoming marriage still worried her.

He walked into the little disco with two of his Air Force buddies from the base nearby. They wore their bomber jackets and their hats back on their heads and they owned the room. Not a single woman in the room could resist them.

When he asked me to dance, I declined, trying not to look at his handsome face. My girlfriend, Paulina, jumped in and he held her in his arms, occasionally looking over at me. Paulina did everything she could to distract him, but he was fixated on me, Sophia.

Somehow he found out where I worked. We tried to speak, but honestly I couldn't think of Italian, let alone the little English I'd learned in school. He pretended to need flowers for someone every day. Every day he'd bring me a cappuccino and we'd talk while I made the bouquet for him.

He'd watch my hands. When I'd hand him the bouquet, our fingers would touch. He knew about the engagement, too. Sophia, somehow I just knew he would become the love of my life, just in the quiet way he waited for me to smile, waited for me to feel comfortable enough to go on one little walk with him on one rainy afternoon I dared to close the shop early.

Sophia looked over the flabby bodies burning in the warm sun on deck. Her dad might have looked like one of these, she thought, if he had survived the plane accident that took his life when she was just twelve.

She glanced over at the Americans in the corner with their beautiful wives. She quickly searched the group, but did not find Mark among them.

"You okay?" Roberto came over and asked, planting a kiss on both cheeks. His hand lingered a bit too long and possessively on her bare waist. He was Matheus's best friend, and would be in the wedding party. But she didn't particularly trust him. The Brazilians were known for being womanizers, though Matheus had denied those rumors.

"I'm not a child, Roberto. You don't have to hover."

"Oh, but I enjoy it so, and I know how anxiously Matheus awaits," he said as he leaned in too close and planted a kiss on her lips, despite her attempt to divert him. She was tempted to wipe her mouth with the back of her hand, but resisted.

"Go. Flirt with all your lovers," she said as she pushed him aside.

They completed the dance demonstration, Sophia engaging the sunburned crowd. She danced with men as well as women, even a few children who were hanging out around the shallow pool on deck with their Brazilian and Italian Bahia Club staff who entertained the youngsters.

Her thoughts about the handsome American were distracting…how he had looked that morning in her bed as she poured water down on him, how his muscled arm behind his head and dancing eyes lit up her insides. How he'd wanted to cover her up earlier this afternoon.

She suddenly did feel shy. Naked. Undressed. Admiring eyes were all around her, and she smiled back, even pretending to flirt. But that wasn't who she was, either.

She wasn't American, although she had an American passport. Even though she had an American last name: McAdams, the one lasting thing her father had given her besides her life.

She wasn't Italian, either, even though her mother was, and had grown up near Savona, and had retreated to Italy upon the death of her husband. Sophia had missed her teenage friends in California, but soon became Sophia of Savona and put most of her American upbringing in the past, because it was easier to forget the pain of losing the first man she'd ever loved, her father.

Though she'd tried for years to forget, when her ears picked up an American accent, she felt drawn to it like a moth to the flame. Her attempts to find adventure in the cities and towns of the world by working for the cruise ship lines had nearly worked. She'd said a temporary good-bye to her mother yesterday, although she'd join Sophia in Brazil for the wedding next month.

Had her mother also felt anything like what Sophia impulsively longed to do with this American man?

She should have just pretended it was a mistake, not told Mark about Matheus, kept her distance, because of her job. The rest of the dancers could be sworn to secrecy, but sneaking around didn't suit her at all.

If you get that itch again, I'll be around. Not going anywhere for twenty days.

God help her, but it was way more than an itch. It was almost like a blood bond, like in those vampire books she loved to read.

Dinnertime was always crowded with other dancers, entertainment crew and some of the tour staff. She retired to the quarters she shared with Li, the Chinese contortionist.

Lying on the top bunk, Sophia stared at the romance novel cover poster from her favorite author that she'd pasted on the ceiling with special adhesive. It showed the torso of a hunky Navy SEAL, taken as the SEAL emerged, dripping, from the ocean.

She was struck by how similar Mark's body was to this cover model. Big shoulders, veins cording over his biceps and the muscles of his forearms. Impossibly narrow waist she remembered hugging with her thighs. His massive body pressing into her and igniting everything that could burn.

No, he wouldn't be easy to forget, but in time she would. Just had to wait out the hours at first, then the days. Eventually the lonely nights in her tiny bed, in the belly of the ship would do their work. Rocked to sleep in a windowless space, as her world got smaller in the darkness, the colorful memory of that sparkling interlude would fade, and she'd forget. Eventually she'd surely forget.

CHAPTER 7

Fredo watched Mia and Jasmine at the slot machines as he, Kyle, and Nick shared a beer in the bar next door. Her graceful arm was mesmerizing. He couldn't stop watching her, really watching her, since she'd laid that gentle peck on his cheek back in Savona. It had been almost like she gave him permission to engage. And he'd been completely charmed by that little touch of her lips. He'd been carefully washing around that spot on his face for the three days since.

What that little kiss told him was that she did have some kind of feeling for him. Perhaps a sisterly thing, but, heck, it was a far cry from the scorn and acid turndowns he'd gotten constantly in the four years since he'd first met Armando and his family.

He didn't mind that she was a wild child. He understood that. She was beautiful, and she could get away with things because she was so gorgeous. She made it impossible for men around her to even think, let alone speak. At least that's the effect she had on him.

What he did mind was that she had made terrible choices in men. She chose men who could not protect her. Who would not love her? She picked them almost at random.

He was fascinated how her shapely legs crossed, how her third toe with the ruby toe ring glinted under the twinkle lights of the casino. The red flip-flops casually dangled, tempting her sparkling toenails. No, being wild was not a problem for him at all. Not one little bit.

If she'd just give him a chance to show her how he could make her feel, he knew he could make her happy. If she'd just give him a chance. If it didn't work, no problem. But the fact that she wouldn't give him an opportunity to demonstrate his devotion was killing him. It had been bugging him for years.

Now, with that little kiss, she'd opened the door a crack. He was going to take the chance. If she still turned him down, he'd stop trying. He needed to move on with his life. He couldn't wait any longer, even for the most perfect woman he'd ever met.

Just at that moment she caught him looking her way. Her heavily darkened eyes smoldered in his direction, like there was a yellow flame dancing behind her deep brown eyes. She gave a sly half smile and turned her eyes back to the slot machine, pulling the lever. Then she glanced at him again. He kept his eyes fixed on her lovely face, her heart-shaped red lips, and didn't move a muscle. He let her see the longing on his face, see how he'd felt about her ever since they'd been introduced. Probably wasn't an occasion she even remembered, but Fredo played it in his mind every night before he went to sleep.

A Brazilian dance instructor came over and said something to Jasmine. The two of them walked off together, leaving Mia alone at the machine. Fredo took this to mean a fortuitous sign she needed protection.

"Okay, guys. I'm gonna go change my life."

Kyle and Nick instantly stopped talking, and Kyle followed Fredo's homing look and nodded. "Got your back if you need it, Frodo."

Nick added, "Go be the man. Every woman needs a good man in her life."

Armed with courage he strangely felt for the first time in years, Fredo stood, took one final sip to finish his beer, and adjusted his shirt, standing up straight and as tall as he could.

The room's lights and background slot machine noise faded. All he heard was the sound of Mia's machine, the little bracelet of Murano glass crystals on her delicate wrist tinkling like broken glass. He knew she could see him approach from the corner of her eye, and...was he wrong, or did her breath catch a bit? Just a little. God, he hoped so.

"I don't like to see you left alone," he said as casually as he could, but it somehow didn't come out that way.

"I'm not alone. I saw you watching over me," she said without looking at him, but smiling to the machine. "You always watch over me."

He had been prepared for the usual sharp comment about him being the lapdog he certainly was, which would launch him into the place where he'd be cursing himself for wanting someone who hated him so much.

But this time it was different. She said something else, and the Heavens opened up for him.

"I'm getting to kind of like it, Fredo." At first she didn't look at him, but then, after she respectfully gave him enough time to adjust to her wonderful comment, she swiveled on the red leather stool and faced him. Turned to him full-on, with her dark hair a tangle all over her shoulders, framing the flawless skin of her face, the dark eyes looking warm and inviting, not biting and huffy.

She licked her lips and scanned what he knew were his train wreck of eyebrows, oversized nose and lips twice the size of hers. But this was all he had, and though he felt naked in front of this incredible goddess, he was going to stand his ground and be the man he was, and not someone else. This was what he'd told himself time and time again. Not to get lost in her, but instead be the person he was and let her come to him.

In slow motion, her hand drifted from the black ball of the slot machine lever to his cheek. She didn't pull at his head and he didn't move toward her. She brushed her fingers over his pockmarked face, as if to heal it. Her eyes scanned what must have been a silly expression on his face. God, this had never happened before and he hoped he didn't look like a goofy schoolboy.

He worked to respond to her admiring exploration from the place of the man he was inside. There could be no hiding the need he had for her on more than one level.

"You have always been there for me, Fredo."

"Always," he answered. It was the truth.

"I have been awful to you, and still you have always been there."

He wanted to say something like, *It's where I want to be,* or *I was hoping someday you'd see me for who I really am,* or something corny like that. But he settled for, "Yes, Mia. I am here for you."

Her other hand joined her right hand on his face, cupping his chin as she rubbed one thumb over his sensitive lips. He was used to giving with these lips, not receiving. The sensation she chose to give him, this tiny pleasure, set fire to his belly. He had to focus hard to keep from allowing his gratitude make him break into tears, but that's the way he felt.

"Sweet Fredo," she whispered.

He was about to burst. His chest swelled, and he opened and clenched his hands, which wanted to reach for her, to minister to her, but he remained still, studying this china doll who was so delicate and careful with him.

Could he trust her? Would she turn him down again, even though it seemed like something had shifted?

And did it matter, after all? Because if he didn't try, he'd spend the rest of his life wondering what might have been. And, in a way, that was far worse than getting shot down. Taking the chance was always the right choice. Always.

He safely put his right hand on her forearm, gently squeezing it, rubbing the softness of her perfect skin. "Mia, I've never met anyone as beautiful as you are. I've always wanted the best for you, like Armani."

She gave him a gracious smile as she removed her hand from his cheek and entwined her fingers with his. Her other hand she placed safely in her lap. "But not like my brother, Fredo. Never like my brother, Fredo. Surely you don't mean that."

She'd left the comment out there on the table, like she was testing him.

This was it. He'd either be man enough to say more, or he would show her his fear. Hell, yes, he was afraid he'd blow it, but he was compelled, by some golden tether he allowed to deliciously encircle them both, to move toward her. Her crossed knee brushed against the top of his thigh as he leaned in and whispered to her ear, "No. Like someone who cherishes the ground you walk on."

He leaned back, but their bodies still touched, and she didn't shrink away from him.

"Then kiss me, Fredo. Here. In front of all these people. Kiss me."

He could hardly wait, but he let the moment drag out, savoring it. The slow bending, approach to her moist skin, the scent from between her breasts flooding his nostrils, the ragged hitch in her breath sending signals to his body that she was fully available to him, unlike ever before.

And then their lips met. He was going to leave it a closed-mouth, gentle kiss on her red lips, but she parted him with her tongue, suckling him, changing positions and exploring all of his mouth. He heard her inhale *him*.

God, could this be? Could this really be happening? To him? Fredo?

His right hand wanted to touch her, but didn't think it proper. Struggling with himself, he brought his hand up to settle on her left hip. Without him asking, she moved closer, as if his fingers had pressed into the softness at the top of her butt, and then he realized he *had* pulled her to him, had splayed his fingers out and pressed the small of her back so that she was against his groin.

He knew she was used to men grabbing and claiming what they wanted. He waited, but found it stirred him the more he waited, the more tentative he was with her. His reward was to feel her flower, unfolding to him, asking for his hand to direct her, gentle her. She was asking for exactly what he could deliver.

One of her hands smoothed up his spine, over his polo shirt. He wished he'd worn a crisp dress shirt, something smooth and silky to match the softness of her palm. Her kisses moved up and under his ear, along his neck, the tip of her tongue tasting him. The hair on top of her head tickled the side of his face as she reached his ear and whispered, "I want you, Fredo."

His first instinct was to jump in with both feet. Grab her hand and lead her off to his room, her room, and any quiet, dark place they could find on the ship. But the years of rejection weighed heavily on him, in spite of how alive and virile he was feeling.

"Mia, are you sure?"

She stopped her little kisses to look into his eyes. "You think I am making bad choices? Have I not found someone who will protect me?"

"Absolutely, I will."

"Then show me, Fredo. Show me how you can do this. Show me your way, since mine has landed me in trouble so many times. Teach me, Fredo."

Teach me? Had she actually said that?

She unwrapped herself from his embrace and led him across the floor. He wasn't hesitant, but he allowed her to pull him, because he wanted to be sure. Needed the confidence, maybe. Loved that she was begging him instead of the other way around. He stole a quick look at Kyle and Nick, now joined by Armando and Mark and got four thumbs-ups, and a wink from Armando.

He didn't want to watch the way her hips swayed in front of him, but damn, he couldn't help it. Was she maybe exaggerating it a little for his benefit? She kept looking back at him, probably at the frightened expression he was trying so hard to suppress. Whatever it was he was showing her didn't seem to dampen her spirits any. Her flashing smile and knowing looks told him, *God*, it *screamed* at him, they'd be naked together in just a matter of minutes.

He had just the trace of a little doubt that perhaps she was toying with his heart, but again, he had to convince himself it didn't really matter. She'd asked him. He didn't initiate it. And he'd let her lead the way all she wanted, until she trusted him enough to lead her, when she wanted to be led. God, he'd give her anything she wanted, and it didn't matter if it hurt afterwards.

She slipped her card into her room door and they entered one identical room to what he shared with Jones. He could hear the blue ocean outside foaming in the ship's wake, since the sliding glass door had been left open.

She dropped her card on the Formica desk and crossed the room to stand in the doorway, lifting her face to the breeze of the warm afternoon. Her perfume wafted to him...and she was a vision, standing there. His hands trembled, and all he could do was watch her for a few stolen seconds together in this, her room, this room that was where she slept, where she showered, where she looked in the mirror. Her inner sanctum.

He'd been focusing on her hair and how it blew towards him when he realized she'd dropped her dress to stand naked, her back still to him. His eyes traveled hungrily over her perfect, heart-shaped ass and firm thighs, her impossibly tiny waist that led to broad shoulders. He was speechless that she offered herself to him this way.

Fredo stepped up behind her, his palms daring to touch the soft undersides of her ample breasts, feel her nipples knot under his touch. He found a bare spot on her neck and placed a soft kiss there, felt her moan in his chest. Stepping still closer, he rubbed against her butt.

He paused, checking, making sure she really meant what it looked like she meant, and was rewarded with her hands reaching back to clutch his ass, and pull him into her. Her torso arched up as her breasts filled his hands, as she angled her head so he could fully kiss his way from her delicious shoulder up that long neck he'd dreamed about for years. Gently pressing his groin into her backside, he allowed himself to show her his need. Her slight push back into him told him everything he needed to know.

His hands skimmed down her flat tummy to the arch of her slender hips. His fingers followed the crease of the triangle of the apex of her thighs. Slowly he glided, until he heard another delicious moan. He answered it with a low growl as his fingers discovered the slit already wet with her own desire. Slowly he ran a forefinger up and down her as she bent her knees, arched backward into him, and allowed him full access.

He one-handedly fumbled with the button and zipper of his cargo pants, keeping two fingers embedded in her silky, wet insides. His cock bounced to life, and immediately rooted at her beautiful ass, tracing the slim crease between her cheeks.

He slipped his shoes off and stepped out of the pile his pants made. He had an eight-inch scar on his chest, curved like the knife that got him there, so he left his shirt on. With both hands free, he rubbed down the length of her velvety thighs, loving the way her head rolled onto his shoulder.

Then she righted herself, raising her arms above her head, holding herself up on the sliding glass doorjamb. She pressed her but into him and leaned forward so he could enter her from behind.

He had a fleeting thought that maybe she would be visualizing someone else pleasuring her, perhaps one of her other lovers with a more handsome face, someone she wanted like he wanted and fantasized about her. She might think of someone else just like he did when he had sex with anyone else. He knew that one well. He wouldn't blame her. And he wouldn't know the difference until it was all over. If she wouldn't look at him, then he would know what she'd done.

He figured it would be worth it. Maybe. Just maybe.

He wanted to say something to her, but held it inside. He bent his knees and felt her warm folds with the head of his cock. He had to watch as he slid into her. One hand lay against the small of her back, the other one at her upper thigh, bracing himself as his gentle in and out brought out her gasps and moans of pleasure. He felt the same way, but kept silent.

Pretty lady, you have no idea how much I love you, have always loved you.

The look of his member disappearing into her made it nearly impossible to maintain his composure. He adjusted his stance, picked her up with his thrusting, her feet gently leaving the ground as she accepted him deep.

She was early to come, shuddering, the tanned cheeks of her ass melting over his thighs as her body pitched. He slowed down, wanting to prolong her pleasure. She was gripping the metal doorframe, forcing her forehead against her forearms, moving from side to side.

As her fluttering ended, she reached around and grabbed his ass with both hands, grinding into him. "God, Fredo, Oh, my god."

At first he wasn't sure he'd heard right. The sound of his name on her lips elicited a growl from deep in his chest as he wrapped his arms around her and buried his face in the back of her neck, needing to have the scent of her hair all around him, urgently needing her deep, needing the lifeline her fine young body gave him.

Save me, Mia.

He wanted it to last longer, but he shot inside her. He didn't want time to slip away. He wished he could fill her forever.

"Yes, baby," he heard her breathe as she arched again, reaching her arm back over her, running her fingers through his hair as he thrust one last time, lifting her again off the ground.

He didn't want to set her feet back on the ground. He held her securely, his arm draped over her breasts as she undulated against him until he was completely spent.

She wiggled free, which at first worried him. Sliding off his cock, her tweaked nipples smashed into him as she turned and drew her thighs up over his hips, planting a big kiss on his mouth. She sucked his tongue into hers. He was emboldened that she would look into his face and not find the flaw of his features. She was as needy for him as he had been—was—for her.

At last he chanced a word. "Mia," he whispered, between her tongue and her lips.

"Oh baby, please, can we go some more?"

Like, more sex? Hell, yes!

He cupped her behind, smoothing over her satin skin, digging his fingers into her soft, all-female padding. She had crossed her arms behind his head, pulling his face into hers, running fingertips through the hair at his temples, and easing the scar on his chest with the warm movement of her wonderful breasts.

He sat on the edge of her bed, looking up at her. Her warm brown eyes consumed him. She adjusted him, running her index finger and thumb in a ring up and down his wet shaft.

"I want you inside me again," she whispered.

"Yes." It was all he could think to say, as she continued to stimulate him, making him even harder than before.

"Why was I so stupid, Fredo?" She found that hollow between his shoulder and the base of his neck and kissed him there. Her left hand massaged down his chest until she found the crescent scar. She ran her fingers up his buttons, and then slowly, carefully undid each one, and eased his shirt off, letting her eyes memorize what her fingers had felt. Then she leaned down, kissing him there, running her tongue over the place where he'd been given the life-saving cut that would forever mark him.

He was overcome with her delicate treatment of his wound.

"Love me, Fredo," she whispered as she snuggled onto his lap and guided him to her opening.

She closed her eyes and he watched her savor the feel of him sliding into her. Her mouth in that perfect "O." He'd never thought he could make her feel this way, and he wasn't an anonymous lover catching her from behind, perhaps enabling her to dream of someone else while he came inside her. She was seeing him, all of him. Feeling *him* inside her, because *he* was the one she wanted.

CHAPTER 8

The road to Marrakesh was a long one, through red earth and clusters of light, olive green patches in between the rocky soil and vast expanses of nothing. Mark saw how hard the farmers worked on their little plots of land, sometimes communally, and didn't wonder for a second why some opted for the city, even choosing a life of begging over the impossible odds of farming with oxen and cart in such a desolate land.

He'd taken on Sanouk as his personal responsibility, something Kyle and the others were too busy to do. All of them were on the same bus.

Mark could see remnants of the Berber culture that felt somewhat similar to the lands and peoples of Afghanistan, especially the minarets and the call to prayers. Part of the tension he felt during deployment crept back. But he was sitting on a groaning bus, along with his buds, men who'd seen battle the same as he had, but they also had Christy, Gina, Mia and Jasmine, Libby and Devon, too. And that was maybe what helped the tension mess with his mind this morning.

He wondered what it would take before he could just visit these places and not have to feel afraid for his life, or for the lives of those around him. He wondered if he could ever have a serious interest in the Middle East without feeling resentment for the loss of those he held in his arms while they died. What the world would feel like if people didn't want to kill each other.

He almost never allowed himself such thoughts. It was his job to just do and not question. Unlike the Crusaders, he was on a mission to stop the killing, the overrunning of an innocent population by thugs and gangsters who used their religion to control them. He wasn't going to convert them, just make them stop killing everyone who disagreed, or die trying.

The Berber driver was speaking in that rapid-fire English with a healthy dose of syrupy sweetness that always raised the hackles on the back of his neck.

"You understand him much?" Sanouk asked.

"About every other word," Mark answered as he watched the bus pass a small cart pulled by a skinny donkey, and piled high with something wrapped in black and blue tarps. The man sat sideways on his cargo, smacking the donkey's rear with a reed. The little animal was skipping down the dusty road parallel to the bus, looking malnourished and scared to death.

They drove by a square with a large school and mosque. Mark didn't have the desire to go inside, and he knew his buds probably felt the same, but they weren't about to be difficult or draw attention to themselves. They poured out onto the hot, dusty street and immediately were assaulted with the same familiar sounds of traffic, minaret callers, radios blaring the calls, several dialects he recognized, and several he didn't. Young, crippled boys hobbled on one foot with plastic water bottles cut in half asking for coin. All of the SEALs opened their wallets and layered small one-dollar bills there, creating a small crowd of followers the tour guide sharply shooed away.

"American? You are US?" the guide asked.

Kyle shrugged and nodded.

"We love Americans," he said as he tried to open his arms and give Kyle a hug. Kyle stepped back and the guide laughed at the rebuff, but Mark could see an underlying resentment there. "You will see, we love Americans in this country. Morocco isn't like the rest of Africa."

The rest of the bus unloaded until they were standing amidst heavyset older tourists.

"In my country," the guide continued, "we have a very good King. He love Obama. He and Obama are good friends," he held up two forefingers side by side, the universal sign for togetherness. The Berber guide wasn't giving up, "You will see, my friends."

As they walked into the large market square they were assaulted by bright-colored clothing, and spices that made Mark want to sneeze. A couple of small boys were holding snakes, asking for money for a picture. Necklaces made out of nuts and shells, plastic gems and knots of colored leather started to look alike. Some had baseball caps with "I heart Marrakesh" logos on them, and silk shawls of every color.

Christy wandered into a stall and was surrounded by a bevy of dark-skinned men draping silks over her body as she laughed, her beautiful long, blonde hair and hoop earrings flashing in the sunlight. Kyle went on instant alert and pulled her away from the quicksand of commerce, earning some disapproving looks from the vendors.

"You don't just do that, Christy," Mark heard him tell his wife.

"Oh stop it, Kyle." Christy wiggled away from his grip and turned her back to him, looking for another stall to explore.

"This isn't Kansas anymore, Dorothy," he said to her back.

She lifted her sunglasses and gave him a sultry smile, but a challenge. "I'm on vacation. I want to experience this place, just a little. Besides, with all of you right here, on duty, we're safe." She joined Libby and they walked ahead of the rest of the Team.

Fredo rolled his eyes as Mia pulled him into another stall to do some haggling.

The tour guide abruptly interrupted any viable commerce. Mark realized the guy had his own ideas about who should benefit from the group's dollars.

Mark saw a beautiful turquoise necklace dotted with amber beads and stopped to inquire. The guide stood in front of him, waving his arms, the sleeves of his kaftan flapping like butterfly wings. The shopkeeper slunk to the background.

"Hold it there, Tonto. I'm interested in that necklace," Mark said.

"Not good quality. I have a place you will find much better quality at a better price. Trust me. Your lady will be very, very pleased."

The guide's defiant brown grin ticked Mark off a bit. He picked the man up by the forearms and placed him three feet from where he originally stood. Mark motioned for the owner to come forward. The black-skinned man's eyes darted from side to side as he bowed and came forward.

"How much?"

The Berber guide tried to insert himself again, but Mark gave him a glare.

"Not the quality. Not the quality."

"I don't care a fuck about the quality. What's the price?" It became a matter of principle. He wanted that necklace for some reason, and was willing to overpay for it. It became important that he have it.

"Your lady will not be pleased," the guide tried to say.

"There is no lady. It's for me," Mark said a little too loudly. Instantly Rory and Kyle were at his elbow.

"Easy there, partner," Kyle said.

"Kyle, get this monk off my ass, will you?" he growled to his LPO.

Kyle occupied the robed guide while Mark negotiated sixty euros for the necklace, which was about half of what he'd expected to pay. The shopkeeper put it around his neck and gave him a toothless grin. Mark handed him another five Euro bill.

"For the dog," he pointed to a skinny mutt asleep on a pile of blue plastic bags. He tucked the necklace into his shirt and felt the cool stones begin to warm from his skin. He thought about what they would look like on Sophia's smooth, tanned body, how perfectly they would drape between her breasts with those full, dark areolas that would pucker when he touched them. The vision alone was worth the five euros, even though he was fairly sure he'd never get that chance again.

Not unless she got the itch.

They watched the twirling dancers, the snake charmers and spice vendors, all calling for coin. There wasn't any way he was going to touch one of the black cobras, didn't matter they had been milked of their venom. Snakes gave him the creeps. He outran one teenager who had picked up on this and was enjoying taunting the overbuilt American with the soft heart.

Get your shit together, Mark.

If the kid got too close again he was fully prepared to use the KA-BAR strapped to his shin and decapitate the squirming black creature, and to hell with the fact that it would be a very stupid move.

Their guide led them through tunnels of makeshift shops, weaving around back and forth, probably in an effort to disorient the travelers. The rest of the group was getting restless because they weren't being allowed to shop. At last the group came to a small metal building and everyone was herded inside, then made to sit.

"The oil will make your skin look twenty years younger," the guide said. That might work on the tourists who were in their fifties and sixties, but one glance at the girls with the Team guys and he realized his mistake. "In your case, ladies, it will help you look young forever." An uneasy tension descended upon the room.

Mark connected with each of the men, and they got up, pulling the girls with them. "No thanks. We'll be outside," Kyle said.

Despite the guide's voluble attempts, the rest of the group followed right behind, so that the whole room emptied in a stampede worthy of a good western, leaving the tour guide in the midst of an argument with the shop owner.

Lunch was served in an old building exquisitely decorated with inlay of agate, marble and sandalwood. The squishy-carpeted hallway led them to a wide room, where several other tours from their ship were already seated around brass tables. They took their places amongst silk cushions while tea was served.

A three-piece group began to perform Arabic music with heavy drums. A veiled woman snaked her way into the center of the room, a silver tray lit with candles balanced atop her head. She took turns in front of all the tables, but stayed especially long in front of the SEAL group.

Mark was transfixed with how she could shake her rear while still managing to shimmy her chest, all while bending backward and balancing the tray. She encouraged him to come dance with her, and his buds gave him the rest of the impetus he needed.

Suddenly self-conscious of his cargo shorts and flip-flops, he attempted to match her grace, but fell short. She took his hand, entwining his fingers with hers, and moved her stomach muscles back and forth, undulating to the beat of the music, encouraging him to do the same. Mark worked as hard as he could, but couldn't be as supple as she was. He felt ill at ease—stupid, in fact.

She sashayed around to the front of him and pulled up his shirt, exposing his abs. The audience went wild with whoops and hollers. Holding the shirt with one hand, she stood close to him—actually a little too close to him—and showed the audience his lower torso. Again, to the beat, with red fingertips holding up his shirt delicately, she undulated her muscles, and he did the same next to her. The crowd of tourists went wild.

The two of them made their way around the room. Several of the SEAL wives ran up and put bills in his belt. The more he tried to copy her movements, the more he was catching on to her gentle rhythm. The beats from the little trio behind him began to get louder and ran faster.

At last the song was over. She bowed, still holding his hand. She removed the silver tray from her head and took another bow, keeping Mark alongside her.

All of a sudden, the trio behind them resumed their ancient beat, as the dancer in white floated away, leaving Mark in the center. He began his retreat back to the corner when another dancer, this one in red, covered with silver coins, her skirt hung low on her belly as she shimmied up to him and danced around him, her dark eyes toying with him, pulling him out to the dance floor.

She arched her beautiful back and swan-like neck, leaning to look at him over her shoulder, getting closer and closer until she turned away at the last minute. Her heavily made up eyes twisted a pain in his gut. He couldn't see her lips from under the veil, but his eyes became transfixed on the lovely tanned flesh quivering as she shook her hips from side to side in a figure eight. The small pillows of flesh at the sides of her belly button shook seductively.

Her slow undulations ended in a swishing from side to side as her hips jiggled the little coins attached to the dangerously low waistband. He found it easy to follow her. As she turned, touching the finger cymbals together, hands above her head; he turned in unison until they had moved a full circle. Instead of using her shoulders or hands as his guide, he followed her stomach muscles, and matched her movement. It could have been his imagination, but he felt a hush fall over the crowd.

The dance ended and she bowed, retreating behind the curtains in the corner. He had the desire to follow her, which of course was really stupid.

Back at his seat he got ribbed.

The little Marrakesh band continued making music with their ancient instruments. Mark and Sanouk were like two clueless travelers on the same path, trying to figure out what they were eating. It was hot, which didn't seem to be a problem for Sanouk, it was colorful, and it tasted unlike anything he'd had before.

"You have bars in California where the dancers do this?" Sanouk asked.

Mark laughed. "There are a few, some Greek and other ethnic restaurants. Not bars, at least not tastefully done like she did. We'll see if we can find a couple for you."

"That would be most awesome, Mister Mark." After a few seconds, Sanouk asked another question. "Can you please tell me what you think of as tasteful? The woman has so little clothing—"

Mark could see the beginnings of a blush rising in the young man's face.

"We have dancers, but they don't do this sort of thing, at least not in front of so many people."

Mark wrapped his arm around Gunny's son's shoulders. His attachment was getting more fatherly every day, even though the two of them could have been brothers. "I know Gunny tried to impart some knowledge before he passed over, Sanouk. One thing I'm sure he never told you—would never tell you in a million years—was that he was a damned good judge of human nature, especially women."

Sanouk's eyes widened as he reared back and away just a little.

"He loved women. He just wasn't the stay at home and take care of them kind. He was always off on one adventure or another. In his own way, I think he fell in love every time he married one of his wives. He just lived in the wrong time, in the wrong culture, in the wrong set of circumstances. You understand?"

"Yes. My mother said the same of him, often. Mark, I think she thought the same of herself."

"So you see, she let her heart do the calling. She probably defied all the advice of her elders, and lived her life with her heart. She knew some day she'd see him again. That you'd have a relationship with him, too."

"Yes, I believe that."

Mark saw the woman in the red costume, now changed into jeans and yellow cruise ship T-shirt, quietly enter the room from a door opposite where she had exited. At first he wasn't sure, but the sultry look on her face as she turned in his direction to get a quick peek before she huddled in with the tourist crowd several tables over was unmistakable.

Sophia

It made for an interesting conversation with Sanouk, as the young Thai knew Mark had been distracted by something, someone. He waited patiently for answers to his questions, sometimes having to wait for Mark to even realize he'd asked something. Mark searched the crowd at her table. Most of the time she hid her face from him.

They finished lunch and everyone was herded out according to their bus numbers. Mark was going to try to jump ship to hers, but couldn't find it, or her.

Kyle was beginning to catch on to what was happening.

"Mark, I told you that was never going to work."

"What?"

"The forgetting the night of great casual sex. You know, that one."

Kyle was right. Mark figured he had that hound dog look that probably gave him away.

"I didn't know she'd be here, Kyle."

"I'm guessing that you didn't know she could dance like that, either."

"Has nothing to do with it."

"Um hum." Kyle replied. "Look, Mark. Don't go chasing rainbows. If she doesn't want to be found, let her go, man."

"After that little dance back there?"

"She's making you pay. Big time."

"No, she wants to be followed. She wants to be caught. I intend to give her what she wants."

"Roger that, Mark. I'm glad one of you will get satisfied, then."

Busses headed in separate directions as the various tours splintered off. Mark figured she'd gone with an Italian-speaking group. Their tour guide told them they had a few minutes before their bus would arrive, so their group decided to wait at a coffee house instead of getting lost in the innards of the souk again. Mark was relieved the guys wouldn't have to try to restrain their girls.

He left their group to use the head. In a dark corner on the way, he saw an older couple kissing. He recognized the woman as the dark-haired lady with a cabin on their floor around the corner. The man she was with also looked familiar. When he returned to his group, the couple was gone.

He walked in on a conversation Kyle was having with the other Team guys. Christy and the girls were going over their purchases.

"See that building over there?" He pointed to a two-story coffee house with a balcony restaurant on the upper floor. A series of colorful lanterns and lights hung from the filigreed metal frame holding up shade tarps in green and blue. "That place blew up about two years ago. Terrorist bomb, right in the middle of the day."

"No shit?" Cooper asked. "The whole place?"

"Well, nearly. About thirty people dead. Mostly native Moroccans, but it was and still is a place tourists hang out at. No one tells them this. They just keep coming back."

"How'd you find out?" Tyler asked.

"Moshe. Kind of warned me where to go and what not to do." Kyle leaned back and examined the ceiling of their the old stucco veranda. "This one is owned by the local Police Chief, and is probably the safest place on the square."

It was a subtle reminder to Mark that nowhere was safe. And that a part of him always felt deployed.

CHAPTER 9

Their bus was the last to arrive at the gangway. The Team always rode in back, so they were the last to say farewell to Mohammed, their guide. The rotund man in his beige robe was short with them, but eyed the women with a special sparkle, especially lingering on Mia. Fredo's protective arm over her shoulder didn't allow their eyes to meet. The grin on the guide's face looked devious.

Mark noticed a group of new crewmembers embarking at the second gangway, burdened with multiple bags with instruments, flags and costumes that overflowed like stuffing on a well-done turkey.

One of the members, carrying a large black duty bag similar to what the Team used, had some stringed instrument and several silver swords extending out two feet from the zippered opening. Mark could tell the bag was heavy. On the guy's other shoulder was slung two stubby drums tied together. But what seemed odd was that he wore a set of full lace-up combat boots. Mark had a hard time imagining a dancer or a musician wearing that kind of gear.

The entertainment troupe disappeared into the bowels of the lower decks just as the Team made their way in. They placed their bags on the metal detector and had their cruise card scanned and verified by the security agents. Kyle chatted with a couple of Moshe's detail, but Moshe was absent.

At zero deck passengers stood in line for the elevators up, but the troupe Mark had noticed earlier turned right and filed down the narrow halls of the crew quarters, past the medical station. The black duty bag was sitting in the hallway and the booted man hitched it up to his shoulder and followed his friends down the hall.

At the last minute, Mark saw the man turn around and eye him carefully, then reverse direction to follow his group.

Mark looked for Moshe and didn't find the security officer at the crew gate, either. Two dark-skinned Indian security agents were assisting the rest of the dancers and crew on board, scanning bags.

Mark's group headed down the narrow rows of cabin doors to the back of the ship on their deck. A cleaning cart was midway down the corridor. Several of the cabin doors were propped open and empty of passengers. The Filipino cabin steward had knocked on a door and then opened it. Inside was the dark lady Mark had seen in the coffee house in Marrakesh, half dressed and being kissed by a man in a single-striped ship's officer's jacket. That's when Mark realized the plain-clothed man in the marketplace had been the same man, and was apparently one of the ship's junior officers.

He looked away before the couple could notice that he saw them. The cabin steward was flustered and making apologies, and they heard the door slam after he retreated back to his cart.

Mark approached Kyle, who hadn't noticed the cabin drama. "You see that?" he asked his LPO.

"What, man?"

"I just saw a couple in one of the cabins. Officer cavorting with one of the passengers? That sound right to you?"

"I think it happens, my friend. You're about to go find that lovely Italian lass, and I'm guessing she'll let you do pretty much anything you want with her," Kyle answered.

Mark blushed. "An officer, Kyle. I know for a fact that's not kosher."

"I'll have to ask Moshe about it, then. He's joining us for dinner."

In the hallway outside their cabin doors, Kyle gave directions. "At eighteen-thirty we meet up at the ninth floor Club Romanza. Moshe has a special table for dinner. Dress up. You've got a little more than an hour, okay, ladies and gents?" Kyle surveyed his Team and their wives. He inspected Fredo standing beside Mia outside her door. Jasmine was next to Christy. "Everyone shows up. Everyone," he said as he nodded meaningfully at Fredo.

Had he not met Sophia, Mark would have been only too pleased to let Jasmine shower and dress in their cabin, since it was obvious Fredo and Mia had made some plans for the next few minutes. He didn't think Sanouk would mind, either. The girl was lean and attractive, with light brown hair and bright blue eyes. She'd have been just Mark's type. Perhaps that's what Christy had in mind when she invited her. He decided to extend the offer.

"You need a place to wash up, Jasmine? Sanouk and I would be happy to oblige."

Rory and Tyler got within earshot. "You can use our shower, too," Rory said with a blush.

Jasmine's cheeks got pink as she smiled and looked down at pink toes that matched her rose-colored flip-flops. Mark liked shy girls, normally. Jasmine had not made a secret that she found him attractive, either.

Christy inserted herself. "Down, boys. She's good, Mark, Rory. Thanks for asking. We got it worked out. But that was very sweet of you." She followed up her words with a gentle kiss to Mark's cheek and a wink in Rory's direction.

Kyle rolled his eyes and followed Christy and Jasmine into his cabin just as the engines sprang to life and the announcement came over the loudspeaker that the ship was leaving port.

Mark wore his shades instinctively, but upon exiting the cabin, found none of his Teammates had done so, so he went back and left them on the dresser. Everyone but Kyle and Christy made their way single file down the long corridor, passing closed cabin doors, including the one with the mysterious dark lady and the officer. The cleaning cart was gone.

Waiting in the foyer by the elevators, they could hear a small combo playing one deck below. They could also feel the rumble of the engines as they headed out to sea. If they got to Deck 9 quickly enough, they might be able to see the receding lights of Casablanca harbor.

The private dining room only had a few tables. Like the rest of the ship, it was swirling with bright colors from Murano glass fixtures in amber and deep red. They were accentuated with strips of green and blue bubble lights that outlined the copper and chrome detail around the windows, ceilings and mirrored columns throughout the room. A large wait staff scurried around the tables, attending to the seated diners as well as working behind the long bar.

While they waited for Kyle and Christy, they were seated at a long oval table in the middle of the room and offered their choice of drinks. Mark scanned the sunset and could see the pilot boat pull away, back towards the shore. He surveyed his group. The good-looking men and radiant ladies could have been preparing for an advertising photo shoot. Tyler sat next to Jasmine, who demurely wore a black sequined sheath dress that showed off her substantial curves. Rory sat on her other side, his red hair flaming toward the ceiling with too much hair gel. Mia was glowing in red, of course, sitting next to Fredo, who almost looked uncomfortable in a dark suit jacket and button-down shirt.

Armando and Gina were locked in a private conversation, as was common these days, interspersed with nibbling kisses and private whispers. Jones was quite the fancy dresser with a white sport coat that matched his bright, white smile, putting them all to shame. Sanouk wore a starched dress shirt, but had not brought a jacket. The boy's shiny dark hair was held back in a ponytail like Armando wore sometimes.

Kyle and Christy entered the room like royalty. She wore large amber and coral necklace they'd bought in town. The large chunks of golden brown stones accented in deep red beads hung precariously low on her chest, drawing attention to her nice cleavage. Mark was sure most the Team guys were trying not to stare, out of respect for Kyle, but it was damned hard. She wore a batik dress in the same hues of orange and yellow, with a colorful wrap that covered her shoulders but left her chest exposed. She was regal, and striking as a Team Leader's wife should be.

Moshe arrived just as they were seated. A junior officer of the ship, Teseo Dominichello, followed him. Mark was impressed that they rated such an important visitors, especially since they were pulling away from shore.

After the Americans were introduced, Moshe introduced Teseo to the group.

"My friend, here, also served in the Italian Special Forces, COMSUBIN, and was named after the great Teseo Tesei."

Mark had read about the elite frogman teams from Italy who actually predated the SEALs. His Team had trained with them on several occasions during joint operations focusing on the North African arena. They were just as tough as the SEALs, although not as well funded. Their centuries-long history of navigating the waters of the Mediterranean was a source of pride and was unequaled by any other fighting force in the area.

If Mark's memory served him, the original Teseo had been a high-value target the Allies had tried to capture during World War II and he died evading them.

"He was a hell of a frogman. We use some of his inventions today," Kyle added.

"The human torpedo," Mark added.

"You related?" Rory asked. Mark had wanted to ask the same question.

"No, sorry to say. But I think my maternal grandmother was secretly in love with the man."

That brought some chuckles from the table.

"He was from our village. I think all the women in town loved him."

Mark asked the next question. "So, how do you go from being in the COMs to working on a cruise ship?"

Teseo and Moshe shared a glance.

"Divorce makes strange bedfellows of us all," Moshe said sadly.

"My wife was unhappy with the lifestyle afforded by my disability pension," Teseo began. "Moshe here helped get me a job with the line, and I thought my Carmella would enjoy cruising with me." He looked down at his mineral water, then took a sip and crunched down on some ice. "I was wrong."

Nobody had to explain the obvious. Being married to a dedicated warrior didn't do much to pay the bills, and there were long gaps in their family life that sometimes were filled with extracurricular activities, on both sides, husbands and wives. It was a hard life, and only the dedicated couples, and they were in the minority, were lucky enough to keep a marriage alive.

"I miss them all," Teseo said before anyone would have the audacity to ask if he had children.

"I'm beginning to think I'll stay perpetually single," Grady added.

"You still dive, Teseo?" Kyle asked.

"Absolutely. I bring my rebreather everywhere."

"Seriously?" Cooper asked. "You don't happen to have another set?"

"I have three. I sometimes accompany dive teams that need to do inspections. Never miss a chance to use my gear."

"So are all your officers Italian, then?" Kyle asked.

"All but one. Maksym Tereschenko, from Ukraine," said Teseo.

"He the tall guy with the pencil moustache?" Mark asked.

"That would be him. A full two meters tall and then some."

"Russian," Jones muttered.

"Not quite," Teseo said. "One of our Ukrainian brothers, a ship's captain without a Navy," he added, "We have a few of them also in the engine room. Very skilled workmen, second to Italians, of course." He shrugged and several of the SEALs laughed.

The kissing scene Mark had seen on shore, and then the quick view of Maksym in the cabin with the mysterious lady, troubled Mark.

"So you are allowed to brings wives along on cruises?" Mark asked.

"Occasionally." Teseo moved around in his chair uncomfortably as the waitress took their wine orders. He continued when they had privacy. "We are not allowed to spend time with our families if they come, except occasionally at dinner, or on shore when we have a few hours here or there. It is forbidden to spend time in the passenger's cabin, so you see, it is no, as you say, 'picnic.'"

Mark had to ask. His radar was springing to life. "Is this Ukrainian guy married?"

Moshe leaned forward, accepted a glass of red wine from the steward and cleared his throat until the waitress left. "My understanding is that his wife and family left with a Russian diplomat last year. So I guess that would make him a single man, but not by choice, I don't think."

Mark was starting to feel like this was the wrong time to pursue the topic any further.

The dinner was delicious, a preplanned meal of prime rib and lobster. The meal lasted nearly two hours, but before they could finish, Moshe and Teseo were summoned to the bridge.

Mark thought he'd discuss his active imagination with Kyle in the morning. His LPO had been studying him carefully all throughout dinner and knew there was something brewing. It was his job to know these things. If Mark didn't come to him first, Kyle would dig it out of him with a spoon.

CHAPTER 10

Sophia rushed through her dinner with a hand towel pinned behind her neck, protecting the skimpy red dress she wore for her upcoming dance instruction session with her Brazilian dance partner, Roberto. She stood during the four minutes it took to wolf down several forkfuls of salad and some pasta.

Roberto came up behind her, giving her a smooth caress over her bare shoulders, ending with a wet kiss at the base of her neck.

"You smell divine," he whispered. His hands slid down her hips—hips that would experience a lot more of his hands during their dance routine. But privately, in the staff dining room, while she was eating, and in front of the Filipino wait staff and the Indian security staff, where they were crowded in like crabs in a bucket, his fingers on her flesh were a little creepy. That and the fact that his palms lingered just a little too long at her sides and his thumbs extended a little too far toward the juncture of her legs.

She wondered how Matheus would take to Roberto's constant need to touch her. The man never wasted an opportunity to show affection, going beyond his natural Brazilian personality, which had confused her at first. In time, she recognized the signs of a wolf waiting for her to have a weak moment.

And that just wasn't going to happen, tonight or any night. At least this was something that hadn't changed since her fling with Mark. In fact, it had everything to do with her own self-respect and not the way her insides ached for the handsome American.

Sophia hitched her shoulders, made her back go limp and inched out of Roberto's reach without acknowledging him. She made a mental note not to wear that perfume again, in case it was something the Brazilian particularly liked. "Meet you on Deck 5," she called over her shoulder as she escaped.

Back in her quarters, her roommate had just finished gluing green rhinestones on her cheekbones. The contortionist from China slipped on a bright, lime-green satin cape with blue and green imitation peacock feathers at the neckline. Her green slippers fit her delicate feet snugly.

"Break a leg, Li."

"You too," she said as she swished past Sophia.

Sophia took out her red flower clip and placed it above her left ear. She removed the towel and closely examined her dress for any evidence of dinner and found none. She walked through another spritz of perfume, this time a lemon scent, recalling gleefully that it had made Roberto sneeze once.

Showtime.

A sullen, dark-eyed male dancer who had just joined the ship stared at her skimpy hemline and scowled. Three of them clung to the shadows as if shy about entering the dining hall. She recognized the guttural Arabic tones she'd become familiar with in Morocco, breaking through whispers at her back as she made her way down the wider hall to the staff elevators.

A crowd surrounded Sophia and Roberto as she stretched back and away from the Brazilian dancer, her head flung back far enough to look in the opposite direction from his. When the music started, the frame of his arms and chest guided her, guiding her to bend and lean at his whim. She normally didn't mind that she had to be so responsive to his touch, to his every direction, even the minute, subtle ones that warned her of a change in direction, a twirl or a tight, inside turn against his muscled torso. But she was more aware of the tightness in his pants than before, and he held her closer, his fingers again approaching areas that were off limits.

She wasn't allowed to show expression as they glided across the dance floor, entertaining an enraptured crowd anxious to imitate them. Flashes blinded her as they danced precariously close to the crowd of onlookers, as they sashayed between them, and Roberto turned her with the command from his first two fingers. Colors of the walls and overhead lights streaked and blended like melted glass. Voices echoed as if coming from a dream.

At last the dance ended. As was their custom, he would bow to her and she would bend over her right leg in a graceful curtsey, but today Roberto held her longer, breathing in her scent, his nostrils flaring. She heard a low rumble deep in his throat, and then all of a sudden he released her and turned to acknowledge the crowd, which overflowed with applause and cheers. She held on to his two fingers as if tethered like a bird of prey, breathing hard and examining the edges of the room, looking for an escape.

But she saw no escape as she examined the distorted faces of the rotund tourists in various stages of intoxication. Their wild eyes and knowing stares pulled at her skin, making her feel like a caged animal.

The dance lesson itself was always led by Roberto. He'd demonstrate the correct posture and angle of the body, where the hands were placed, how she was to lean, where she was to look, how he was to give her the signal to do his bidding. She stoically demonstrated everything he explained, avoiding eye contact. A couple of times he dropped their stance and he shook her arms to loosen them up, asking her in a low, purring tone not be so tense. The more he begged her to relax the more the hair at the back of her neck stood on end. She even managed to take a 'horrible misstep,' which she never did, and land hard on top of his right foot.

Roberto examined her, peering down from his six-foot frame in what could only be called a sneer. She remained committed to showing no emotion. No smile, no flashing eyes, and no sad lift of the eyebrows. She thought of herself as a porcelain doll on display.

And then she saw Mark. He was leaning against one of the shiny columns in a pair of faded blue jeans, canvas slip-ons and a light blue long-sleeved V-necked T-shirt. It wasn't fair that he could to stand there and stare at her, those blue eyes traveling all over her, challenging her to concentrate on the dance while knowing she was affected by his gaze. She made a point to avoid looking directly at him, but watched him from the corner of her eye so Roberto wouldn't catch on.

But it was no use. Minutes after noticing the American who watched them dance, Roberto swung them very close, almost brushing against Mark's chest and nearly causing them to collide with several older dancers as he whirled her around in his powerful arms. Roberto's cheeks tightened as tiny lights in his dark eyes looked excited, but menacing. Fear crested up from her waist and scattered over her shoulders and arms, dissipating into the air above the dance floor.

The end of the music couldn't come too soon. She floated to the side of her Brazilian partner, free from the grip of his fingers on hers, and felt like a piece of wrapping paper flung to the side by an impatient gift recipient. Until he grabbed her fingers, yanking them down, cracking one of her knuckles. Of course he wouldn't look at her, but he let her know most emphatically that he was royally pissed, and, she would have to say, possibly violent.

But she wouldn't let him see he had hurt her. It would only add to his pleasure in the debasement she'd experienced at his hand. Her eyes fluttered with demure elegance she'd seen Li manage after a bad fall from the ropes during her routine. Like the brave smile her mother always gave her when they talked about her American father, the husband she missed now more than ever.

The pain radiated down her wrist as Roberto curled back her entire hand, spun around quickly to the rapt applause from the audience who oblivious to what he'd just done. The smile plastered on his face was downright evil.

Tears streamed down her face as the pain began to get unbearable, and her arm got limp. Perhaps if she fainted, she thought, then he'd stop. But it would be just her luck, the Brazilian monster would carry her off to his room and do unmentionable things to her.

Does Matheus know about this, his best friend, and how he treats his fiancé?

The answer both puzzled and worried her. Surely he must know what Roberto was capable of? And if that were so, why would Matheus trust him to be on the cruise with her?

Roberto gave her a brief gloat just before he released her hand with a devilish grin and a flourish, extending his arm straight up into the air. She was going to say something when a hulking body pushed between her and her dance partner.

"Find someone else to torture, you son of a bitch," Mark said, pushing her behind him.

For a brief second everything was hushed, quiet. Even the music stopped. Sophia knew Mark was leaving it up to Matheus decided how far he wanted to escalate things, and she could read in the American's clenched jawline that he'd take it all the way if he needed to. The man was fully engaged.

Roberto was a smart man, she thought. He took a couple of steps back and bowed ever so slightly to Mark who now had completely blocked her from Roberto's reach.

"She's my partner," Roberto hissed, but kept it low, just between the two of them.

"Not any longer. She quit," Mark said without checking with her. Sophia wasn't sure that was wise. "For now. Perhaps you can get yourself a French hen or a German polka dancer to abuse. But she's done for the evening." Mark stepped toward the Brazilian to emphasize the point.

Sophia looked down at her wrist, which was now getting black and blue. He had hurt her far more than she realized at the time. She hid it behind her back and was glad she had, since Mark grabbed her other wrist and led her off the dance floor. Behind her she heard Roberto instruct the crowd about what they'd just witnessed, trying to put them at ease.

"You see, ladies and gentlemen," he almost shouted. "Dancing the Tango requires passion. The dance floor is a stage where love is explored in all its extremes."

That seemed to satisfy the masses.

As Mark whisked her away from the crowds, she dared to ask the question, "Where are you taking me, Mark?"

"As far away from that bastard as possible."

"Mark, it is my job."

"No, it *isn't* your job," he said without looking at her. His cheekbones had tightened. He looked almost sick. "You don't have to put up with that."

He stopped abruptly, faced her, and for the first time looked in her eyes. "Are you hurt?"

Her tears still trickled down her cheeks. She couldn't answer him, keeping her wrist safely behind her back.

"Show me, Sophia. Show me what he did to you."

"I'm okay."

"Show me," he demanded. He wasn't smiling. Then, as if checking himself, suddenly softened. "I want to see your hand, please, Sophia." His palms gripped her cheeks as he drew her head to his face and touched her lips with his.

She tried to wrestle free, since it was forbidden. She didn't want to get fired.

"I can't. I can't be seen with you, Mark. I'll lose my job."

"Then take me some place where no one else is, or, so help me God, I'll drag you to my cabin."

CHAPTER 11

Mark was breathing hard. She'd insisted he follow her, but at a distance, so it wouldn't appear he was pursuing her. Hell, yes, he was running after her. He never wanted to let her go. His protective nature had swelled to unrealistic proportions, and they could both get in trouble, but he would make sure she was safe, and then sort out the consequences later. So, if she said follow behind, some twenty feet behind, he'd do just that. He knew how to follow orders.

She almost disappeared down the stairwell by the elevators. He raced to catch up with her and spotted her rounding the corner to the left and down another corridor, past the internet station, past the chapel, to a meeting room of some kind set up with tables in rows facing a small lectern.

No one else was in the room, so he slowed down, expecting her to take up a chair, but she passed the lectern and exited a doorway onto a deck at lifeboat level. He checked the handle before he let the metal door close behind him to make sure they didn't get locked out. The gray-painted surface of the deck felt spongy beneath his feet. It was eerie to see the ocean pouring past them sideways, while they were lulled by the rumble and noise of the huge ship's engines. Looking right and then left, he reassured himself that they were completely alone.

She was still looking to the sides, making sure no one could see them, when he grabbed her arm at the elbow and urgently pulled her to his chest. It became the most important thing of his life, holding her in his arms again. And she struggled at first.

"Don't fight it, Sophia. Let me hold you. Please. Let me hold you," he'd whispered. He hoped his voice was soft enough to calm her down.

She hesitated at the request, and he knew she had caved but didn't want to show it. Her little body was shaking like a leaf. Her backbone was rigid, until he put his hand at the top of her spine and massaged her neck. Then he felt her melt into him and even bring her arms up around him, her hands smoothing over his back. There was no mistaking her need.

He let her rest her cheek against his chest. Wanted her to feel the beat of his heart, how she excited him, how he needed her close to him, how he needed to protect her from the whole world if need be. He prayed that was the message he was giving her. He was careful not to make it sexual, in case she couldn't go as far as he wished they could go.

Until he heard her little moan as she squeezed her chest against his, her hands coming around to the front of him and reaching up to his neck, and then his face.

What he saw when he leaned back and scanned her pretty face surprised him. She had tears running down her cheeks, her makeup was smeared, the dark eyeliner and shimmering eye makeup migrating down from her eyes and over her cheeks. His thumbs removed her tears.

"Shhh. You're safe, Sophia. You're safe, sweetheart."

He expected her to feel reassured, but instead another flood of tears filled her eyes, and that's when he realized she was confused and in a lot of emotional pain, if not physical pain.

"Show me where he hurt you," he said as he kissed her wrists one at a time. He felt the angry warmth of her bruise as he kissed the injured wrist and hand. He held it gently between his palms. Without him needing to pull her, she leaned against him and watched as he ministered to her injury, her eyes spilling over, as if his kisses would heal her. He even started to believe it too.

"So sorry, baby," he said, looking at her mouth, hungering for the touch of those lips.

Her eyes also studied his mouth as he slowly crossed the threshold and closed the distance between them. His tongue ran along the seam between her lips, and she opened to him with a little moan. The fire in his belly ignited something more than lust. No question he wanted her, but it was more than that.

He nibbled at her mouth, careful not to go too deep or too far, but she pulled his head closer and sank her tongue deep into his mouth. Her legs parted and he could feel her pubic bone rub against the hardness of his erection.

The conversation they'd had in the little abandoned bar came flooding back. Was this the itch that she wanted scratched? Or was this something else?

For him, he wanted to soothe her, protect her, show her how he felt about her, and give her some sense of how she'd made him feel for that stolen afternoon in Savona. It was important he show her with his body that it wasn't just sex. He wanted to give her more than just his sperm, he wanted to give her the tenderest part of him, whatever that was.

It didn't seem right to just go full tilt into each other's arms without something being said, without something being understood fully. Mark knew his intensity scared away most women. He had the control to hold back if she wasn't ready for what he could give. But just what did she want? His body? His protection? The safe haven of his arms? Or was it something else?

And then he started to have those doubts again. Was he good enough? Was she just interested in his body, or something else?

What the fuck are you doing, Mark?

Something made him stop. He carefully peeled her arms from his neck, placing his forehead against hers. He kissed her injured wrist again, her palms, and her fingers, and noticed she was not wearing an engagement ring.

That set off all the bells and whistles, all the questions he knew he had to ask before he'd get nekked with this beautiful woman. She smelled fresh and lemony. Her breathing was intoxicating. Each time her chest heaved, he felt the delicious soft pressure of her breasts against his pecs.

He was going to let her set the pace. No way was he going to take advantage of her, even if he thought that's what she wanted.

"You want to talk?" she whispered.

He nodded, still pressing his forehead against hers.

"I'm not even sure what's going on, Mark."

Well then, all the more reason to talk, sweetheart. "So we talk, Sophia, until you can tell me what's going on," he said. He tucked errant strands of her curly hair around her ear. He kissed her there, let her hear the hitch in his breathing. "I think I can handle anything you tell me, Sophia."

She relaxed a bit at that.

They heard some scuffling at the end of the deck and saw two white-clad cooks step outside a doorway to have a smoke. They didn't expect to see anyone else on deck and so hadn't looked, engrossed in their Italian conversation.

She urgently found his hands and pulled him toward one of the large, orange lifeboats. She unsnapped the thick plastic covering on the doorway and slipped inside. He followed.

The boat was big enough for about thirty people, with bench seats, life vests and equipment hanging from secured clamps along the walls. Several large boxes were labeled with various kinds of safety supplies. The seats were covered in orange vinyl cushions.

Checking to see what was visible from the deck, she brought him to a private corner diagonal from the doorway. When she reached the shadows, she sat and pulled him down next to her.

She kept hold of his right hand, smoothing fingers over his arm. She stroked the frog print tat that peeked out from under his sleeve.

Drawing in a deep breath, she held it a bit before releasing it, like she was resigned to revealing something. He wasn't sure he was going to like what she said, but there was no way he was going to go anywhere with her until he got some answers. He rubbed her fourth finger with his and looked into her eyes. He didn't have to ask her why she wasn't wearing the ring. He could see she was thinking about it as he rubbed her there, as she studied him with that liquid gaze that he'd lost himself in that afternoon as the sun was setting. For just a second he felt like he was back there, in her tiny apartment, drinking water and feeling the wonder of her hot and sweaty sheets full of the smells of her body mixed with his own.

He could see she was struggling.

"Take your time. I'm not going anywhere." He put his arm around her shoulders and held her safely, secretly loving the feel of her hair against the underside of his chin, against his neck. He held himself gently against her shaking body. God, how he wished he could turn all her pent-up emotion into passion. He knew he could love her until her body until she shattered beneath him and set them both free.

"I'm confused," she whispered.

"No crime in that."

"I thought I'd feel different."

"Um hum," He wasn't going to touch that one. His thumb rubbed against her shoulder in a lazy figure eight pattern. He worked to bring his breathing in line with hers, in tandem.

"I love him."

"That asshole upstairs?" Mark asked chuckling softly. He knew the answer, but was trying to make light.

"No. Roberto is Matheus's best friend."

"Some best friend. I'd kill someone who treated my woman like that."

She jerked at this comment. He'd hit a nerve.

Good to know.

"It bothers me too."

"It should. No offense, but, Sophia, how well do you really know your fiancé? I mean, if this is his best friend, what are his lesser friends like?"

She pulled away and he removed his arm from her shoulder. Okay, so he'd crossed a line there.

"Mark, I know it sounds crazy, but that afternoon we had—" she stopped and drew in a big breath again.

He was all in at this point. It was either going to be really bad or pretty freaking good. He was hoping for the freaking part.

"That afternoon," she began and looked up at him innocently.

God, he wanted to kiss her again. She kept staring at his lips, too. The lady was driving him nuts. Her body was a furnace, sending constant messages to his body parts that of course had now waked up and were screaming for more.

"It changed me."

There it was. Did he want to hear this? Hell, yes, he did. He'd go down in flames, but he'd let her finish and take as damned long as she wanted to. Every second he could have with her thigh against his, her arms lightly brushing against his, the way her hair smelled, how good it felt to match her breathing. He elongated the breaths and she followed. She followed his lead. He was pacing her. Holy shit, she was getting aroused!

Into the abyss he plunged. Her eyes longed for something he knew he could provide, and it didn't belong to someone who would have such an asshole friend as the prancing Brazilian stallion. It belonged to a guy who grew up driving pickup trucks and worked on his body quietly, who knew how to dish out pain, but was sent in to stop it. Who could blow up a bad guy but tenderly console a child. There were no dance floors for that kind of person, no cheering crowds or intoxicated fans.

He found the strength to say it at last. "It changed me too, Sophia. I only wish I'd met you before you got engaged. And I know that sounds crazy, but if you're not sure, then my personal opinion is you should think about it further before committing your life to someone."

He had to stand up. He stared out the plastic windows at the sea beyond. Something about this wasn't fair. No mistaking the attraction. But he couldn't take another man's woman, no matter how much he wanted her. He braced himself and turned to face her. Looking down on her beautiful face, he knew he had to do the right thing.

"Sophia, I feel like I have to apologize. It was one thing to hook up when I didn't know you were already taken. But now that I know you have a fiancé, it would be wrong to take advantage of you, indulge in something I know we both want, but shouldn't. I don't want someone that way. I don't want any regrets afterwards."

She examined her crossed ankles. The red dress had hitched dangerously high on her thighs. The red flower clip over her ear was askew and in danger of falling out.

"I'm going to break it off, Mark. I know now I wouldn't have so many doubts if it was right to go ahead with this marriage."

"Not because of me, you're not."

"No. Yes. Well, partly. I don't think I'd be as attracted to you if I truly loved Matheus the way—"

It was way too soon for her to be saying things like this. He willed her to keep her mouth shut, no matter how much he wanted to hear that she felt for him even half of what he felt for her.

"It's more than chemistry, Mark. It's like one of those paranormal books I read, like a fating. For some reason, meeting you has turned my whole world on its axis. Does that sound absolutely crazy?"

Mark turned and looked back out to sea. *Damn.* The right thing was still the right thing. He was going to have to get away from her or they'd be fucking their way from Italy to Brazil. Not that that was an unpleasant thought, but it wasn't right. She was going to have to convince him. He didn't want to talk her into something she'd regret later.

He dropped to his knees in front of her. "No, honey, it doesn't sound crazy." He didn't touch her, but she leaned over and kissed him on the lips anyway.

"Do you—" Her stopping was a good thing. Safe.

"I'm a sailor, Sophia. He stepped up to the plate and gave you a promise, and you gave yours. I can't promise that kind of thing, sweetheart. I've got to be totally honest with you."

"But maybe we could just be together without promises. I'm not sure I want anything with a date and a ring, either. I think you helped me realize I don't want that anymore. I'm not ready, Mark."

He held her hands in his, continuing to kneel in front of her. "Now you're talking my language. But all this is up to you. Your call. Your decision completely. I don't want you to have any regrets, and I don't want to feel like I got in the way of something that would have worked for you, do you understand?"

She nodded, and then gave him that little smile, just like the one that had warmed his heart that day at the café with the sounds of traffic and footsteps on cobblestoned streets in Italy. As ancient as love stories in the Bible and before, that little smile from this woman filled his heart with hope. Perhaps he had found someone after all who could handle his ways. Perhaps she could handle his sorrow and loss. Perhaps she could soften and heal him.

"I want to give this a go, Mark. Not so I can go back to Matheus. Because I get the feeling if I don't let myself have this time with you—no promises, here, because it might be a very short time. But if I don't give this to myself, I know I'll regret it for the rest of my life. I truly believe that."

He was overcome, staring down at their entwined fingers. "Then baby, I'm your guy. For today, for the time until we get to port, and then we'll see where it goes. If you're sure."

She didn't hesitate. She kissed his fingers and smiled back at him. "I'm sure."

CHAPTER 12

She ached for him to touch her, and she wasn't trying to hide her longing for him. Her body felt alive in his presence. She'd grown up loving to dance growing up, feeling she could follow a partner's lead, be compliant and acquiesce to his movements. That's what good dancing was, following the man, always following the man, regardless of whether or not he kept time with the music or took even steps. Whatever he did she would mirror.

It was no different now. She wanted to follow Mark's lead, hoped he'd take her in his arms, play her body like an instrument. Command she lean and turn, command her to show him what she wanted. When he reached out and put his palm on her cheek, she turned her head and kissed him there. She held his muscled forearm with both her hands, sliding down to his elbow and up his arm to his shoulder, over the corded muscles there and up to the strong muscles at the base of his neck. She traced the shape of his ear, moving his hair behind it, rubbing behind his ear and down under his jawline, tickling him and beckoning him to lean into her.

And he did.

The kiss was delicate. The taste of his tongue made all her lady parts ache for the feel of that tongue on her sensitive sex. She felt herself swell, becoming moist, and needing him inside her.

He removed his hands, pulled at the vinyl she was sitting on, and found it would move. She pulled the long pad next to her as they simultaneously dropped them to the floor of the little lifeboat. He guided her to lie back on the soft surface while he covered her with his body.

Their hands explored each other, his finding room under her red dress, beginning to peel down her dance stockings, smoothing over her backside, flesh on flesh. She helped him remove her underthings until she lay back naked from her waist down, watching him.

"You sure you're okay with this?" he asked again.

She nodded her head, watching the way a few strands of his hair fell forward at the sides of his face. She tucked them behind his ears. "I want you, Mark."

He slammed her with a deep kiss and she heard and felt the guttural groan deep inside his chest that vibrated hers when she softened to accept him. The sound of his passion made her skin tingle. She bent her knees to the sides as he rode her mound and pressed himself against her through his cargo pants.

"Baby, I've been dreaming about doing this practically twenty-four-seven," he whispered to her ear as he gave her lobe a gentle bite. Her hand felt the ripples of his forearm muscles tense as his fingers found purchase under her skirt, between her legs. He gazed into her eyes and swallowed, like his mouth was parched, just as he slipped two fingers inside her.

She was filled with need, though his fingers deliciously coaxed her juices. Another deep groan emanated from him as he felt the slickness and ease with which those fingers moved in and out of her.

He began kissing her neck, down lower to the space between her breasts, then carefully lifting her dress up, kissing over the red satin bra she wore underneath. His tongue found its way under the fabric to suck on her nipples, first one and then the other. The delicious sucking sounds he made caused her to arch, pushing her breasts further into his mouth. Her legs wrapped around his waist and she moved up and down against his bulging package.

Her fingers breached his waistband, smoothing down his backside. With one hand he undid the button and zipper on his jeans. With his large hand over hers, he guided her to his shaft until she felt the smooth surface of his cock, then reached further to take his balls and squeeze them.

Her hand worked on his shaft, moving up and down as he groaned into her chest. He began kissing her lower, until she held his head between her palms, sighed, arched up to him. He was looking at her bare sex. With a quick inhale he dipped his head down and allowed his tongue to travel the entire length of her labia, lazily pushing aside the delicate tissues and then rubbing inside and against the walls of her channel as he pushed inside and sucked.

Her body jerked as he ran his teeth over her nub, coaxing it into a stiff little peak, causing her to hiss with delight.

"You like that, baby?" he whispered, watching her face, his lips glistening with her juices.

"I like all of it, Mark. All of it."

"You taste so sweet," he said before he bent and lapped at her again.

Her fingers sifted through his shiny brown hair, squeezing and then releasing his scalp. At last, the shuddering inside her belly overcame her and she arched back into a loan deep moan as the beginnings of a powerful orgasm began to take hold. He fed on her passion, his face full of the delight at her taste, which turned her insides molten.

Through half-closed eyes she watched a glistening smile consume his face.

"God, Mark, I've missed this."

"Me too," he said as he sucked at her quivering peach.

She needed him to ride her orgasm, let her fly, and as if he'd read her mind, he quickly shimmied out of his pants, climbed over her and lay back down against her chest. She pulled her dress over her head but left her red satin bra in place. Mark reached around her back to the clasp and released her to his waiting lips, to his callused hands that kneaded her pillows of flesh. As he moved higher, she could reach his cock, and she stroked him, covering him with a condom he hadn't noticed she held. Then she guided him, raised her knees and her pelvis to receive him.

His shaft lay in wait at her opening while he brushed the hair from her forehead, kissing her face, her eyes, and her ears and under her jaw. But his clear blue eyes searched hers as he began to thrust inside slowly at first.

She arched back and gasped as he filled her to the hilt, pushing deep, stretching her pulsing and swollen channel.

Her hands felt the juncture between them, ringing his cock, squeezing his balls as he rooted inside and then pulled out and then pushed back in again. There wasn't anything in the world she wanted to feel more than his hardness impaling her and demanding to be fed.

The slow rhythm he began was setting her insides on fire as he undulated his hips. She felt the muscles of his butt cheeks flex and soften as she pulled him deeper into her, and she heard the guttural response from deep in his chest. He pulled her legs up, folding her knees at her ears pressing down on the backs of her thighs as he fucked her deep. She began to clamp down on him with her internal muscles, her involuntary spasms making him writhe and moan into her ear.

"Baby, baby," he whispered.

"Oh, God, Mark. Oh, God—" but her words were cut off as he sucked at her mouth, consuming the low, guttural scream forced from her breath to his.

"I want all of you, baby," he said between kisses. His tongue was demanding, his body hard and wound tight but performing controlled and fluid movements as he claimed her in every way possible.

His heavy pace ignited a blaze in her belly as she felt on the verge of shattering in his arms. She needed urgently to squeeze his waist with her thighs, hug his torso into her chest, clutch the hard muscles of his buttocks and grip his back, massaging and clutching the muscles she felt underneath her palms. He picked up the pace and, just when she felt like she couldn't take any more, she fell into a deep rolling orgasm that sent her flying over the waters of the sea.

Her body rocked, as he responded to hers, as he hurried to join her, plunging deep in several long strokes and matched her pleasure with his own, tensing and pushing, deeply into her core.

Before he could search her face, before he could wipe the sweat from her forehead and give her that lopsided smile and say something really soft, which she knew he would, before all of that, she realized she wanted him all over again.

Her addiction to his body was seated, fully positioned, blooming, pounding in her head, her belly and between her legs. She'd never desired someone so completely in her whole life.

CHAPTER 13

Roberto searched everywhere in the shadows of Deck 5 and realized she'd probably gone back to her cabin. He doubted she'd go with the American to his room, but secretly, in a twisted sort of way, he hoped she had. Then he could get her fired. She'd be his captive until Brazil. He could complain about her to Matheus, who then wouldn't listen to her protestations about how Roberto had mistreated her. Served her right. He'd lusted for her since before she'd met Matheus. In fact, on a fucked-up twist-of-fate day, Roberto had introduced them and they were soon off like a couple of fuck puppets.

He'd had to endure the detailed descriptions of how hot she was, how she liked to scream and exactly what else she liked. Matheus must have known how it made his dick lurch when he told these stories. All he could do afterwards was either drink to oblivion, work on himself, or find someone to use immediately. Did he know what a fucking bitch it was to be the Latin Lover's best friend, when he owned a piece of woman he was incapable of riding hard and long? Matheus was too gentle for the likes of her. She needed pain, and she needed to feel the full dominance Roberto was sure only he could provide.

He pushed aside two of the darkly made up dancers with the strange instruments, sending one to the floor of the crew deck at zero. He was glad he didn't understand their Arabic, these Middle Eastern pricks.

"Yeah? Well your mother fucks pigs, you donkey dick," Roberto spat in Portuguese at the little troupe.

The hatred in their faces mattered little. He used it as fuel to stoke the fires of his need to possess, to conquer and, if he was completely honest, destroy. He'd destroy his friendship, all right. But Matheus was from a rich family, and could pay for all the therapy.

All Roberto could do was get thoroughly lost and fucked, perhaps if he got angry enough, find solace between Matheus's woman's thighs, and then run like hell to avoid the police. Revulsion at the thought of living in a cage for the rest of his life kept him from going over the top. Didn't mean he didn't fantasize watching her beg for her life, or seeing Matheus watch as he demonstrated how to thoroughly pump a woman senseless. And about how after he'd seen her debased that way, no way would Matheus love her. That's when Roberto could fuck her good and proper, and hope that it hurt.

The shouting behind him intensified and he turned just in time to see one of the sand people come at him with a sword. His fluid training in Capoeira, which he'd studied since early childhood in the dirty favelas and back streets of Rio, kicked in immediately, and he focused his need to punish on the little Arab, turning the sword back on the guy and slamming him down on the floor with the blade to his neck.

He pressed the silvery blade against the sweaty dark skin of the dancer until a line of red blood appeared.

"How hard do you want me to push?" he asked as he made sure to back up the question with a wild grin. "Yes, I'm crazy. Do you know how many people I have killed with my bare hands?"

The Arab was rolling his eyes, trying to find his buddies, who had taken off down the hall screaming, trying to get someone else to intervene.

Roberto spat to the side.

Cowards.

He enjoyed the tiny trickle of blood that found its way to the dirty gray metal floor. He halfway wanted to slice all the way through the guy's windpipe, feel the crunch of the blade as it shattered his upper cervical vertebrae and severed the head. The expression on the man's face would remain in death. He'd seen it before.

But not today, he decided. He threw the sword behind him and almost hit a cook carrying a tray of dishes, which came crashing to the ground. The little

Italian's eyes got wide as he bolted down the hallway as if chasing the bowls rolling and bumping along the floor.

Roberto picked up his attacker by gripping his shirt and righting his body. He'd peed and shit himself, and Roberto didn't want anything more to do with his stinky, shivering body. The guy would be ruined, Roberto thought, almost as surely as if he'd been raped in the ass.

For a second the man didn't know whether to run for cover, which way to run, or to wait for Roberto's next move.

"Boo," he barked to the Arab. That was all it took for the man to waddle at high speed down the hallway and disappear around a corner.

Crew had begun to gather. Whispers and pointing didn't bother Roberto. He searched the faces and didn't see an officer or the ship's entertainment director, who was a spineless gay Frenchman who never liked to confront anyone. He already knew Jacques was afraid of him, and probably didn't care for the Arab dancers he was forced to hire. It was the first time Roberto had ever seen Arab dancers, too, who had been brought on at the behest of one of the junior officers. The Arabs were worse than Chinese when it came to blending into the harmony of the staff.

"What? You have something to say?" he shouted to the crowd. "He insulted me, pulled that blade on me," Roberto screamed. "And he was damned lucky I didn't really hurt him. Movie's over. Go back to your work."

With that, Roberto went to his room, deciding it was best not to go after Sophia, slid the keycard down the door lock, and slammed his cabin door shut behind him.

Helena heard the radio beep with a danger signal. Maksym's lovely body was draped across her bed, naked, a dark trail of hair leading down below the top sheet he'd used to cover his giant cock and impossibly long legs. He jerked to life before she could turn the damned machine off.

"Thought you had a couple of hours, Max. You'd think one of the other officers could steer the ship, even if the captain is drunk again." She held the small radio behind her head, her eyes hungry for the sight of his naked body again, especially if he wanted something from her. The tease was turning her on.

Again.

Maksym's bright, white smile made her heart dance. He was the most exciting sexual partner she'd had in several years, harkening back to the days of her youth when the Russian soldiers liked to entertain pretty girls in Praque with orgies, liquor and porn. She'd received enough favors then to have her mother and their family relocated to a top floor apartment. Those were the happy days, when she thought every problem could be solved by a sexual favor. Before the Russians killed her sister and mother and took away the family store. It didn't matter how many men she had to screw. Her family was never coming back.

"Helena, I need my radio."

She placed it between her legs, hitching it up against her sex. "Come and get it." She jumped to the side as he lunged for her.

The little squawk box buzzed again and Helena squealed as the vibration sent pulses in all the right places. Maksym's wide smile was the only thing he wore. His huge frame was trim and lithe like a runner's, his cock enormous, just like she liked them, and he was dark in a pirate kind of way. The cruise line allowed him to wear his hair long, and he frequently had to brush it out of his eyes, unless she did it for him, which she loved to do almost as much as she enjoyed fucking him and kissing his entire body.

"And now it's going to smell like you all evening while I'm up at the bridge, when I need my concentration."

"Steal me up there, Maksym. I'd like to fuck you on the map table."

He laughed. "Helena, that's not going to happen. Now give me that damned radio," he said in Russian, which was their signal that he meant business.

She walked to him and put her forefinger in her mouth, twisting her body from side to side as he reached down and retrieved the radio.

He held down the button at the side and they heard the device crackle to life. Helena dropped to her knees and took his cock into her mouth. He groaned and pretended he'd just hit his head on something to the person on the other end of the radio.

"....need you down at the crew deck immediately..." The words, spoke in a clipped Indian dialect were scratchy and going in and out of range. She was vaguely aware something had happened down below, and Maksym was wanted as a police presence. He was being summoned by one of the security guards.

Helena'd managed to get him fully primed and erect again. She was beginning to straddle him, trying to push him back on the bed for round three or possibly four. She'd been dreaming about dressing herself up as one of the dancers or a maid so she could sneak into his cabin and have him all to herself all night long.

But Maksym held her wrists and stopped her forward advance. "Helena, not now. I have to go." He didn't smile so she slipped one hand free and ran her fingers up and down his shaft and gave his balls a healthy squeeze, pouting, which usually got him distracted enough to forget anything else he was doing.

But not today.

"I'll come back when I can. I have to go there. Someone's been hurt. Blood shed. Only an officer can make an arrest."

"Blood?" She asked as she stood quickly.

He reached over and grabbed his white pants, putting them on commando style. "My jacket will cover my hard-on until you can take care of it, my kitten." He wiggled his eyebrows and put his white ship-issue knit shorts on top of her head like a hat.

"Do I wear this around, now? Can I tell everyone that you have claimed me? That I belong to you?"

"No," he said as he changed his mind and pulled the shorts off her head. "Where is my shirt?"

"This one?" she said as she turned around, giving him a good view of her ass as she bent down, grabbed his cotton V-necked T-shirt and rubbed it between her legs, peering over her shoulder at him. "You've got me hot and sticky with your come, Maksym."

"That's what towels are for, kitten," he said as he pulled the shirt from her fingers and slipped it over his head, pulling it down. He sniffed the front of the stretchy cotton by holding it out with two of his fingers, and then smoothed the stained fabric over his breast, and shook his head. "You'll be the death of me, Helena."

"I like dangerous love," she said. She'd said that once to one of the Russian officers who knew she was underage and would be relieved of his command if caught. That's how a lot of the young girls were killed in those days. Raped and sexually assaulted and then robbed of their young lives so they wouldn't become a liability to the men who abused them. She'd decided right then and there that she'd perform things for this man that would make it impossible for him to ever forget her.

And while it worked for her, her mother and sister had not been so lucky.

"Stop it. I must get back to work right away," he curtly said in Russian.

"Don't tell me what to do with that tongue. Don't order me around while using that filthy language."

Maksym had tied his shoes and, before putting on his white jacket, he stood for a moment tenderly holding her naked body. He touched her chin and tilted her face up to his.

"Sorry," he whispered. He kissed her tenderly, leaving her desperately vacant inside, and left the cabin.

CHAPTER 14

Kyle and Christy were seated at the slot machines next to Fredo and Mia when Moshe ran past them, shouting something in his radio. Kyle noticed that two Indian security guards followed, having trouble keeping up with Moshe.

His Israeli friend didn't see them sitting there. For a second Kyle considered running after him, so sure that it was something important, something he should know about. But Christy sensed it and laid her hand on his forearm.

"Not your fight, baby," she whispered so as not to embarrass him.

"Right. But doesn't satisfy my curiosity." He glanced over at Fredo, and the look they shared said volumes.

Fredo stood up, gave Mia a kiss on the cheek and said to both the girls, "I think we gotta go."

Christy frowned. "Kyle, we're on vacation."

"Not if something going down. I've seen that expression on Moshe's face before. Something's going on, and I need to know about it," Kyle replied. He kissed her on the forehead. "You find the other ladies and have them go back to the cabins, okay?"

"Kyle, this is ridiculous," she started to say, but the glare he gave her stopped anything further from coming out of her mouth. She sighed in resignation, nodding as she took Mia's hand. "Come on."

Kyle and Fredo raced to try to catch up with Moshe and the rest of his security detail.

"You have Teseo's number, boss?" Fredo asked.

"Damned if I did. I left his card back at the room, so no fuckin' way to get hold of him."

"You want me to go up to the bridge?" Fredo offered.

Kyle considered it. "Let's see what's going on first, and then we'll decide. Can you get hold of Mark and Nick? I'm going to try to get Coop."

While running, they tried to text the other Team members. Mark didn't answer, but Cooper said he'd check to make sure the girls got to their rooms, and Nick and was with Armando playing poker at the other side of the casino. They abandoned Sanouk, who was on a winning streak, and soon caught up.

"What's going on, Kyle?" Armando asked.

"Not sure, but something. I need to know," Kyle answered.

"Moshe know we're following him?" Nick asked.

"Don't think he saw us."

Just then he saw Moshe flanked by the other two guards block the entrance to the elevator, sending guests out onto the landing and commandeering it for their own use. As the doors began to close, Moshe noticed Kyle and the Team, shaking his head from side to side to tell him not to follow.

But of course Kyle wasn't going to listen. They ran down five flights of stairs until they got to the zero deck, which was a beehive of activity. The shows had let out and dancers in full-feathered costumes pushed their way past, speaking Portuguese. A wait staff was kneeling on all fours picking up broken pieces of pottery from a food tray that had been dropped. Kyle attempted to follow Moshe's path but was stopped by two very large Indian security agents wearing navy blue suits, walkie-talkies and earpieces.

"This is off limits to passengers, sir," they spoke to him in clipped English.

"I'm with Moshe," Kyle began. "I'm here to help him."

"You are not going anywhere down here. Now, go back up to your cabins. Everything is under control."

Like hell it was. Loud voices punctuated the air, the festive dancers stopped their chattering and their flutter of laughter and everyone focused on shouts and rants coming from the sick bay.

"What's happened?" Kyle asked the large security man, wearing a badge that read, *Kumar,* from India.

Kumar held his palms at Kyle's chest. "You must not go in there, sir. This is not allowed. There is no problem, no problem at all," he said in his singsong dialect.

Moshe walked out of the sick bay, looking dazed and confused, scratching the back of his head. A metal bedpan came flying from the doorway, hitting him in the small of his back. There was no mistaking the Arabic shouts, including some invectives to *Allah,* from someone who was clearly very angry with him. The tall junior officer Kyle recognized as Maksym Tereschenko came toward Moshe from the other side of the hallway and stopped to whisper something to him, and Moshe nodded.

The tall Ukrainian officer briefly looked up at Kyle, Fredo, Armando and Nick, and then disappeared into the doorway under the red medical sign.

Moshe approached Kyle and directed the security officers back to the sick bay. He gave the SEAL a quick smile after the men were out of earshot.

"We've got ourselves a rat's nest here. All these nationalities, and sometimes they don't get along."

"And someone got hurt," Kyle said, nodding to the sick bay.

"Not really. I'd say more a hurt of the pride." Moshe spoke tentatively, indicating he had more on his mind than he was letting on.

"What's the injury?" Kyle asked.

"A glancing knife wound to the dancer's neck that will heal just fine with butterfly bandages. No stitches needed."

"Dancer? What dancer?" Kyle asked.

"They are part of a Moroccan dance troupe and they speak a dialect I don't understand. They are Berbers."

Kyle knew Moshe was fluent in Arabic as well as other languages in the Middle East including Pashto, Urdu, Turkish and Persian.

"What was with the bedpan?" Fredo asked.

Moshe flashed a smile. "I'm used to having things thrown at me, but that was a first. I'm guessing he recognized my accent."

The muffled shouting began to die down. The hallway emptied and the normal bustle of a busy crew quarters resumed.

Moshe placed his arm on Kyle's shoulder. "Thank you for your show of support, but I have a report to make and another dancer to interview."

"Another dancer?" Nick asked. "What the fuck's with the dancers all of a sudden?"

"The other dancer turned this gentleman's blade back on his neck. He's our Brazilian tango instructor." Moshe shrugged. "I'm guessing he was feeling rather passionate about something. Apparently he's a trained street fighter in addition to being a great dance instructor."

Nick and Kyle shared a look. "One of our Team is kinda sweet on his dance partner."

"Who? Sophia?"

The SEALs nodded.

"Get in line." Moshe winked and waved goodbye as he stepped back a few paces, then turned and headed down the hall. Before he rounded the corner in the crew quarters, Kyle saw him report something on his radio.

Fredo texted Cooper. No one had seen Mark all evening. The SEALs took the elevator back up to their cabins on Deck 6.

Roberto let them pound the door. He was in a foul mood. The evening had been comfortably normal, until everything went to hell when that damned American shoved his way between him and Sophia, whisking her away for a little private conversation. He could only guess what they were doing. He'd turn her in if he caught them so much as holding hands.

But now he had bigger problems than Sophia and her attraction to the American. *He* was the one in danger of losing his job, not Sophia.

Whoever it was banging on his door was about to break it down, so he gave up and opened it. The dark Indian security guard, an acquaintance of Roberto's named Kumar, at first seemed surprised to see Roberto, his suspended the air with his brass buttons glinting in the hall light. He'd consoled Kumar when the tall Indian crewmember broke up with his Swedish girlfriend.

"Roberto? This is you?" Kumar asked. His eyebrows bunched together and his lips formed a thin line across his face.

"This is me," Roberto said and waited for Hell to freeze over.

Kumar turned to another security officer, the frizzy-haired Israeli. "There must be some mistake," he said. "I know this man."

But Moshe wasn't listening, entering the tiny windowless cabin and instructing Kumar to stand in the open doorway.

"Sit," Moshe demanded.

Roberto did so. Moshe sat on the bottom of the bunk Roberto shared with another Brazilian dancer.

"I've tried to talk to Azziz. I'm hoping you and I can have better communication."

"Yes, well, that man's an animal," Roberto returned.

"That may be, but he's the one with the injury, unless you're covering up something."

"He's a stupid animal who doesn't know how to fight. He should stick to dancing or playing those awful drums made out of dead snakes. He should learn not to pick a fight if he hasn't the stomach for it."

"You could have killed him."

"Exactly. And I didn't."

"May I ask what all this was about?"

"He came after me with one of his swords." Roberto decided to tell a little white lie and see if Moshe picked up on it. "I thought it was part of his costume, you know, plastic."

Moshe immediately frowned. "And when did you discover it wasn't a plastic blade?"

"When I put it to his neck."

"And that was after you slammed him to the ground?" Moshe continued frowning, making notes in the small spiral notebook he pulled from his breast pocket. "Roberto, that your story?"

He had to think about that. "So he's claiming back injury as well?" Roberto couldn't believe the bastard would have the nerve.

"I'm not quite sure what he's claiming. But I'm pretty sure you're going to have to make sure you're never alone with any of that troupe. It seems your indiscretion has taken on a *holy war* type of importance. Do you understand what I'm saying?"

"So now he's declaring a *jihad*?" Roberto wanted to spit at that, but didn't want to insult his unwelcome guest.

"Roberto, I'm still trying to understand how it was that you overcame him and put the sword to his neck, the *heavy* sword that was made out of steel. The one you thought was plastic. Just before that happened, what was said or done? That's the part I'm afraid I don't understand and, frankly, Azziz was not willing to tell me."

"I called him a name, but in Portuguese. I don't think he speaks Portuguese," Roberto responded. As he replayed the scene over again in his head, he realized Azziz, if that was his real name, had reacted as if he *did* understand his language.

Another miscalculation. Fuck it.

"And what did you call him?" Moshe asked, staring down at his lined tablet.

"Something…something like your mother loves pigs and donkeys—"

"It was a slur, in other words. You insulted him. Why?"

Roberto thought about this. Why had he said it? Probably because he was angry with Sophia, at the American, at the humiliation he'd received at their hand. He could still see the clown-like expressions of laughter on the faces of the beefy, weaving crowd of tourists he was supposed to turn into dancing elephants. He was pissed about his job, pissed that he had to babysit someone he wanted to fuck senseless. Pissed he'd given his word and had no intention of keeping it. And then some Arab guy had looked at him sideways, and that was all it took.

"Why did you insult him, Roberto?"

"Because he accidentally stepped on my foot," he lied. "The guy thought he owned the corridor. Why can't they walk single file like the rest of us? No. They have to walk side by side, not paying attention. We bumped into each other and he stepped on my foot, and it hurt."

It was such a good story, Roberto even began to believe half of it. He was rather proud of that.

Moshe stood up and exhaled, hitching his pants up, tucking his shirt in and nodding to Kumar to close the door, leaving the two of them alone. Roberto saw the young Israeli officer was angry, but controlling it very well.

"Listen, Roberto, unless you want to die with your throat slit, I mean a real cut, because I don't think they'll give you the same break you gave them. It's a matter of honor that you didn't kill him. That has further enraged him. So, unless you want to volunteer for their knife-throwing act or want a knife in your back when you're not looking, I suggest you stay far away from them. *All* of them. Do I make myself perfectly clear, Roberto?"

Roberto didn't like the Israeli's tone. He wasn't a grade school boy, and he could handle himself, he thought.

"Roberto," Moshe said as he locked a serious stare onto him, pricking some fear. "I can see you're not paying attention to me, so let me just tell you this." Moshe cocked his head and looked thoughtful before he blurted out, "I am responsible for the safety of nearly thirty-four hundred people on this boat, including eleven hundred staff." He cleared his throat for emphasis. "I cannot be everywhere at once. In addition to all the issues that normally come up on a cruise, I now have a war between ten Moroccan dancers and fourteen Brazilian ones. I don't care what those guys say to you, you stand down, Roberto. Do it like your life depends on it, because it just might."

"Fine," he said timidly. "You'll not have any more problems with me."

"Glad to hear it."

But Roberto knew in his heart of hearts he wasn't going to obey. The holy war Moshe mentioned was nothing compared to his injured pride.

Everyone always underestimates me.

He had told the truth about the Moroccans. They *were* stupid animals. He'd be prepared next time they tried to accost him, and no, he wouldn't be merciful. In fact, he might even enjoy the fight and watch their surprised faces just before he sent them back to Allah, if that's what it took.

CHAPTER 15

Maksym looked at the blood on the paper covering the plastic patient table, noting there was quite a bit of it for a simple flesh wound. The dancer Azziz sat shirtless, yelling at two of his troupe, who hung their heads.

I have to babysit assholes.

He wondered why they didn't use more of his own people, there were so many disenfranchised Ukrainians these days, people who had played the game with the Russians, as well as the West, and found themselves caught in the middle, not trusted by either side. Dangerous people, he thought, without a loyalty to any country, like him, others who had lost everything they'd cared about.

His children would be attending the finest Russian schools, taken care of by the older rich Russian they would soon call Papa. Maksym would always be their father, but his wife's sugar daddy, at least for as long as her looks held, would ensure the girls had a nice education and a beautiful home, and, most important, would be safe from interference from others. It was smart of the diplomat to choose a woman who had daughters she wanted protected. It ensured her complete loyalty.

But it still gnawed a hole in his stomach. He'd have laid down his life for them, something he doubted either his ex-wife or the diplomat she ran away with would ever do for anyone, including each other. Even though she'd cheated on him, he'd still have done it, if she'd come back to him.

What he shared with Helena was intense, which was what he needed, did not contain strings, which he really needed, and had a future involving a beach, an island somewhere and lots of sex with her, which he needed most of all. He just wanted to disappear.

But that meant he had to work with zealots who couldn't keep their feelings to themselves, who hated everyone, including their own families. Maksym couldn't understand those kinds of people. And he guessed they'd never understand him, either.

"So, Azziz," he began in Tachelhit, the man's Berber tongue, "I'm sure the Gray Wolf who set us up forgot to tell you the part about you keeping your mouth shut and not attracting attention. So I apologize for this oversight on his part."

"The Brazilian said my mother fucked pigs and donkeys. That's an offense that deserves the blade of my sword."

"There are worse things than death, my good man," he said to Azziz.

"Yes, living a dishonorable life."

Maksym leaned forward and hissed, "So is having your skin peeled from your flesh a strip at a time and watching it being eaten by pigs and donkeys, Azziz. So help me, if you mess up this mission, I'll make sure that is your fate."

"You keep the Brazilian away from me."

"I might let him kill you if you don't behave. The man is dangerous. *You* stay away from *him*."

"But we have the strength of Allah."

"I think in Brazil they aren't afraid of Allah. In fact, I don't think Allah goes there very often."

Azziz drew himself up, attempting to slide off the table and go for Maksym's throat, but was restrained by his two friends and the Italian medic who had brought a tray of butterfly bandages. The tray flew to the side and hit the wall, scattering the little strips intended to help Azziz's flesh heal.

Maksym quickly zip-tied Azziz's hands together. "You'll behave until we can get more bandages on your neck, and then you'll spend tonight locked in our cell. If you calm down, you can dance for the passengers tomorrow night, understood? Just like the trained monkey you are."

Azziz reacted to this by screaming, "No! I will not be caged like an animal."

"Azziz, you *are* an animal."

"You cannot do this." He began to rattle off some invectives Maksym could only imagine.

Maksym stole a look briefly at the medic. "How long will he bleed?"

"You mean without the bandages? About an hour. But he won't heal right. It will leave a scar, and might get infected."

"Perfect," Maksym said as he hoisted Azziz up using one hand on the man's bound wrists and the other on his belt at the back of his pants.

"You want me to calm him down?" the medic asked, holding up a syringe.

Maksym could probably handle him, he thought. But he didn't want to get his uniform bloody, or get scratches he didn't need. "Please."

Azziz struggled, but the little dancer was no match for Maksym's long arms and strong hands. He pulled his wrists up and over the Moroccan's head backwards until Azziz began to stream. Within seconds after the medic administered the injection, the dancer began to get compliant.

"You two," Maksym pointed to the other dancers, "help me with him, please." He could have slung the Moroccan over his shoulder, could have sent him overboard without a bit of a struggle, but that could soil his clothes. He took the dancer's callused brown feet encased in leather sandals, letting his friends take his head and shoulders, where all the blood was. He led the way down to the security office and the double jail bays. He opened the one on the right it with a passkey and they placed the near-comatose Azziz on a cot, covering him up with a scratchy, green blanket.

"Now, you have a show to prepare for?" Maksym asked the two friends, who avoided making eye contact with him.

"Yes," one of them mumbled.

"I'd better hear reports it was the best show of the cruise, understood?"

They nodded.

"You talk him out of being violent tomorrow, or I'll drop all three of you off at Tenerife and let you worry about how to get home."

"But..."

"He has to be controlled. Can you do that?" Maksym asked. Seeing one of the Indian security guards come into the office, he lowered his voice and whispered. "When is your next contact with the Wolf?"

"After the third stop. When we are on our way to the Equator."

Maksym had no such timetable and he wondered why the man who had hired them all chose to be in contact with the dancers by prior arrangement, where he had received only a loose, "I'll be in touch with further instructions."

"I will be watching him very carefully," Maksym added. "You prepare for your entertainment, and the other entertainment as well. If I don't see a marked improvement, I'll tell the Wolf, and I think it will piss him off. I might be kind and let you go. But the Wolf might want me to end your miserable lives. Do you understand?"

The dancers were shaking as he delivered that last piece. Maksym was almost a foot taller than either of them. He knew even his whispers were feared. And that was a good instinct on their part. That might keep them alive for another five days or so. Until they could get to the Equator.

After he got his money, he and Helena would be off someplace warm, never to be found again. It would be like dying and being reborn.

He'd have his own full-on religious experience.

CHAPTER 16

Mark and Sophia exited the lifeboat discreetly, watching for crewmembers using the deck outside. They re-snapped the door in place. Mark patted the letters stenciled on the outside. In white fluorescent paint it said No. 26. It was going to be his new favorite number.

"I rather like cabin number twenty-six," he said to the side of Sophia's face. She giggled, which thrilled him. He loved hearing her laugh.

"It could do with a little decorating. A little more padding might be better as well."

"Agreed. Wine. Some candles. I'll bring them next time," he said watching her try to straighten her hair, her clothes. "Just leave yourself mussed up. It turns me on, Sophia."

"But I could get fired."

"But if you get fired, then you could be my guest and we'd have my room."

"No. That's a violation of the contract I signed. They could send me back home if..."

He put his fingers on her lips. "Shhh. You talk too much. I liked it better when we let our bodies do the talking, before I knew you could speak and understand English."

"I can talk dirty in Italian. You'd like that," she whispered and kissed him.

"Nope. I want to know what you're saying to me. The imagination I can handle all on my own, thank you very much. I want to know what you're saying when you talk dirty to me."

"We can text."

"Not if you do it in Italian. Besides, why can't we meet here in our cabin? I want to do more than texting with you. Texting just isn't going to be enough for me, honey."

She frowned after his kiss.

"Oh, Sophia, are we having our first fight?" He couldn't help himself. He felt great. Nothing could dampen his mood.

"Mark, we have to be extremely careful. Roberto—"

His mood quickly shifted dark. He didn't like that she'd stopped telling him something about her fiancé's—her *ex*-fiancé's best friend.

"Who cares about Roberto?" he said casually as they opened to door to the meeting room. He was glad it was still vacant. "You're going to break it off, right?"

"I'm not worried about my soon-to-be-ex. But Roberto is a crazy person. Something not quite right about him."

"He's just very full of himself. Jealous, I'd say. One of those guys who doesn't like to lose."

"I think you are right." She faced him and placed her palms on his chest, giving him a quick, soft kiss. "Look. I want to play like we're not a couple, just keep it from Roberto."

"Why, baby?"

"I don't know. Self-preservation? I mean if he gets wind that I'm not going back to Brazil to get married after all, he'd insert himself into my life—he'd feel like he didn't have to be careful around me."

"You think what he did tonight was careful? How do you suppose he shows affection? To his best friend's fiancé? The guy's not stable, and therefore you can't count on him acting rationally."

"But I think he'd be on better behavior if he thought he would get in trouble when he gets home to Brazil."

"He's already demonstrated his dislike of you. Sophia, why are you protecting him?"

She stared down at her feet.

Mark pulled her face up with fingers under her chin. "Hey, what are you not telling me?"

"He has a past, Mark. He's killed people before."

It wasn't lost on Mark that he had as well. He decided not to remind her of that fact.

"Not sure I'm following your logic, Sophia."

"I don't think he dislikes me, Mark. I think he wants me for his own. If he thinks I'm free, he'll do everything in his power to keep me close to him. He'll be dangerous for you."

"He doesn't scare me."

"He should. Don't ever be alone with him. He'd kill you without thinking twice about it. Tonight confirmed what I've believed for some time now. My fiancé's family is very rich and powerful. Roberto won't cross them until he gets what he wants. He wants something. So he's delivering me, and then he'll ask the favor of them. I need to let him think he's still winning this game."

He didn't like it, but Mark agreed for now to go along with keeping their affair private. He'd tell his Teammates, of course, but he wouldn't be affectionate in public with her, or do anything to inflame Roberto any further. And, since he couldn't protect Sophia day and night, he wanted to do anything that would make her safer.

"But it's a requirement that I see you every night, you got that? We can meet here on the boat."

"Yes. It will be our secret hideout, then," she agreed. Her warm smile tugged at him. He almost begged her to stay with him a little longer. They exchanged their cell phone numbers for messages. Afterwards, she was all business. "I'll walk out of the room first. You wait about two minutes, then you go, okay?"

He reluctantly let her slip away.

On the way back to their cabin, Mark passed the doorway of the dark lady he'd seen in Marrakesh. She'd opened it and stepped out into the hallway, almost bumping into him. Her dark eyes appraised him quickly. He could see she noted his muscular build, the fact that he could handle himself and react quickly. He'd been able to dart out of the way just in time to avoid a collision.

"Scusi," she said with a slight bow, her long lashes falling on her cheeks and then drifting upward as she gave him a flirtatious look. Mark saw the danger in her gaze and the promise that she had some sort of dark secret. Years of interviewing and assessing tribal leaders overseas made him quick to discern when he could trust someone, and when he could not. And he didn't trust her in the slightest.

He let her pass, but just before he rounded his corner, he glanced over his shoulder at her fine frame undulating down the hallway, and saw her sneak back a look at him as well.

That was the telltale signal for him that she had an agenda of some sort. Did she know he'd already seen the two of them together?

Kyle and Armando were in his cabin when he returned, counting Sanouk's winnings.

"Looks like he's made just over $4000," Kyle announced, examining the chits Sanouk had accumulated. "Sanouk, you take good care of these, okay? No way to prove you won this. Anyone who walks into the teller with this paper can walk away with your money." He held the fistful of white paper slips in front of him, waving them back and forth. "Don't lose them."

"I should go do it now," Sanouk replied. "Mr. Mark, would you accompany me?"

Mark was tired, but he wanted to make sure Sanouk got his fair share.

"Oh, I'll go," said Jones as he walked through the adjoining doorway from the cabin next door. "Mark here has been exerting himself, if I have my geography and real estate down right."

That earned him some catcalls and whistles. He was beginning to think maybe someone pulled sentry duty to keep an eye on him and Sophia in the little boat. In spite of himself, he blushed and couldn't help but smile.

"I'll tag along too," Mark said.

"I was going to meet Kyle upstairs, so we'll join you," Armando said.

Six members of SEAL Team 3 accompanied Sanouk to the teller box to the side of the poker room, just beyond the slot machines. He wanted to get the cash, rather than have it added to his onboard bill for the ship. Mark guessed Sanouk was frugal, and didn't buy much of anything for himself. But with more than $3,400 now stashed in the kid's cabin, Mark had some concerns for Sanouk's safety.

"You don't go walking around any of the ports carrying more than about $100, hear?" Kyle instructed the young Thai. "And you don't brag."

Just then, several Brazilian poker players who had lost to Sanouk sauntered over to congratulate him. The SEALs made a barrier around Sanouk, who tried to shake hands, but couldn't because the Team wouldn't let him.

As they walked away, Mark added softly, "You got that much money on you, Sanouk, and you watch out for anyone. Anyone you don't know. Someone bumps into you, and then someone else relieves you of your money."

Sanouk agreed to be careful. "Holy cow, guys. Never knew having so much money was such a complete drag," Sanouk replied. "I mean, it's more money than I've ever seen before."

"So how did you learn to play poker without money, kid?" Jones wanted to know.

"We played for cans of soda. Once I won a $50 Starbuck's card and a set of golf clubs."

Everyone laughed.

Kyle and Armando headed over to one of the bars at the end of the Deck 5. "We're meeting Moshe for a drink, gents," Kyle said. "Make sure Sanouk gets back safely, hear?"

"I'm on it," Jones said. Fredo nodded and was joined by Rory. Mark drifted towards Kyle and Armando.

"Mind if I join you?" Mark asked.

"No problem." Kyle said and plopped his massive arm over Mark's shoulder. Together, they watched their Teammates amble up the stairway to Deck 6, and hopefully to the safety of their cabins.

"You missed some action today, Marky Mark," Armando quipped. "Your ears burnin'?"

"I'm just doin' what you'd have been doin', if you get my drift," Mark said.

"Roger that, Marky. I'm happy for you, but there's a complication, and I think Moshe will be able to fill us in. Something's not right about the dynamics down below," said Kyle.

As if on cue, Sophia's dance partner, Roberto, rounded the corner, giving Mark an appraisal straight from Hell itself. He was wearing jeans and a tight knit tee stretched across broad, muscular shoulders. Mark noted his arms and chest were nearly as big as some of the Team guys. Roberto fisted his hands at his sides, locked his jaw and passed them like it required great effort to do so without a fight.

"And that's the complication," Armando whispered as they watched the Brazilian's backside moving down towards the casino with sinewy grace.

"Looks like a street fighter, not a dancer," Mark said.

"And I think you'd be right. I don't think he's a dancer at all," said Kyle.

Moshe was waiting for them at one of the tables in a corner by a large window that was covered by padded window shades. The boat was rocking heavily. Mark noted the ship's captain was probably trying to make up time. Kyle and Armando sat down, while Mark went over to the window covering and pulled one corner of it aside, staring out at the moonlight reflecting off the churning waters of the sea.

"Hey, Mark," Moshe raised his voice. "Keep that closed. We're not that far from shore."

"What's up with that?"

A young server with a pretty face and dark hair done up in a bun added her explanation, "We have an agreement with some of the African countries not to bother them at night with our lights."

Kyle wrinkled his nose. Mark didn't understand how their lights, just like the lights from merchant ships they'd been passing, would bother anyone.

"That just doesn't make any sense at all," Mark said as he re-secured the padding and came back to the table. Moshe had a meaningful look on his face, but said nothing until after the server left with their orders.

"It *doesn't* make sense. That's just what we tell the passengers," Moshe began. "Truth is, at night, we make a pretty huge target."

"No shit?" Armando asked.

"Just a precaution. Nothing's ever happened, you understand. But everyone is extremely careful, as required by the insurance carrier for the line. That's the reason for a beefed-up security detail—about double what we usually have. You know that expression, better safe than sorry? That's why they hired me. They love Israeli special forces guys." Moshe frowned and held off saying anything more while their beers were served.

That's when Mark noticed that Moshe's nametag identified him as coming from the U.S., not Israel. He decided to ask him about it. "You a U.S. citizen, Moshe?"

The Israeli officer tilted his head and gave a kind smile. "Fewer complications that way. But the whole crew knows. Not many know my background, and I want it kept that way."

"Agreed," Kyle said and clinked glasses with him. Armando and Mark added their glasses to the toast.

"Which brings me to something I must discuss with you all. The situation today, while I'm not at liberty to divulge the details, is troubling to me." Moshe took a small sip and pushed his glass away like he was abandoning it nearly full. "I've got a small war going on downstairs, and I just want to give you a heads-up."

Mark knew that somehow this involved the Brazilian tango instructor, if that's what he really was.

"I've tried to reason with Roberto. We had a scene earlier today that Kyle and Armando here witnessed, between our Moroccan dance troupe and the Brazilian." Moshe swallowed, searching the room before he continued. "Roberto is a hothead, but he's bitten off the head of a cobra, only to find the babies are more deadly. I've got nine Moroccans performing tonight for the late show, and one in the hold with minor injuries."

"He going to be all right?" Kyle asked.

"There is no *all right* about this situation. It's a powder keg." Moshe stared down at his hands, fingers linked and resting on the yellow resin tabletop. "I'm going to try to get them tossed in the Canaries. I have to speak to our representative onshore when we arrive there day after tomorrow. You can't just kick someone off the ship without making sure the host country will take them."

"I hear that. Sounds like a plan. Less for you to have to manage," Kyle nodded and sipped his beer.

"There is no managing these people sometimes. I wish they'd leave some of these decisions to us. We are involved in the screening of the crew and staff, but the entertainment is hired by the entertainment director, and I'm afraid he isn't quite the man for the job."

Mark was concerned for Sophia's welfare. "Moshe, I know there are rules about getting involved with the staff and crew. But I—"

"I don't want to hear it. If I didn't hear it, it didn't happen," Moshe returned.

Mark's belly began to do flip-flops. He felt sweat dripping down the middle of his back. "Is she safe?"

"As long as she stays out of the crossfire." Moshe's serious face alarmed Mark even further. "You don't want to do anything that will upset the Brazilian. It's safest for her that way."

"I want to protect her. That's my only motive," Mark said shaking his head.

"Bullshit, Mark. It's *one* of your motives," Kyle grinned.

Armando and Kyle shared a chuckle at his expense.

"Then what happens when a crew member gets fired? For something like breaking a rule?"

Moshe sat back into the bright blue vinyl of the bench seat. "They get flown home immediately at the next port."

"What if—" his LPO interrupted Mark.

"You're a dumb shit, Mark. Don't even go there. She can't just change her mind and then be your fuck bunny, sharing your cabin from here to Brazil. It won't happen."

"You're playing with fire, my friend," Moshe added.

"But I see that big officer, Maksym, he's having a fling with a passenger on our floor," Mark answered.

"You *think* you saw them," Kyle corrected.

"No, fuck sake, Lanny. I saw them on land, too. They were all over each other." Mark then addressed Moshe. "He's been to her cabin. I saw them myself."

Moshe shook his head. "Unfortunately, the officers have a bit more leeway, just like this meeting here. We are supposed to be strategically placed amongst the passengers. We even have security posing as passengers, just to be sure. No women, though. So this would be forbidden, but not, unfortunately, uncommon. And I think Maksym is a decent guy. I don't trust him like Teseo, because I don't know everything about his background. I didn't hire or vet him for the company."

"Who did, then?"

"Someone in Florida. All the ship hiring is done there. And they contract with local employment agencies in other countries, like the Philippines, Brazil and Italy."

"So that leaves us with Roberto. Hired by the entertainment director, then. A Frenchman, unless I'm mistaken," said Armando.

"Who also hired the Moroccan dancers," Moshe added.

"And you didn't vet any of them?" Kyle asked.

"No. I have their passports in the safe. That's the extent of my involvement, other than trying to keep them from killing each other."

"It doesn't change the fact that I'm worried for Sophia's safety, Moshe. I really am. You should see the bruise on her wrist. That guy looked like he wanted to cause her pain for my benefit. Did it right in front of my eyes. I just couldn't let that happen."

Moshe's brow furrowed. "You must be exaggerating."

Kyle piped up. "Maybe that's what set him off tonight. Ever thought of that?"

"She has a fiancé. A very well liked Brazilian dancer, and it is my understanding she is completing her contract, and then staying in Brazil to be married. Why are we even talking about all this?"

"Because she's going to call it off," Mark said and immediately regretted it.

The three other men groaned.

"You a fuckin' idiot, Mark?" Kyle barked.

"Doesn't explain why Roberto is so pissed about it," Armando said, agreeing with Mark. "He's not the groom, after all. I think Mark's got a point. Sophia is in some serious danger."

"That's right," Mark added. "Something's wrong with the guy. Even Sophia said so."

Moshe shifted and then stood. "Okay, this is getting too complicated. I'm going to ask you to stay away from her. And all of you, stay away from Roberto. Hopefully I can keep an eye on him, and Sophia," he nodded to Mark, "and Maksym will keep an eye on the Moroccan hotheads. Maybe, just maybe, we'll get through this cruise without another incident."

"Wow. Had no idea about all this," Kyle sighed.

"We have fifty-three countries represented here. We usually get along much better than our world leaders do. We try to instill the 'one family' concept, which results in a lot of multicultural marriages, and that's good for the ship. Normally it's pretty harmonious. But this cruise almost seems like it's cursed."

Kyle, Armando and Mark shared that *oh, shit* look that happened sometimes when they got the feeling something really bad was about to happen. Mark knew his two mates were assessing threats, determining their options, searching their minds for tools to help them keep their families safe. Advance planning saved lives. Even on a cruise ship.

They watched the handsome Israeli walk out of the bar. The heaviness of Moshe's final statement hung like the smoke from a firefight. There was no way Mark would leave Sophia alone, even if she begged him to. Just like the rest of the Team. No one would leave one of them behind, or leave any of the ladies unprotected. She wasn't entirely his yet, except in his heart. Didn't make any difference, though. His honor and commitment to her settled in on his shoulders, and he felt his chest swell with the knowledge he had someone else to live for.

He just hoped he could do it without making an international incident out of it or get them all in trouble.

CHAPTER 17

The next day, Sophia submitted to Roberto for their pre-planned midmorning rehearsal in the vacant auditorium. They had a dance class to teach that afternoon, and then would be the highlight dancers for a mini grand review involving much of the dance staff from all countries. It was supposed to show the unity of the international crew of the ship.

It was a total lie.

Roberto was back to being well behaved and charming. Sophia knew he was working hard to get back on her good side. The pattern for him seemed to be to show his nasty side, then show his soft side. Dr. Jekyll and Mr. Hyde. She warned herself not to trust this courteous Roberto, knowing the evil Roberto was lurking, ready to pounce, especially if she didn't give him what he wanted.

She was becoming more and more convinced his plan was to take her at any cost. His hands held her waist a little too long, they slipped down previously avoided body parts in casual caresses. His sighs and little grunts, not perceptible to anyone but her, were dangerously obvious. Did he think this sort of behavior was desired? If Mark weren't around, she'd be going to Brazil to meet Matheus and his family. Roberto, even if she had been interested, and she never had been, would have been at best a distant second. As it was, he'd never been on her radar. What, she wondered, made him think he ever could be?

She'd felt this cruise was a big mistake. The wedding was being planned by people she hadn't met. "It's the way we do it here. My mother would never forgive herself," Matheus had said in his soft, Brazilian accent. She'd loved that part about him. His gentleness was what had attracted her to him. And the promise of an exotic life in a foreign land.

And then, just a dream, Mark had appeared on that cobblestoned street, near the place where Matheus had proposed last year. That's the day her whole world had changed. She impulsively decided the handsome American would be her goodbye kiss to all the men she'd loved, a goodbye kiss to her single life. She'd be taking the path away from everything familiar, from where her loving father had lived, and replacing it with an exciting new adventure in Brazil with her handsome new husband.

She hadn't expected that Mark's ways would charm her so completely. The simple, direct way he'd tried to talk to her when he didn't know she understood, with that casual American drawl and straightforward honesty that had gone straight to her heart. Just the way her father had been, the airman with the bomber jacket her mother had fallen for in Italy those years ago. Had she fallen for Mark because she missed her dad?

She knew the answer was no. But being in Mark's arms felt like coming home, like remembering the way the Central Valley looked in the early morning hours when the tule fog covered everything with a gray blanket. She knew what it smelled like to drive past orchards of blooming peach trees, or fields where you could almost see the corn grow. She'd remembered the picnics they'd taken at Doran Beach, when it was really too cold and windy, but she didn't care. Her daddy was there and that was all the warmth she'd required. She remembered holding his hand while riding the cable car or visiting the aquarium in San Francisco. She remembered going to apple farms and pumpkin patches with her grade school classes, so proud her father was a soldier, and couldn't always be there, but happy when he could be.

She'd worked hard as a young girl to not let her grief make it harder on her mother. America had not been her mother's home. But now Sophia realized it was hers, as surely as the name on her U.S. passport.

She wasn't ready to put that image of her father and her American life away forever. That's what had opened the door a crack, why she'd taken the chance with the American that afternoon.

And all Mark had to do was walk in. She couldn't let him go. She couldn't say goodbye to her past without one more dalliance, one more flirtation to help her remember what it meant to be a California girl and proud of the uniform her father wore. She'd forgotten what that service and sacrifice had meant to her.

Roberto's touch on her shoulder made her jump. It was more like a flinch so she plastered a bright smile on her face and spun around to greet him. Her private indecision and pain would be just that: private. She wasn't going to share an ounce of anything going on inside her with Roberto.

"I'm ready," she said as she pulled her wet towel from her neck and placed her hands in position in his before he'd set his form up. She felt he'd wanted to talk to her, not resume their practice. She wasn't going to give him the chance.

Roberto drew her tighter against him, and she felt his arousal. With her gaze focused off to the left at a point on the wall between columns, she allowed herself to be pulled into him, allowed him to press further, felt his eyes on her, saw his little smile that quirked up at the corners of his mouth. He was pushing to have it register with her, to have her recognize his intent, but she remained the graceful ice queen who was his dance partner but never, ever would be his lover. She focused on perfect turns, being responsive to his direction, not reacting when his hand slipped between her legs in a fluid movement before he released her.

She curtsied to the audio tech, to the invisible bodies sitting in the rows of seats out in the auditorium, to anyone who might happen to be watching them. No one would be able to tell the loathing she felt for her partner, not even her partner himself.

"Again," he said to the side of her face, his hot breath on her neck, his need growing. The handler dutifully replayed the set. She was grateful the good workout would relieve some of the tension in her legs, smooth over the soreness of her sex as she traveled over the dance floor, deliciously recalling the way she'd wanted Mark deep inside her. The way he'd kissed down her neck, and numbingly kissed her beneath her skirt and licked her nub, which stiffened under his tongue. She drew energy from the simple, direct ministrations of the American hero she knew would always be there for her.

The thought of him going off to war triggered a quick reaction, and for just a second her lapse created a tear that Roberto must have noticed. She felt his grip tighten on her fingers, squeezing them until it hurt. She tried to relax, willing the salty shimmer to dissipate without running down her cheek and giving away. Miraculously, the tear evaporated and she could see the room clearly again.

This time, when the music ended, he dropped her hands like a hot poker, without the practice bow. She allowed her arms to float back to her sides and then braved a glance into his angry face.

It is what it is, Roberto. Sophia returned his hard glare without apology. She didn't back down. She didn't cower. For the first time she stood close to him, her own chest heaving, but standing tall and unafraid, just as if Mark stood right behind her.

Roberto broke off the eye contact first, which was new. He picked up his towel and blotted his sweaty face and the back of his neck. His nostrils were flaring, his lips pursed and his jaw muscles bunched as he clenched his teeth. She saw understanding sink into his face.

He wouldn't be able to get to her anymore. She had something Roberto would probably never have.

Someone who loved her so much he'd do anything for her. And for the first time in her life she felt the same way.

CHAPTER 18

Mark learned that Moshe's request to have the Moroccans removed from the ship was denied. Moshe had been rather upset to discover that Maksym had negotiated with the office in Miami without consulting him first. Teseo explained to them over dinner that technically Maksym outranked Moshe.

What Mark feared most was that this would bring additional pressure on Roberto, increasing the likelihood that he'd do something irrational. The more Mark watched him, the more convinced he was that Roberto made enemies wherever he went. Sophia told him that his close connection to Matheus's wealthy family had served to protect the volatile Brazilian dancer so far.

Mark had seen men filled with their own bravado become blind to danger. So, while Roberto was focused on competing for Sophia, he might underestimate the danger the Moroccans posed. He could find himself ill prepared, regardless of his extensive street training. Those kinds of fighters were good at the spur of the moment, but ill equipped to handle a well-coordinated and planned attack. It was always their undoing, and something the SEALs specialized in.

"That's fucked up, man," Armando said. "You'd think they'd take the word of their security officer over a junior officer."

Kyle and Cooper agreed. "Maybe the night in lockup has set the Moroccan straight," Cooper offered.

"Not likely," Kyle replied.

Christy, Devon and the rest of the SEAL wives wanted to watch the multi-country extravaganza after dinner, which meant the men had to accompany them. The Team settled in on an upper-level, unoccupied corner next to an exit. The sightlines were excellent, Mark thought.

It was going to be a long night as the ship barreled down the east coast of Africa for its planned stop the next morning in Tenerife.

Mark had arranged to meet Sophia in their cabin after the show. He hung back from the other SEALs and their wives, and already had his backpack equipped with a bottle of champagne, two glasses and some desserts he'd confiscated from the dining room earlier. Sanouk, Rory and Tyler left for the casino to see if they could improve Sanouk's winning streak.

Devon and Christy were looking through brochures for island the tour they had scheduled. Gina had her head on Armando's shoulder, their fingers entwined. Mia sat next to them, with Fredo by her side. Libby claimed not to be feeling well after dinner, so she and Cooper went back to their cabin. Jasmine and Malcolm Jones had peeled off to listen to a singer at the jazz bar downstairs.

A spotlight shone overhead and soon the undulating body of a Chinese contortionist unpeeled herself from a green fabric pod that hung from a trapeze. Her face was covered in bright blue and green peacock-like designs dotted with rhinestones. She did a controlled roll down a swath of red silk, joining the rest of the Chinese acrobatic team who erupted in bright circus animal costumes. Dancers from various countries followed them, including Roberto and Sophia, who danced a smooth, sensual tango that made Mark's hands clench. He nearly tore the arm off the padded auditorium seat. Kyle and Nick were having trouble keeping a straight face. Mark noticed Sophia was careful not to look anywhere near their little group, but he sensed she knew exactly where he sat.

The large samba number incorporated everyone, including the Moroccan dancers with their ancient, reedy musical instruments. Azziz was playing an odd-shaped, tiny, single-stringed base guitar with a small belly. Their rhythmic chanting was backdrop to colorful, rippling dancers showing lots of leg and midriff.

While the production showcased the blending of music and dance from all around the world, and at the end of the grand finale Roberto and Sophia were at one end of the stage, while the Moroccans were all the way at the other.

The audience loved it and demanded an encore. Mark was getting impatient to see Sophia, and get her away from Roberto. The effeminate entertainment director had his face heavily made up like a woman, but sported a tux. He bowed to the side as Roberto acted as the master of ceremonies at the end, introducing the other talent. In a well-aimed display of poor manners, he neglected to introduce the Moroccans. Kyle, Nick and Fredo swore under their breath.

Here we go again. For someone supposedly trying to be on his best behavior, Roberto had pulled off one of the most obvious insults possible. He treated the Moroccans like they didn't exist. Before the curtains could close Roberto looked up into the balcony and waved to the SEALs and their wives. Christy and Devon waved back.

"I'm outta here," Mark said as he hoisted his backpack and quietly ducked outside the exit door.

He came out onto the gray painted surface of the lifeboat deck. He'd already made one trip earlier in the day to leave a couple of soft blankets, a thick bedspread from his own bed, and two pillows. If she wasn't allowed to sleep in his cabin and he wasn't allowed to sleep in hers, he was going to insist they spend the night together in the boat.

He unsnapped the plastic door, carefully setting down the backpack. He heard the glasses clink, and carefully pulled out the French champagne, pushing aside the vinyl padding on the bench seat next to the bed he'd created, and setting the champagne bottle on the emptied framework. He set the two glasses next to it, and then took out two pieces of apple pie he'd pilfered from the kitchen, four chocolate-covered strawberries, and a couple of clean forks. He'd wanted to bring candles, but didn't want to advertise the location of their love nest.

He heard a metallic squeak and then quiet closing of a door that led from the meeting room to the chilly outside. He saw her beautiful face through the clear plastic doorway.

Beads of sweat still clung to her upper lip. Her chest sparkled with glitter, the cleavage of her ample breasts shiny with moisture. Her dancing had released a wonderful womanly scent, her pheromones, which hit him right across the chest, making his breath hitch.

He was going to show her the goodies he'd brought, but she ran to him and held him close.

"What's this?" he asked.

"I've missed you. It's been over twenty-four hours, Mark."

He smiled at her urgency, at her need of him. "I've been thinking about nothing else all day," he whispered just before he covered her mouth with his.

She was mewling into his lips, sucking his tongue as she slid her fingers under his shirt to palm his nipples and then pinch him.

"Ouch."

She giggled, but didn't stop her exploration.

"I've brought champagne, Sophia."

She lazily leaned backward, allowing his arms to support her lower lumbar zone. Her dark eyes, lined in heavy kohl and shimmery green and blue shadow, explored his face while her pink tongue darted out as she licked her red lips. Best of all was the feeling of the warm, feminine triangle at the juncture of her legs, which she slid slowly up and down his upper thigh.

"Wonderful. Feed me some champagne, then," she whispered.

He sat her down on one of the covered benches, sat beside her, propped the champagne bottle between his thighs and opened it. The cork's *pop* echoed off the plastic and metal walls of the boat, and the champagne began to fizz out over the top. Instead of holding a glass underneath it, Mark drizzled the cool bubbles into his mouth, and then held the bottle over hers so she could enjoy the froth, too. Champagne bubbles spilled down her front, making the tops of her breasts glisten in the moonlight.

He pulled her hair clip away, releasing her beautiful curls to tumble over her shoulders, and then he grasped her upper arms to pull her towards him. She smiled and he was filled with need. His hands roamed over her back until he found her zipper, and peeled the red dress from her delicate skin, leaving it pooled around her waist.

He dipped his lips to the place beneath her chin, and kissed his way down, lapping and sucking the champagne tracks. His hands moved to the back of her red bra and he released her pillows of flesh to his waiting lips and tongue.

Again she arched backward as he held her with one arm splayed at her shoulders, bracing her in place, as she separated her thighs and allowed his palm to rub and press against her pubic bone. He could feel the heat of her moisture gather underneath the satin.

She inhaled as he hooked a finger in her panties, pulling them aside to expose her peach. Her nude lips were fondled and separated by his thumb and fingers as he made a slow, circular exploration of her nub, watching her eyes flutter, watching the way her pink tongue darted out between her red lips, calling to him to taste her. He coated his fingers in her milky moisture, feeling the smooth slickness of her ready channel. He removed her panties and slid his two fingers in and out of her opening slowly, rubbing and massaging the delicate petals of her sex.

He liked that she wanted to speed it up, but he planned to take his time with her. He could do this all night, if it came to that. He'd make sure her fire was fully stoked before he plunged in.

She begged him with her eyes, spreading her thighs further. He bent down and licked the length of her, nibbling on her lips, curling his tongue over her nub and sucking her to a stiff peak as she jolted with pleasure.

Sophia was balanced precariously on the padded bench, so he gently slid her down to the floor, on top of the doubled-up bedspread, her head propped on the two pillows he'd brought from his own cabin. Her soft body sank into the light gray fabric, her head into the clean, white cotton of the pillows. Her hips rolling, she bit down on her lower lip, and reached up to spread her hair out to the sides. She held herself, inserting a finger into her own opening, while he undressed without taking his eyes off the way she pleasured herself. Her red dress was still draped across her waist. When he got naked, he lifted her legs by the ankles with one hand and with the other smoothed the dress over her soft bottom and up off her thighs.

He threw her dress behind him and covered her nude body with his own.

She pointed to the champagne bottle and her eyes widened, the crinkly laugh lines expanding at the sides in devilish play.

"You want some champagne? Like I wanted the water?"

She nodded her head.

"Are you going to be quiet tonight?" he whispered.

She shook her head from side to side as he brought the bottle to his lips and drank. He leaned over her and allowed the bubbly to pass from his mouth to hers. He licked the trickles of delicious bubbles down her cheeks, into the hollow at the top of her shoulders at the juncture of her long, graceful neck.

"Sophia, you are the most beautiful woman I have ever met," he said.

"I like the way you make me feel, Mark. My Marko. My mysterious American lover. The man I dream about every night."

"Really? You dream about me?" he whispered to her ear as he nipped her earlobe.

She nodded, one forefinger tracing the line from his lips, down his neck, down the middle of his chest down, down to his package. She reached for him, squeezing him, moving her hand gently up and down his shaft and fingering the moisture at his tip.

Suddenly she sat up, pushing him back onto the spread. Taking the champagne bottle, she took a big sip, then bent down, her breasts touching his chest, her perfumed hair falling all around his face. Her red lips descended over his and she allowed him to drink from her mouth. She followed up what he had done, licking the errant ribbons of champagne down his cheek and neck.

She sat on him, rubbing her mound slowly up and down against his shaft, coaxing him to stiffen and harden even more. He could feel the soft tissues of her sex as she rubbed herself lazily over his crown, teasing him.

She took another sip of the champagne, and with her mouth full, slid down his legs and slipped his cock between her lips, bathing it in the cool liquid, rubbing him with her bubbling tongue. She sucked and lapped at his sensitive skin, suckling his balls, then drawing his shaft deep down her throat, fully enveloping him, then squeezing her lips, encircling his cock as she sucked and pulled him straight up, as hard as a concrete lamppost.

Mark was getting so engorged he thought he might spill prematurely. She purred as she licked him with the sandpaper of her tongue on his underside all the way to his tip, pulling and sucking.

He launched himself up to meet her, chest pressed against chest. "My turn," he said. He held the back of her head and gently helped her back down to the bedspread. He took a big swig of the champagne and leaned over her sex, pouring the champagne over her labia, lapping her as he did, then trickling the liquid slowly down her slit, saving some for her opening, and, with his tongue swirling her insides, let the golden liquid drip down inside her.

Her hips rocked, her abdomen rippling like when she danced. She squeezed her own breasts. He followed up by placing his hands over hers. Taking one last look at her pink folds, he positioned himself at the entrance to her ripe, quivering peach. Her beautiful abs pulled as she gasped in anticipation his rooting. He slowly moved into her, watching her eyes, the way her breasts raised and fell with her heavy breathing, reveling in the feel of her thighs hugging his. Her movements were as liquid as the champagne they'd poured all over each other, the places where their flesh touched igniting the flame inside his soul.

When he was fully seated, he angled back and forth in slow, deliberate motions, moving inside and out of her all the time, watching her face to judge the effect his filling her had on her. Her fingers found his nipples and she twisted one. The pain was delicious. He smiled down on her. She slid her hand between them and ringed the seat of his penis, feeling the place of their joining, squeezing his balls as he filled her delicious cave with his girth, and then stroked back and forth against her internal walls. He couldn't get enough of her. He couldn't touch enough of her softness, her rippling body that wrapped itself so deliciously around him, accepting him, loving him.

He pulled up one of her legs, his palm cupping the soft bend behind her knee and forcing her thigh back to the side of her chest. He twisted his body to move at a slight angle, adjusting his knees until he was perpendicular to her. She rolled to her side as he pumped her in deep rhythmic movements eliciting rolling moans. He pushed into her as far as he could go, desperate to encase himself fully in her warm channel.

She kept turning until she was on her belly. He was still buried in her channel, and spread her cheeks wide as he moved to his knees. He pulled an orange life vest from under the bench and slid it under her lower abdomen to raise her hips, allowing him deeper penetration. She groped for the blanket, squeezing as she moaned into the fabric, pushing her sex up and onto his shaft. She reached back, leaning on her shoulders and reached behind, finding his butt cheeks. She pulled him into her, grinding him deep, squeezing his flesh until his ass burned.

He leaned forward, smoothing a palm along the ridge of her spine, tracing a finger along the indentation all the way to her neck, all the while pumping into her, forcing her knees apart further. His other hand went underneath her, pressing a thumb on her nub. He ran his thumb over and over her clit, feeling the juices flowing from her.

She buried her head in her hands, using her knees to prop her little sex up against him. Spreading her legs outside his, she pressed herself against him. Her jerking motions told him she was ready to shatter. He became desperate to taste her.

He flipped her over. Sophia wore a dazed expression, already fully engulfed in orgasm. He pulled himself out and placed his mouth on her sex and sucked while she vibrated against his tongue. She came for him, moaning his name over and over again as he tasted her.

"Yes, baby," he said between kisses. "I've got you. Come for me, baby."

She raised her pelvis up to his mouth again, watched his face as he devoured her pleasure.

"You taste so good, Sophia. I've never tasted anything so wonderful. Ever. Come some more for me, baby."

She writhed, moving her hips in figure eights. His tongue darted in and out while her lips swelled. He felt the hot, pulsing squeeze of her insides.

"Inside, Mark. I want you inside."

"Yes, baby." He inserted himself again, felt her delicious ripples, and the friction of her swollen lips, and the pulsations coming strong. She spilled over the edge, her ecstasy exploding all around him. He felt the tightening in his balls as he began to spill seed inside her, riding her orgasm, stoking the fire of her desire, which engulfed both of them.

CHAPTER 19

Kyle was told Mark hadn't slept in his bed the night before, and that some of his sheets and pillows were missing. He hoped his buddy had been careful, staying out of sight from Roberto and any of the other crew or staff.

Christy returned to the cabin after a workout with Gina and Devon. Kyle knew they were supposed to get ready for the shore excursion on Tenerife, but he'd decided to take of this rare opportunity—he was being lazy and not feeling one ounce of guilt. He watched the blue sky and deeper blue-green waters of the ocean, furrowed by white caps in the wake of the ship.

Christy climbed into bed with him and they looked out the window together.

"What's wrong?" He knew when Christy climbed into bed with all her clothes on, even if they were skimpy workout clothes, that she wanted to be close to talk to him. Close enough that she could kiss away any concerns he might have.

"I think Libby's pregnant again, and she's just as sick as the last time."

It had been hard for all of them when she lost the baby at almost four months, even though Coop had been around to console her. The wives took turns cooking for Coop, cleaning their house and letting Libby sleep until she got her strength back and her head cleared. She'd taken it as a personal failure that the baby didn't survive the early pregnancy.

But this time things could be worse. Coop would be gone, since the Team was going to deploy shortly after they returned to San Diego. All of them had seen what it did to a man who had troubles at home. Wives and kids could get sick. Parents and grandparents passed away. Life didn't just stop because they were overseas. It was a hard fact of life in the military, but especially for the SEALs, since they would frequently be out of communication for weeks at a time.

Christy was the one to organize the help, and he was proud of her for it. He brushed the hair off her forehead with his fingers, and let her slip her arms around his waist and snuggle close to him.

"I think she'll do fine this time, Christy. She's stronger than anyone gives her credit for."

"I'm worried, all the same."

"Not everyone can crank them out as easily as you can, babe."

She was quiet. He reared back on the pillow and twisted to take a look at what he could see of her face.

"What?" he asked.

"I want another one. Brandon needs a little brother or sister."

Kyle was thrilled, but didn't want to make the load any heavier than it already was since the Team was leaving so soon. He didn't like the idea of Christy being pregnant when he couldn't be home for it. He'd loved being able to watch every part of the process when Brandon was born since they flew him home just in time for his birth.

"We talked about waiting until I get back." He watched her eyes. Unspoken was always the consideration he might not come back. She wouldn't be the first wife to want to retain a little piece of him stateside, just in case.

But in matters of the family, and their having children, Christy was the boss. She gave him a warm, shy smile.

"All right, then," he said. "Suppose we work on that before breakfast." He kissed her neck and upper chest, following a trail between her breasts until he encountered the stretchy fabric of her sports bra.

"Can't I take a shower first?" she asked.

"I think it's completely unnecessary. I plan to get you good and sweaty all over again. Besides, I love the way you smell right now, Christy."

"Yes," she said as she sighed into one of his long kisses. "When you come home, from the gym, I feel the same way," she whispered as she smoothed over the seam between his lips with her fingertips.

"So what'll it be?" he asked. He pretended she would automatically know what he meant, and loved watching her beautiful brain struggle to come up with an answer.

As she turned her head slowly from side to side and furrowed her brow, she said, "I don't know what you mean."

He tasted her lips, and then kissed her slow and went down to tease the place she loved beneath her ear. She arched to him, her thigh seeking the bulge between his legs. He rubbed himself against her knee and upward against her muscled thigh.

Into her ear he whispered, "We do it slow and sensual, make it long and make it last. Or, we do it rough and urgent."

"Ah," she said as a knowing smile crossed her face.

"So what'll it be, girl, or boy?"

"And you can serve me up a male or female child by the way you make love to me?"

Kyle angled his face and winked, then shook his head, "No, *we* make a boy or a girl." He kissed her again, this time pressing and searching with his tongue.

His face migrated down her chest until he sucked her nipple through the stretchy fabric of her workout bra, and then nipped her through the cotton. Her reaction was immediate, always what he loved best about her. She threw herself into whatever mood he was in, and he cherished every moan, every sigh, and every gentle thigh on thigh stroke, every time she showed him how much she wanted him. She bit her lower lip, her eyes sparkling.

"So, how do you know that slow and long makes a girl and urgent and rough makes a boy?"

"Because, my love," he said as he lifted her sports bra and sucked the nipple bared to him until it knotted, "when I'm with you, anything is possible. *Anything.*"

Most of their group ate on the ninth floor deck, where Italian rock videos blared on twenty-foot-high screens. Mark joined them, picking up two glasses of the fresh squeezed orange juice from the machine behind the bar. He finished the two glasses in barely two gulps, and then went in search of the omelet maker inside. It was going to be a very warm day, even though it was still winter, and most the passengers were in tank tops and sleeveless dresses, applying sunscreen to their pale arms and wearing floppy hats. He noted that the Germans liked to carry walking sticks, while the French and Italians preferred zippered fanny packs.

He and the rest of his Teammates who planned to go ashore wore knee-length kakis, flip-flops and white T-shirts. All wore sunglasses, and most of them wore a baseball cap of some kind, none of the caps with any logo identifying them as Navy, or any sort of military. Though they had them, they never wore their dog tags.

He felt eyes on his back and checked over his shoulder to see Roberto deep in a discussion with two older Brazilian passengers seated at a table by the window. Though Roberto seemed fully engaged in the conversation, Mark saw he didn't miss anything. He watched everyone around him, and when the Brazilian dancer made eye contact, his skin pricked. Perhaps Roberto knew she hadn't slept in her cabin last night. Mark could smell her on his skin still, had been reluctant to shower off her flowery scent , but hoped no one else could smell it.

He'd known the dance instructor search for them. Eventually, he would find them. It was only a matter of time, and Mark slowly began an assessment of the threat. He decided he might risk stashing a weapon on the lifeboat just in case their spot was discovered and things became violent, especially since he was some distance from his Teammates when he and Sophia were alone on Deck 5. Preparing and arming himself suddenly seemed prudent. He wasn't going to tell her about it, though.

Libby sat closest to the railing, nursing a glass of ginger ale along with a piece of Cooper's toasted bagel. Mark thought she looked pale and preoccupied. Cooper hardly left her side, rubbed her back, her neck and shoulders, asking her questions and barely getting her attention.

Mark set his tray of oatmeal, omelet, hash browns, sausage and bitter black coffee down across from Coop and Libby. Immediately, Libby turned and looked out to sea.

"She's not well?" Mark asked quietly.

Coop studied the side of her face before answering. "We're not quite sure what is making her so sick, but we think she's pregnant. Won't know until we can get to a lab."

"But I was sick as a dog the last time," Libby said as she turned to face Coop.

"I remember that," Mark said gently. He also remembered Cooper being concerned last time that her violent vomiting might harm the baby, a concern that might have been justified.

"You're going to be fine, babe," Coop said a little too cheerily. He'd forgotten to tell his face to support his words, and the worry line above the bridge of his nose was deep, pulling in the skin around his eyes, as he squinted.

Mark decided to try to be more helpful. "The ship was really rocking and rolling last night. I think you may just be a little seasick."

The comment sent Libby dashing for the automatic teak wood doors inside.

Coop gave him a deadpan stare. "Thanks." He curled up the side of his mouth.

"Maybe if she gets sick she'll feel better."

"She's been throwing up all night and she still doesn't feel better. She has practically nothing in her stomach." He held up a half bagel that looked like a mouse had nibbled on the outsides, barely touched. Mark saw the ginger ale was still half full.

Cooper's phone buzzed. He checked the screen. "She's gone to the cabin. I gotta go."

Mark moved over to a long table where Fredo and Mia sat across from Armando and Gina. Armando was studying Fredo, a wide smile plastered across his handsome, tanned face that Mark recognized as a taunt. Fredo had been avoiding eye contact with the Puerto Rican SEAL, and looked pitifully grateful when Mark joined them to take some of Armando's focus off him.

"Hey, Marky," Fredo said eagerly, punching his left bicep. "Where'd you sneak off to last night?"

"I was on patrol."

"I feel you," Fredo said. Mia wrapped her arms around his bicep, squeezed herself to him and leaned her head full of curls against his shoulder. Fredo avoided looking at Armando, and wiggled his unibrow at Mark instead.

"Fredo here's been on a mission of his own," Armando said.

"Stop it Armando," Gina chided, playfully smacking his arm. "You're terrible."

"No," Armando said as he nodded and stared at his coffee cup and empty plate. "Terrible would have been what I'd be if anyone but Fredo was cozy with my sister."

Mia straightened. "There you go again," Mia huffed. "Why do I always feel like you're my father? You don't approve, just say something."

"Like it would do any good," Armando returned quickly, but he was still beaming, showing he didn't really object to any of it.

Gina sighed and shook her head, crossing her arms. "I can only imagine what it was like in your household growing up," she said.

"Damned straight. He practically taste-tested my food, too."

"Well, Mama did hire that voodoo cook, you remember that? When she took on that extra job that one summer?" Armando said, pointing his forefinger at her.

"Oh, please, how could I ever forget? The one who liked meat practically raw?"

"I'm sure glad Libby isn't listening to this conversation," Mark interjected. On that they all agreed.

Mia slipped her hand into Fredo's lap and squeezed him in front of everyone. "Ready, hon?"

Fredo looked up, as if he was asking for help from Mama Guzman's God, and then stood.

"It could be worse, my man," Armando said, grinning up at him.

The two of them finally smiled cordially. "Wasn't complaining, just that—"

"He likes me to surprise him, but pretends he doesn't." Mia winked at Gina. "But he does...trust me, he *really* does."

Mark watched the little SEAL and his bombshell walk away, their arms wrapped around each other. He was happy for Fredo, who was finally getting to exercise his protective nature. Mark knew he'd lay his life down in a heartbeat for Mia, and would have done so even before she returned his feelings.

He longed for the day he could openly show his affection to Sophia, bring her to breakfasts and dinners with his Teammates. He didn't like that she spent so much time in a windowless cabin on zero deck, or sliding down the hallway anywhere near the Moroccan dance troupe, or around Roberto with his frustrated, third-grade libido.

CHAPTER 20

Two of Azziz's friends went with Maksym to the holding cell to let the Moroccan dancer loose. The Ukrainian officer didn't mistake the hatred that flared in the dancer's eyes. He decided to do a little diversion as he unlocked the cell.

"Are you even a dancer?" he asked.

He heard some Arabic dialect he couldn't understand. Someone was translating for someone else.

"We all dance in our village. We have for centuries," Azziz returned in Russian, with icy coolness.

"But you've been carrying a rifle more than your one-stringed, sorry-looking guitar," he said in English. Maksym's surprise that the dancer knew Russian stuck in his throat like a fishhook.

"It could do serious damage if I fucked you in the ass with it," Azziz said in Russian again. The two cohorts rattled off something between them and laughed.

"Seriously," Maksym said, sticking stubbornly to English. "You juveniles are going to ruin the whole mission if you don't get your souls right with God."

The Moroccans jabbered among themselves again. Maksym knew he should have learned Berber, but had wondered at the time if he'd ever need it again. He was hoping for an island in the Caribbean or someplace else warm where he and Helena could retire and explore their passions without interruption.

He'd be as far away from the Middle East or Russia as humanly possible, basking on a sandy beach as white and flawless as the insides of her thighs. He'd be some place that was a tax haven, with more money than he could spend in his lifetime, buying fish and coconuts and occasional beers down by the wharf.

He heard Allah's name. English was such a much better language to swear in, he thought. He regretted the Moroccans could understand it. It robbed him of the satisfaction of spewing his venom in a way that kept the meaning private, but still making the public display. Nothing better than telling your enemy you despise him while robbing him of the translation. Made it extra sweet. The world was getting to be a smaller place. Harder and harder to do now.

Patience, Maksym, Helena had said many times. He was looking forward to not having to be patient, cordial, nice, or in charge of anything but the way she moaned and pleasured him. How often he could fuck, where he could fuck and with whom, and how often he could just get drunk and lie on the beach. He wondered why, in the bowels of the ship with three smelly Moroccans, he was suddenly filled with lust for the busty and vibrant Helena.

The SEALs darted wary looks at the three dancers as they sauntered down the crew hallway. Maksym rounded the corner toward them, but he was watching the dancers over his shoulder like he was bracing for an explosion. Mark noted how troubled the junior officer looked, in his dark and brooding way. The North Africans were speaking in clipped shouts to each other, flailing their arms about, far from settled. In front of one of the doors, the tall one, the one Mark saw as the leader of the group, stood and spat at the floor in front of the closed door to a cabin. The man arched his chest like a bow as if challenging the metal and plastic door itself.

Mark saw Maksym react quickly, shake his head and rub his chin, absorbed in some dark thought. When Maksym glanced up and their gazes connected, he saw the officer's dark eyes widen and challenge him. Mark looked away, not because he was afraid, but because he didn't want Maksym to know he was on to the guy. Something had set off alarm bells in Mark's gut, and he needed space to consider what it actually was. It all stemmed from what he'd seen. He'd learned to trust his instincts, know when something just wasn't right.

He wondered why Kyle had given permission for Christy and the other SEAL wives and girlfriends to stray further than Mark thought safe. Surely his LPO could pick up on some of the dangers lurking all around them. Maybe he'd had a private talk with Moshe and had some inside knowledge that left him feeling unconcerned. It would be like Kyle to check things out, do the advance survey of the situation.

Mark pretended not to notice Maksym hadn't stopped drilling a stare into him. "Kyle, shouldn't we wait for the ladies?" he finally asked, hoping to get the attention off him. It was his way of telling Kyle he was worried.

"We're hiring our own bus. I want to make sure his creds check out before I'm letting any of the girls get on it," Kyle answered. "And Moshe said he'd accompany them."

"Thought he wasn't on this tour," Fredo barked.

"He wasn't. He's agreed to accompany us," Kyle replied.

"So we got the fuckin' bus all to ourselves, then?" Coop asked.

"Roger that. You do your sweeps, Coop and Fredo," Kyle added as he nodded to his two trusty gadget guys.

The shiny silver and red bus was in much better condition than the buses the rest of the passengers were herded onto. The driver was an acquaintance of Moshe's, who came bouncing off the ship with all the ladies in tow, looking like he was thoroughly enjoying himself.

Mark leaned into Kyle and Cooper. "Somethin's wrong with that picture, gents."

Kyle pushed his baseball cap back off his forehead and repositioned his sunglasses. "Way too much fun for him," he said and grinned.

Coop was frowning.

"She not there?" Kyle had turned to Coop, his voice barely a whisper.

Coop shook his head. He faced his LPO, holding his arms out to the side. "Don't know why she didn't text, but guys, I gotta stay back."

"Sure, you go, Coop. Take care of your woman."

Cooper jogged past the ladies surrounding a delighted Moshe, tipping his cap to them. He ran up the gangway, but was stopped and asked to go back down and up the other side. Mark was grateful he'd been stopped. He would have run into the Moroccan dancers, who burst from the bowels of the lower deck. Each sported matching new-looking black backpacks and sunglasses.

Their small, skinny frames made them look like high school kids on a field trip.

Coop disappeared, ducking inside the ship just as the dancers made it out into the morning sun from the other gangplank. They gingerly swerved around the Israeli and his harem, one of them looking over his shoulder at the girls. The other two squinted at the group of SEALs gathered next to the shiny red bus. Mark could tell Azziz had no intention of getting anywhere near the Team guys, or any of the other passengers. They quietly vanished into the crowd of taxis and small delivery trucks littering the pier.

Kyle wrapped his big arm around Christy, hauled her into him to give her a penetrating kiss as he, and then practically carried her up the bus stairs. Devon pulled Nick up the steps right behind Christy. The two had been pretty inseparable, since they both worked in real estate and had similar all-out shopping habits. Jones and Jasmine stood close. Mia and Fredo were walking with their arms around each other's waists.

"Boss, where's Armando?" Mark asked after he stepped up into the darkened bus.

Kyle gave his movie star smile, complete with the white teeth and dazzling blue eyes. He winked at his wife. "Mark, I didn't think I'd have to spell it out for you. You see, when a man and a woman—"

"Shut the fuck up." Mark was getting irritated. The whole world was in love and could show it. Here he was, in some form of love or lust, and he had to keep it a secret *for the good of all.*

All is a fuckin' killjoy. It felt like politics, just like the directives handed down telling them when they could or could not engage, and which sometimes cost good men and women their lives. Because of a decision made by someone who would never see a war zone and didn't know what it felt like to put his or her life on the line.

But that had always been the way of it for the warriors of the world. Most days he accepted that. He didn't like what was happening today, though, with innocents being exposed to crossfire.

Even if the crossfire was imaginary.

CHAPTER 21

Tenerife was quaint. The weather was perfect, with a wide, cloudless sky and views out to sea from the narrow switchback roads to the top of the volcano's caldera. The air was slightly breezy but temperate, and Mark could see why European settlers had stayed up in the hills, away from the hot, crowded beaches below.

Cobblestoned streets adorned by upper-story windows with flower-laden balconies curled along rows of buildings built hundreds of years ago by Portuguese merchants. Birds chirped in the blooming bougainvillea vines that covered several cathedrals and storefronts. Sailboats looked like toys on the blue water sprinkled with whitecaps.

Mark felt time stood still here. He could easily come back to this place, spend a month in one of those upper rooms with the flowers on the balcony, watch the boats, eat and sleep and make love to Sophia all day long. Scanning the groups of tourists disembarking from busses, he was glad to know some people still got to live that way.

Maybe someday. Maybe when my work is done, when I am no longer on the front lines, maybe there'll be something like this in my future.

He'd been pushing so hard for so many years, he wasn't entirely sure it was possible. Just look at this cruise, for instance. He was more tense right now than he was sometimes in the killing fields overseas. Of course, the women weren't there, like they were here. He was aware that violence in a place where you least expect it is even more shocking. It bothered him that he was expecting it and didn't think anyone else on the Team was.

Kyle was walking hand in hand with Christy.

Nah, he's got to have the same radar I have.

One of the buses backfired as it headed up the hill after spilling its content of tourists. His group's immediate reaction was to cover the women because the echo sounded like gunfire. As the men straightened their muscular frames, Mark saw Sophia standing amidst a cluster of adults. After temporarily lowering a yellow sign with the number 5 on it, she extended her arm up and stood straight, like a beacon for the confused tourists who had scattered into the courtyard.

Their eyes met. He felt his delicious attraction to her, the need to protect her, go to her and give comfort and aid. And of course, more, if he was totally honest.

Kyle brought the group into a cooperative artisan studio while Mark headed straight for Sophia. He checked with his LPO before they could disappear through the doorway of the shop, and all he saw was Kyle's three-finger salute.

Frantic Italian was being spoken all around him, but everything faded as he came upon her, giving her a hug. "You okay?" he asked before he could let her go. She wasn't squirming, but God, the urge to kiss her was overwhelming.

"Happens all the time. I've got the jitters, I guess, just like everyone else," she said in a whisper back at him. "Thanks." Then she leaned in close to his ear. "Tonight?"

He nodded. She held up her hands, making five on one hand and three on the other. *Eight.*

Mark stepped backwards to follow Kyle and the rest of his group, and motioned with one hand and a single digit. *Six.*

She frowned as her group of tourists charged him, headed for the shop opening as well. She held her hands up again, and shrugged. *Eight.*

He blew her a kiss and nodded, disappearing inside before her enthusiastic group overran him.

Mark slipped around the corner just inside, behind a display of hanging tablecloths. As Sophia crossed the threshold, he pulled her arm, yanking her into the private space beneath the bright yellow and white, hand-embroidered tablecloths. Amid lace and fresh linen smell, he claimed her lips, holding her tight against his package. He was rewarded with the little whimper he now dreamed about just about every waking second of the day.

"Baby, we gotta get you fired. I can't handle this," he said as his hands roamed over her ass, as he felt the delicious juncture between her legs press against the ridge of his erection. Sophia's sighs and smooth skin were adding fuel to the fire that was ignited because this was something they were not supposed to do, but couldn't help themselves. She giggled as he quickly reached inside the back of her pants and squeezed the flesh of her butt cheeks.

"Marko, Marko, il mio amore, ho bisogno del tuo tocco così tanto che non lo sopporto." she whispered.

"Don't know what you said, sweetheart, but liking love that you used that word *amore*—that one I recognize, at least."

"Marko, Marko," she said breathlessly into his mouth, "I am consumed by you."

"Well that I love, too. You're best in English, but I'll take whatever you can dish out, baby." He hugged her close, kissing the side of her neck, loving the feel of her urgency for him. He usually found himself holding some woman off, usually felt smothered. With Sophia, he wanted it all. Wanted even more. Being wrapped up in white linen and flowers didn't temper his libido. Her tiny growl like a small bear cub was such a turn-on, he couldn't focus on anything else.

Until Kyle pulled back the tablecloths and exposed them.

"Gezuz. Fuckin. Christ." he barked, "Just get a room, would ya?"

Sophia's eyes widened as she pulled her hand from the front of Mark's pants and held her own up, since Mark had unbuttoned her top two buttons.

Mark wasn't sure what to say. He was embarrassed for Sophia. Several of her charges were peering at her above Kyle's shoulder, with nods of approval.

"Don't think you two realized you were not nearly as under cover as you thought." He pointed down to their feet. Mark could see that even though most their bodies were hidden, anyone could have seen them from just below their knees to their tennis shoes. His insides smiled at the thought that he hadn't noticed something he would have had eagle eyes for in the arena. Her proximity was changing him, and he actually liked it.

"All right, kiddies. Just didn't want you guys to properly embarrass yourselves. My job is done," Kyle said, grinning and throwing Sophia his blue charm. He let the tablecloths fall back around them.

"I guess we better wait for 8 o'clock, then, baby?"

"I think so. But I won't be thinking of anything else but what you're going to do to me in that little boat at eight."

"Count on it."

Mark watched her thread her way through the rows of leather purses, through displays of necklaces and lace shawls. Her little smiles thrilled him. She was sighing as she talked to people, a blush on her cheeks. She'd scan the room, looking for him, and he'd hide, only to pop out when she least expected it. He'd walk in front of her, trying to cut through a line, and brush against her, leaning down to whisper, "Excuse me, darlin'," in front of her group, who seemed to be enjoying it as much as he was.

He'd not felt this preoccupied by a woman in his entire life. Just being goofy, playing little tricks on her, finding any excuse to get his fingers on a sensitive body part of hers in some totally inappropriate but hidden way, was so much fun he didn't want to join his group on the bus when Kyle signaled him.

"Remember what Moshe said, Mark."

"I don't fuckin' care," he said. The rest of their group had mounted the bus steps. "I'm in love with her, man."

"Sure you are. Who wouldn't be," Kyle said.

"Fuck you, Kyle. It isn't like that." He was looking for Sophia's group, since their bus had also arrived.

"Come on, you sick puppy. Maybe I can get some beers into you at lunch and then you'll wise up."

Mark frowned. "Like when you met Christy? That kind of wise? You fuckin' almost forgot to pull your cord one time, I'm told."

"That'd never happen and you know it," Kyle said as he patted Mark on the shoulder. "You're gonna need your strength, so let's hit the road. "

Mark did as instructed. As they pulled out of the parking lot, he waved to Sophia, just before he saw Roberto come barreling out of a private taxi and head straight for her.

"Wait! Wait!" he called out to the driver, who stopped. He began to run down the aisle, Kyle right after him, trying to restrain him.

"No you don't. You stay right here."

"That Brazilian dick just drove up in his taxi. Not leaving her alone with him." Kyle shrugged his shoulders, resigned to letting him go. "We're waiting, then," but he turned to face a sea of groans. "Okay, I guess we're not."

Mark ran toward Sophia. Roberto had hold of her wrist and, just as he had done in the dance demonstration, had twisted it back painfully.

There was only one course of action, and Mark knew it wasn't smart at all. The Brazilian immediately crouched for the blow he thought he was going to get. At the last minute, Mark landed a kick to the dancer's knees and watched as he nearly collapsed on the cobblestones. But the guy was like a cat, pushing off with his hands and righting himself, throwing Mark a roundhouse kick that sent him back into a flowerbed.

"Stop it!" Sophia shouted. Several tour bus drivers stood by watching stoically. No way would there be assistance coming from any of those rotund gentlemen. A shopkeeper was on her cell phone. Mark figured she was calling the local police, and he didn't want anything to do with them.

"You leave her alone," Mark said as he righted himself. Roberto had a wild, almost feral look in his dazed eyes. His grin and squint were pure evil. "She's not yours to abuse and play with. Especially now," Mark added.

The wide smile he got back would have been sickeningly sweet, if it hadn't been for the hatred shooting from the dancer's eyes. "She is not yours."

Like hell she's not. I own every cell in her body, and that's the way she wants it, you cretin.

Mark backed up, trying to look compliant in case the police were just around the corner. He didn't mind that he looked weak to the emboldened Brazilian, who was still going to come after him. Sore loser didn't even begin to describe the man. *Deranged* was closer.

The sound of the two-toned police or emergency vehicle pierced the sunny late morning. Roberto rubbed his palms on his designer jeans and sneered at Mark, who still stood in the flowerbed. Sophia was distraught.

The shopkeeper ran to meet the little blue and white car, and entered into a heated discussion. The two police got out slowly and sauntered over to Roberto, who didn't appear to notice them, his glare was so focused on Mark.

Although Mark wasn't sure, it appeared the shopkeeper had told them Mark had come to Sophia's aid. He decided it was safe to walk over to her, but she met him halfway and flew into his arms.

The signs of a budding love and a third wheel were probably obvious to the police, who took Roberto away in the car without handcuffing him. The diabolical laser look he shot from the rear window as he was being driven off would have been exciting, if it didn't mean more problems for them all aboard the cruise ship.

"What was he so pissed off about?" Mark asked her.

"I was supposed to help him this afternoon. But the tour won't get back in time. I left him a message, because I knew he wouldn't let me go."

"He can't do that, baby. He doesn't own you."

She wept into his chest. "He scares me, Mark. He really scares me now."

"I know it's not what you want to hear, but maybe it's about time you called your fiancé and told him what is going on."

"I can't do that."

"Why? Sweetheart, maybe he could help."

"He'll know. Matheus will know. He'll dig it out of me."

And there he was. He was fucked in so many ways. He knew this was the woman who could rock his world, not a replacement for Sophie, but her Italian twin, the fun-loving woman who would bring him back alive.

Although it was confusing, he loved the being totally at the mercy of this little woman. The urge to protect, keep safe, and claim her for himself alone was clouding his judgment. Yet he willingly went there. He'd fallen for her so easily it made him dizzy. Some common sense drained into him as his little head settled down for a nice nap.

So, even though it wasn't wise, he had to ask her. "Just when were you going to tell Matheus? Or is that not in your plan, Sophia?"

Her confused look broke his heart.

Just great. She hasn't gotten to that part yet.

So was it going to be like this? She hadn't made up her mind. She needed him, but was it in the right kind of way? And, once again, had he jumped in and fallen for a woman he couldn't have? One he'd met too late and she'd died on him. And this one, with her whole life deliciously ahead of her, achingly alive and so full of the spirit of life itself, a life that was something he wanted to be a part of in some way, this one had made a different choice. Who was he to question that choice? Make her come to a decision for him, when she hadn't convinced herself?

The sad look she gave him was just as hard as watching her die in front of him like Sophie.

"Ah, I get it. You're going to use the cruise to make up your mind. I mean, why tell him about us if you might still want to marry him when we get to Rio, that what you're saying?"

"No, Mark. That isn't it."

"Then what is it, Sophia? 'Cause I gotta know." He held her delicate pointed chin with his thumb and two forefingers. Her warm brown eyes were moist with the early signs of some serious tears. She was filled with the lust for him, he could see that. Hell, he could almost smell it. But she was on overwhelm, confused.

And that wasn't any good for him. Not that it stopped his heart from wanting to reach out from his chest and pull her to him. Not that it was going to soothe the ache he felt at, once again, not being able to have something he so desperately believed was right on so many levels.

"I need a little time to think. This has all happened so fast for me, Mark."

"Me too, baby." Anything else he would say would be just bullshit. Like, "Oh it's okay, take as much time as you want. I don't want you until you can commit a hundred percent. No sense getting involved if it isn't going to go anywhere."

Those were the lies he would have said, if he'd not cared so much for her, and for himself. If he couldn't be honest, he'd say nothing. She was going to have to come to him, because he didn't like the man he'd be to take her away from someone else. He'd told himself she'd made the choice already.

You fuckin' miscalculated.

He realized how his timing sucked. Finally free from having to worry about Roberto, so they could spend the entire night together, anywhere they wanted, not just on the little boat, now he couldn't do that because it would be wrong.

He thought about her all the way back to town as he rode in Roberto's taxi, even having to bear the humiliation of paying for the Brazilian's ride up the mountain, as well as his ride down.

Yeah. Your timing sucked big time. And now you're going to go back to the ship and gamble too much, ogle someone's ugly daughter or be the fantasy come true for some older woman sitting at the bar.

There was nothing honorable about the way heartache felt.

Or about the way it could be medicated.

But he was going to give it the college try.

At port, he found the Moroccans lined up in front the glass picture windows of a port agent set up to handle requests from the crew. A bank of phones was on one wall, occupied two and three deep with people of every nationality. Bundles were being shipped home, mail retrieved. The Moroccans carried a box so heavy that required two of them to manage, and after they went out the doors without seeing him, they headed for the belly of the ship.

Mark wanted to know what was in that box and why it was so heavy. He knew it wasn't costumes or an instrument.

One of them tripped on the gangway's bottom rung and the box landed on one corner. The tall one was shouting so much he drew lots of attention. When he saw Mark watching them, he shut up and bent his shoulder and all his attention to the task at hand. The three of them worked as one crab-like unit, doing something in unison they all clearly felt was important.

That worried Mark the most. He would have to tell Kyle about it and see if Moshe could take a look inside that package. Just in case something was about to go down. He had that sixth sense.

Maybe it was good Sophia wouldn't be wrapping her thighs around his waist tonight. Maybe he needed to think, too.

CHAPTER 22

Maksym was restless and didn't like the news he'd received today, delivered in clipped Russian, even though the Moroccan knew how much he hated it and could speak almost perfect English.

The Wolf had delivered a package to the shipping station at Tenerife, and Maksym was told to arrange that the dancers, or whatever the hell they were, be allowed off ship to claim it.

He'd had conversations with the Wolf back in Genoa, and then again in Savona. But since the ship had left port, not a word from him, except through the Moroccan mob. He wondered where the guy had found these yo-yos. He didn't doubt that they could fight and fight hard. But did they fight smart?

The answer to that question was a resounding *no.*

So why, then, would the Wolf put his trust and faith in them, and not in him, an experienced Ukrainian naval officer. Who was now third or fourth in line to run a cruise ship, of course. But no matter, he still was plenty busy being responsible for more people than these skinny terrorists would meet in a whole lifetime. He'd been a war hero, for chrissakes. He had medals, even though he couldn't show them off now. He'd given them to his girls as a parting gift, the only thing, other than his DNA, that he could leave them. Before they left his left forever.

Helena had come into his life at just the right moment. He'd been morose and spending time at bars in Prague, where he enjoyed the flow of the city, where he could get drunk every night and not be hated. He liked to take his medicine down at little dives by the river, since being close to any waterway was soothing for him, and so he wouldn't make a spectacle of himself at some expensive restaurant in the old town square. He liked the city before they painted all the buildings yellow and bright rose. The Russian period. And, of course, the waterfront girls were more grateful. A little bit of money went a long way for a weary seaman away from home and family, such as himself.

That had been a mistake. He'd fallen in love with a dancer, Eniko. Her long, shapely form was a thing of beauty. He watched her and, for a bit, didn't worry about what his wife was doing late at night, working for the Russian Embassy. The girls were safe. He was making good money. And he needed a little release.

Eniko had first fucked him in a farmer's field after one of her gigs. He drove her there, and she didn't ask. She gave the best head he'd ever experienced, but her hot, lithe body made him hard again almost instantly and they fucked like rabbits so hard, his knees had bloodied.

She was a fun girl with simple needs. He must have looked to her like a knight in shining armor. He'd forgotten to tell her about the wife and kids, and when he came home one day and found her sitting in his living room, across from his wife, he knew he'd seriously messed his life, or what was left of it. He suspected it would cost him his family, and it did.

Of course, what he didn't know at the time was that his wife was already banging the diplomat and making her exit plans. He'd lost his wife that day, he'd thought, because of his own stupidity. Truth was, he'd lost her nearly six months earlier. All he managed to do that day was break Eniko's heart, too. The sweet little dancer who naively thought she would surprise him. She deserved way more than she got. Way more.

Afterwards, he'd tried to call her, to make things right, but each time she rebuffed him. And who could blame her? She was a beautiful girl, a good girl, and he was a dog of the first order.

So when Helena came into his life, he already considered himself a flawed man with needs all the women in the world couldn't satisfy. What he'd really been looking for was someone who could command *him*. He didn't care if it wasn't love. He just liked that she enjoyed pushing him around and surprising him to death and back. The sex was like glue that held them together until maybe something else could show up.

No, life with Helena was what he deserved now. He'd played by some rules and gotten caught breaking some others. She was a perfect match for his appetites, and he made her feel like she wasn't with someone too dangerous. Underneath all her bravado, was a scared little girl with daddy issues. She knew how to take care of herself by riding men to the top of their careers and getting out just before the fall, switching ponies so she never had to worry about being dragged into some despicable lot in life. Maksym thought of her as smart.

Smart women made him hard.

He had an hour's leave from the bridge since they were still in port, and he needed to check with his chief of engineering. The bowels of the ship were usually hot and sweaty. Didn't make it easier that the laundry was also nearby and fresh soap and moist air mixed with the smells of the huge diesel engines made it almost feel like home to a seaman. He knew many engineers who would rather stay all day with their equipment and didn't care a fuck for where the ship was headed or where it docked. His guy was like that.

Anton Boiko had served under him in the Navy and had been the best chief engineer he'd ever had. He didn't know much about the man, except for his all-consuming hatred of the Russians, which was one of Maksym's top requirements for Maksym. Only thing better than hijacking an American vessel would have been to hijack a Russian vessel. But the Russians placed no value on the passenger's lives, like the Americans did. And the American companies had insurance, something that was problematic in Russia. It did keep the lawsuits down, however.

Boiko was cleaning a metal part with a dirty, oil-stained rag. He'd taken to wearing red bandanas around his neck like a pirate. His little act of defiance, if anyone had looked too closely. Though it was forbidden, Boiko also smoked like a chimney. One look from the ruddy red-faced hulk of a man, who easily outweighed Maksym by more than thirty-five kilos, nearly eighty pounds, and whoever was going to ask him not to smoke quickly changed their minds. Boiko didn't allow anyone else to smoke, though.

"I trust myself not to blow us all up. I have no such trust for anyone else," he'd told Maksym one day when he questioned it. He liked that his engineer didn't smoke while the ship was fully powered up, something he found rare on the crews. Anton kept his mouth shut and was loyal, keeping to himself. But Maksym could always count on him to let him know if trouble was brewing.

His engineer knew what their plans were: to stop the ship, allow pirates to take over, and hold the entire contingent of passengers hostage until ransom was paid. When they received verification the funds had been deposited in the Maltese bank accounts they opened before they set sail, they'd be transported to the coast of Brazil and left to find their own to find their way to the Caribbean. Boiko was the only person Maksym would allow to travel with him and Helena.

The simple plan was relatively risk free, since Maksym wouldn't be identified as one of the terrorists. He just had to make sure the ship stopped where it was supposed. He'd allow himself to be taken hostage on the pirate vessel, like he was sacrificing something. They'd somehow get Helena there, too, and his engineer, so none of them would have to answer questions when the plot was discovered and the secret negotiations he knew would take place with Wolf's team in Miami were made public. He'd be long gone. Kicking back and counting his money, and how many times he could make Helena come that night.

"Everything set?" he asked his engineer.

"Set, boss," Anton answered in English.

"Anything out of the ordinary?" he asked.

Boiko set down the piece he was cleaning. "As a matter of fact, there is." Maksym didn't like the tone of his voice.

He gestured for Maksym to follow as he opened the door to a storeroom with his key card. Inside, Maksym saw a large, white, oddly shaped box large enough to smuggle a body.

"How come you never told me about this?" Anton said, pointing to the box.

"What is it?"

"How the hell do I know? I was told you wanted it left here. Going to be damned inconvenient starting tomorrow. We'll be taking on some parts in Cape Verde and I'm going to need the space. Can't you put it somewhere else?" Anton's disapproving glare worried Maksym.

"I knew nothing except they were expecting something and I was supposed to let them bring it aboard. No one told me it had to stay *here*. I thought they'd keep it with them. Who put it here?"

"A couple of your dark-skinned teenage messengers of death, you ask me."

"Teenagers?"

"They're an odd bunch. North Africans. Don't mix with anyone. Don't understand any language I put in front of them. All sign language, except for the English phrase, 'He will be joining us before Brazil.'" Boiko scratched his scalp.

"Who?"

"They said the man we all work for."

"They use any names?"

"Wolf. They knew I was in on it."

Maksym went back to peering at the box. "I've never seen this before in my life. Knew nothing about it being stored here." He turned his head at an angle, seeing some light pink liquid seep through the white porous packing crate.

Boiko followed his gaze. "I'd say this box is bleeding," the engineer said.

That is what it looked like. Maksym was thoroughly confused.

A box big enough for a body, bleeding like it contained an injured body, the man was joining them soon...and what?

Maksym was going to take out his utility knife and rip it open above the stain, when he heard unmistakable sounds of something moving inside the box. Something with a tail that flopped around inside the cavity. Something that hissed. More than one thing that hissed.

"Mother of God," he whispered. "They've brought snakes on board my ship."

"Well, I didn't notice *that* until just now, Maksym. But there's something *else.*"

Boiko leaned over and placed his ear near the surface and begged him to do the same. When Maksym got close enough to the crate surface he could hear the unmistakable sounds of ticking.

Fucking Moroccans.

He wondered what kind of diabolical scheme they had hatched. Smuggling snakes on board his ship for what purpose? To sell on the side to make some kind of sick profit? Or were these part of the plan?

A plan that was looking like something he knew fuck-all about.

"Maksym, are you planning to blow up your own ship?" Boiko asked.

"Fuckin' not if I can help it. No. This. Definitely. Isn't. The. Plan."

"You better call him."

"You don't let anyone in here until I've had my talk with the Wolf. No one, understood? Especially not the Moroccans."

"With what kind of force?"

"Deadly. Until I know what the hell is going on, I want it contained in here."

"Yeah, until it blows us all up."

"Anton, there's not going to be any blowing us all up. My guess is this is the decoy, the thing that makes them believe the ransom demand is serious. I don't think there's a real bomb in there. But I'm going to find out."

He tore out of the engine room and caught the freight escalator. His last view of Anton was of the old engineer peering back up to him with worry like he'd never seen in the man's face before. It mirrored his own fears.

On Deck 5 he found the outer walkway occupied by mostly cook and wait staff, their favorite place to stand outside and have a cigarette. He chirped open his Sat phone and dialed the three-digit number.

The ringtone sounded slightly distorted, he thought.

"You promised never to call me unless it was an emergency," the deep Italian voice on the other end of the line said quickly.

"Well, it is an emergency. You had the Moroccans smuggle snakes and a bomb on board my ship."

"First Maksym, it isn't your ship."

"How about some answers, Wolf?"

"Well if you'd be more patient, Maksym. Maybe Azziz would be able to talk to you."

"Never agreed to take orders from a Moroccan."

"You don't take orders from them. You take orders from me. And I've told you to cooperate with them."

"A fuckin' bomb, Wolf? And snakes."

"Snakes?" the voice asked.

"So you don't know anything about that? Or about the ticking?"

"The ticking, yes. That's supposed to happen at this stage of the operation. But there is plenty of time. This is not a life-ending event, Maksym."

"Will be for the souls in the bag."

"Well then, perhaps they deserved it?"

"Listen, I was never told about a bomb."

"It's a delivery device. Not a bomb."

Maksym hesitated. The Italian was being evasive. Years of training and interrogating prisoners told him this trained Italian knew exactly what was going on and had decided, for some reason, not to level with him.

"You can call it anything you like. It's making noise and getting attention. Somehow I didn't think that was part of your plan, sir."

"All in due time, my son."

"I'm not your fuckin' son. And I don't want to die. I want to live long enough to spend my money." Maksym was seeing Helena's naked body on the white, sandy beach, writhing beneath him. The sun on his back. She had sand on her boobs, oil and sand mixed into her shoulders that smelled of coconut and vanilla...

"Everything is going according to plan. Now that we have the box on board, the success of the mission is almost one hundred percent assured."

"I never heard about a bomb," Maksym said, still smelling the coconut, her imagined moans so loud he thought perhaps Wolf could hear them too.

"Again, let me correct you. Everything is going according to plan. In the end, you will be rewarded your fair share. Don't worry. Now let's hang up and discuss this another time, shall we? Call me in twenty-four hours, exactly."

Maksym recognized a cold shoulder when he ran into one. He was being played, and he didn't like it one bit. It was about thirty hours until the big event.

He hung up the phone and found a doorway to walk through to the main quarters of the ship.

Mark heard the door slam and peered out the clear vinyl door opening to the lifeboat. He'd brought a sidearm and hidden it at the bottom of the life vest box. He was going to take a nap on the bedspread and pillows where she'd lain with him. Where her naked body had sent him to heaven. He'd been hoping that wrapping himself in her scent would calm him. Just his luck he was awakened by angry speech from the officer he didn't trust, and, of all things, he was talking about a bomb on board the ship.

His interest became laser-focused right quick, while he tried to memorize everything the officer said to the person on the other end of the line.

He wished he knew what that voice said, but from the sounds of it, Maksym wasn't pleased.

He mulled over what he'd heard. There was a bomb on board. There was some kind of plan and other accomplices, since Maksym seemed to be upset he wasn't the one in the know. So Maksym was a stupid soldier, an expendable soldier. Mark wondered if the man realized this. He got the idea that some blinding hatred of something, someone, was causing Maksym to stop being the hero he must have been at one time.

And that made him dangerous to both sides.

Mark wished that even though Maksym was the enemy in this rotten little game now threatening the lives of all the passengers—including the wives of his best buds, and Sophia—he wished that Maksym would grow eyes in the back of his head.

And be careful. One misstep would kill them all. Or trigger the loss of innocent lives. That just wasn't going to happen on his watch. Not while he had all his faculties.

CHAPTER 23

Sophia was numb for the rest of the tour, unaware even of the gentle hum of the diesel bus as it rode the twists and turns of the two-lane highway down the volcano, around and through the demonstration farm and the vineyard. She watched people making commerce, going to work in offices and holding school children by the hand. Nothing interested or appealed to her. She didn't pay attention to the bus guide, who spoke horrible Italian anyway. Several of her group members slipped closer to her and asked for translation. Half the world thought Greece and Italy were the same country, so naturally their Greek guide was someone's idea of customer service.

Her sadness rode on her shoulders like a tattered shawl until four o'clock, when they headed back to the ship. Her duties were over once her group was delivered to the arms of the terminal's little tourist shops. Hucksters were older women with no teeth and young teenage boys wanting to sell handmade bracelets and plastic trinkets that had been made in China.

She pushed by them all, saying a brief goodbye to her charges, some of whom dropped coin in her hand. The Greek guide saw it and looked disgusted. He hadn't gotten any tips from the passengers. She reversed course and went back to the man, who was arguing with the bus driver, who was probably supposed to receive a share of the tips. She deposited every penny she'd been given into his palms.

"Have a nice day," she said in English, hoping they didn't understand.

The gangway was sparsely populated. At the top, she said hello to the handsome Indian security officer, Kumar.

"Miss Sophia, Miss Sophia. We were most distressed when we didn't see you or Roberto for the dance instruction this afternoon." He was a good catch, with his dark skin, beautiful white teeth, and striking build, with a height over six feet something. She and Kumar had consoled each other over cappucinos during a few late nights on prior cruises. She actually was pretty fond of him. The guy was decent, with a heart as big as the ocean that had been trounced on pretty regularly.

Poor Kumar. Maybe this was to be her plight as well. One lonely cruise after another. Daring to find a brief love that was really just a sexual hookup. Confused. Making promises and then breaking them. Not sure what world she lived in. Missing something of her American side while not feeling as comfortable and carefree as her Italian side. Her mother's family's secure, exuberant way of life was usually something that brought strength. That, and the travel. She'd told herself constant travel didn't remind her so often of the fact that she didn't belong anywhere. At least it was better than staying in one place and knowing you didn't belong there. That would drive her crazy.

And she was crazy. Crazy for the American SEAL. Crazy for everything he was that she was not. Crazy to believe in a hero. God, he'd laid his heart at her feet and she'd had the nerve to tell him she wasn't sure. On which continent was she sure? On an island off the coast of Africa? Was she surer in Savona? In Sacramento, at the funeral of her dead father? With her mother in the little piazzas in Savona, where she pretended she was happy? Would she be happy in Brazil with a wealthy husband who insisted she stop traveling? No doubt he had plans to keep her pregnant and all to himself. Locked in a gilded cage with things most of the world's women would want.

But that's not me.

She'd rather be penniless with the American with the strong blue eyes that she saw ignite whenever she kissed him, as she played with him, and yes, as she enchanted him. It wasn't fair, this effect she had on him. But she loved being his muse, his fantasy love. Surely that wasn't a bad thing.

Or am I being selfish?

Kumar handed her the cotton satchel she'd brought with her as it came off the metal detector. He slung it over her shoulder and softly spoke to her so no one else could hear.

"You okay, Miss Sophia? I am worried for you."

"Thanks, Kumar." She glanced up at the grinning officer. He must have been a cute little schoolboy with doting aunties and elderly Indian family members, as he'd lost his mother when he was young. He obviously felt more comfortable in the company of women. "I'm just tired."

"The cruise director is most distressed. Most distressed." Kumar pushed his dark-rimmed glasses back onto his nose. Sophia knew he'd be even handsomer if he could get contacts. She decided to counsel him about next time they were spilling out their painful heart stories.

The cruise director can go fuck himself.

"Roberto's had a little altercation and will be detained. I'm not sure he's coming back to the ship." As she said this and watched Kumar's surprised expression, she hoped it was true.

Then it dawned on her. If Roberto wasn't on board, that left the time available for Mark. They wouldn't have to slink around and be careful to avoid Roberto and his temper. She was grateful the evening demonstration would now be cancelled. Or was that wise?

"Kumar, do you dance?"

"Most definitely," he said as he handed bags to two people behind Sophia. She stood to the side so she wouldn't block the passengers streaming onboard.

"I mean Latin dancing."

"I'm afraid I do ballroom, but no tango. I can do the cha-cha," he said moving his hips and snapping his fingers. She could see a budding dancer in the man's movements.

"Then meet me at the theater at six thirty, can you?"

"Most definitely, Miss Sophia. Are you asking me out on a dinner date, please?"

"No, Kumar, I want you to be my dance partner tonight for the show."

"I speak no German, Miss Sophia. My Russian—"

"Not your language skills I'm looking for." She leaned into him and whispered, "It's your body I want."

She swore she could see a blush surge under his coffee skin. "Oh, my golly, Jesus. I cannot believe you are answering my prayers, Miss Sophia."

"Not what you think, Kumar. I just want you to do your best as my dance partner, for one night."

"I shall endeavor to be your partner every night." The man was grinning from ear to ear, standing up straighter, his eyes were wider and he showed more big white teeth than a person had a right to.

"Bless you. See you at six thirty, then."

"Most definitely. Most definitely. Your humble servant. I shall look forward to it…" she heard as she walked down the crew hallway, past the medical office, to her room.

She wondered where Mark had gone, if he was back on board or caught up with his group. Li was in the cabin, stretching out from an earlier rehearsal. Sophia knew nothing about the little Chinese contortionist, since language was somewhat of a barrier.

"Shower?" Sophia asked.

"Please," Li said. "I use later."

She washed her hair and indulged in a long, hot shower. When she emerged from the little cubicle, Li was gone. Sophia put on her old, favorite terry robe, the one her father had bought for her mother and was a hand-me-down, the go-to piece of clothing whenever she needed a good cry, and climbed the bunk. With lights off, she might be able to get an hour's rest before the rehearsal and demonstration. Rest was what she needed now.

She drifted off to sleep hearing the water lap against the side of the ship. How the bright light sent crystal shards dancing around the walls of the little red lifeboat. She heard him speaking to her, whispering things in her ear. It was a pleasant dream. He was begging her to share his bed, and his life. She forced everything else out of her mind and just went with it.

When Li opened the door, Sophia was startled.

"Excuse me, Sophia, but I must get ready," Li said as she turned on the light over the desk.

"What time is it?"

"Nearly six."

"Oh. My. God. I have to be down at the theatre at six thirty."

"You first, then," Li said, pointing to the bathroom.

"I'm showered, just need a moment for the hair dryer and some makeup."

"Certainly."

Sophia emerged from the cabin ten minutes later and ran down the hallway to the zero deck elevators, punching six.

She rode with several of Mark's buddies returning and their wives to five deck. Kyle cleared his throat. She avoided eye contact.

"Mark on board, do you know?"

"No. Haven't seen him. He did not finish the tour with us."

Kyle looked slightly alarmed. Several of the other members of their group exchanged glances. When the elevator unloaded them to Deck 5, Kyle stood in the doorway, holding the elevator.

"He all right, Sophia? What happened after we left?"

"They got into a fight. Nobody was hurt, but Roberto was arrested and taken by the police." She looked down at her black dancing shoes with the one-inch heels. "We thought it best he should come back in the taxi."

"I know he's back. He texted me. But did he hurt Roberto in any way?"

"You don't know Roberto. He's been hurt so many times he now brings it on himself. Mark did come to my defense, and then we thought it would be best if I stayed to complete my job."

Kyle was assessing her. She felt the stare into her soul, all the way down to her toes. He was an honest man. A true hero. Thinking about everyone else first. Maybe too caring. But she knew Mark would die for this man, and that gave her the courage to be honest with him.

"I was foolish, I'm afraid. I'm confused." She couldn't help but show him the tears she hadn't shed during her nap. "I think he's a little angry with me. He deserves better."

Kyle motioned to a couple dressed in formal attire who waited by the elevator, indicating they needed to find another one.

"Mark is one of those guys with a sixth sense about character. From what I saw today, he's pretty hung up on you, Sophia. He's not often wrong."

"I'm not sure I'm good for him."

"Well if he is, you have a problem." Kyle started to smile. "A problem most the female population of this ship and the entire world would love to have. But you gotta do what you gotta do."

She found it in herself to smile back.

"I do have to go. Meeting someone for rehearsal at the theater. If you run into him, you can tell him I'll be there, or at the dance instruction in the Kasbah bar from seven to eight for the dance lesson."

Kyle nodded. "Know where he is, then? Any guesses?"

She wanted to tell him about the lifeboat, but thought better of it. "Maybe text him?"

Kyle stepped back and allowed the beeping, complaining elevator doors close, to close as he waved goodbye with two fingers.

Sophia got to the theater five minutes early, but Kumar was already there. He had showered and had put on a pair of black slacks and a white satin shirt, buttoned a couple of buttons too low. He wore a gold chain with a medallion around his neck. She saw shades of *Saturday Night Fever* in his eyes.

Upon seeing them both, the engineer began playing some disco music, getting Sophia's drift. She smiled up at the Ukrainian disc jockey in his sound booth.

"Very nice, Kumar. Not sure your costume will work for the waltz, but I'm sure our students will love it."

"Do you love it, Miss Sophia?" he said eagerly.

"Yes." She had to admit he made her smile, and the welcome distraction of dancing would take her mind off her troubles. "I like," she said as she stood in front of him and extended her arms in dance position. "We start with some basics, and then we'll have some fun."

Kyle got a return text and met Mark at his room, as directed. Everyone else had gone to wash up for dinner. Armando and Gina were dressed for a private dinner and were going to take in a show beforehand. Fresh from what Kyle knew was an afternoon of lovemaking, the glow on Gina's cheeks was unmistakable. He'd never seen two people so into each other before. But then, he hadn't been the observer when he and Christy first got together, either.

He checked in with Coop, who had just emerged from his cabin.

"How's Libby?"

"Pretty sick, man. I'm a little worried, to be honest."

This wasn't good news. "Maybe should take her to the medical office?"

"Fuck, no. Not letting anyone else touch her. If she can get through the next couple of weeks, I think she'll be fine. Guess we underestimated the effects a bobbing ship would have on her stomach."

"Roger that. Perhaps you should consider cutting early and flying home?"

"She doesn't want to. She keeps thinking she'll be okay."

All their women were tough and extremely stubborn, Kyle reminded himself.

"Can she sleep?" Kyle asked.

"Barely. I'm going to go get more ginger ale and some dry toast."

"When you get back, meet us in Mark's room. Something's happening you gotta know about."

"What?" Cooper asked.

"Take care of Libby and meet me back in Mark's, okay?"

"Sure thing."

Coop nearly ran down the hallway toward the lobby elevators. Kyle knocked on Mark's door and walked inside when it was opened.

"What's this about a bomb?" Kyle demanded. Jones, Tyler and Fredo were already there waiting.

"Just what I overheard, man. This guy Maksym, the Ukrainian Moshe talked about? He was on a cell phone call with some dude, and he was asking him about a bomb like it was a surprise to him. Like there was some plan to take over the ship, but he hadn't been aware there was a bomb involved."

"Go on."

"Well, that's it. Just a two-minute conversation. Couldn't hear the other side, but Maksym sounded pissed."

"I say we do a high-level target interrogation," Fredo said. "And we get Moshe involved right away."

"I intend to call him. I guess I'd like to learn a little more about the plan until we get all Snatch and Grab on the guy. Any idea when?"

Mark shook his head.

"I don't understand what their motivation is," Kyle said to the floor. "This is a fuckin' cruise ship, man. Mostly international passengers, not a lot of Americans. Not exactly a military target."

"Sounds like this Maksym's motivation is money. Like a hostage for ransom. That's why the bomb has him spooked."

"It'd spook me too. Any idea where it is?" Jones asked.

Again, Mark shook his head. "The Moroccans brought it on board today. I saw them do it, Kyle."

"No shit. They brought it from shore?"

"Yup. Sucker was heavy, too. They came through the crew gangway. That cargo container was too big for the x-ray machine."

"Moshe has to tell us who was on security at the gate. What time was that Mark?"

"About fourteen hundred hours."

"Kyle, there's something else, too. Maksym told the person on the phone the box was ticking. And it had snakes in it."

"Snakes?" Fredo wrinkled his nose. "I hate snakes!"

"Me, too," Jones said.

"You let me handle them snakes. They don't scare me none," Tyler said. "My uncle used to have them in his church in Louisiana growing up. You get 'em from behind and you be quick about it."

"Good to know, Tyler, but right now I'm more concerned with a possible bomb," said Kyle.

They heard Cooper knock and let him in. They decided to separate and collect information, as much as possible, on Maksym. Kyle and Cooper would start with Moshe. Fredo would go speak with the cabin boy about Mark's sighting of Maksym with the woman down the hall. Jones and Mark were going to find Teseo and ask him about Maksym. Tyler said he'd go look for Armando.

The Team left, agreeing to rendezvous at the Kasbah in an hour. Kyle winked at Mark as he left. In parting, he said, "We'll see if we can repair a little heartache along the way."

"Sir?" Mark asked.

"Your lady will be there. She told us. I think you owe her an apology."

"Me?" Mark protested. Fredo and Cooper shook their heads and exited the cabin.

"Come on, lover boy," Jones said as he hauled Mark out by the shirt collar. "We got this. You just need to sit back and let your LPO hook you up."

CHAPTER 24

Mark was seriously annoyed that his love life was front and center with the Team. He'd have been more comfortable with it strictly his own business. But he was encouraged that Sophia had reached out and offered Kyle information, and to somehow convey that she still cared for Mark. That part was more than okay.

He and Malcolm Jones walked up to Deck 11 and then traversed the metal stairways toward the bridge level. This new, modern ship had an extended bridge with windows that could see in three directions. It took a full crew of eight to run it, not counting the crew below decks. Even at port the skeleton crew of four was needed, just to make all the required inspections.

A gut-wrenching blast from the large smokestack above them nearly broke their eardrums. Mark always thought it was odd passengers liked to be outside and right under the damned thing when these big ships sailed. He was certain they would clock some loss of decibels in their hearing. But an adventure was an adventure. He'd also seen his share of stunts, even on Navy ships, where people mimicked the famous Titanic scene, "I'm king of the world."

To hell with that.

Jones swore creatively, covering his ears with both hands. "You'd think they'd give some warning."

Of course, Mark then realized they'd also heard loudspeakers announcing the missing passengers who had failed to make the gangway in time. There were always a couple of them. Seemed like the same ones, too.

That's when he recalled hearing Roberto's name.

Damned straight.

The asshole was probably the guest of the Policia Local. He hoped Roberto had been stupid enough to argue with the famously hair-trigger gentlemen who wore the blue uniforms. He knew they had a special distaste for foreign cruise ship workers who often ripped off locals by not paying their bills while on land and then disappearing. Mark knew they'd exact some pain on the Brazilian for all the workers they hadn't caught. And it didn't matter what form of martial arts you had, if you were restrained in a small room with five or six bullies intent on doing harm, you were toast. In fact, any knowledge of basic self-defense would sometimes inflame them.

So that part was working. Now he needed to get with Teseo and warn him about what he'd overheard.

The gate to the bridge was locked, and there was a guard posted.

"Scusi," Jones began, "Abbiamo bisogno di parlare con il responsabile junior Teseo in una sola volta. È più urgente."

Mark looked with new admiration at Jones, who shrugged.

"Un momento. Dovete stare qui, mentre io verifico. Un momento," the guard said as he pointed to the bridge the next deck up.

"So you coulda saved me all that embarrassment back there with Sophia's letter and all."

"And miss the excitement? Hell no," Jones grinned. "Besides, I did language school. I'm good with the conversations, not so much with the written word."

"Man, I could have used you for—"

"Not on your fuckin' life. I don't interfere. Besides, I think you two communicate pretty damned well, you ask me. But of course, you're not asking."

They chuckled as they looked up when they heard sea birds making alarmed noises and noticed the chopper flying overhead. Although small, it looked expensive, and possibly military. It faded into the darkness that was overtaking the sky. A bright peach sunset was imminent.

"I'm getting a bad feeling about all this," Mark said as he cracked his neck and rolled his shoulders.

Teseo Dominichello followed the uniformed crewman down the steps two at a time. Mark shook his hand.

"Can I have five minutes of your time, in private?" Mark asked. "It's important."

Teseo turned to run back to the bridge but Mark stopped him with a tug on his elbow across the metal gate he could have easily scaled. "We have a medical issue with one of the wives we need your help with. Tell them that."

Mark looked at the guard and didn't see anything register there that led him to believe he'd understood anything.

Teseo returned a moment later and the three of them walked back to a little platform marked with a circle.

"This a helipad?" Mark asked.

"Yes. We occasionally have celebrity passengers or emergency head of state offloads. Sometimes people like to travel anonymously."

"So some of those overweight passengers—" Jones started in.

"Could be ministers of defense or World Bank officers, yes. We have all kinds."

Mark stepped close to Teseo so quickly the man jerked back in reaction.

"We believe you have a bomb on board."

He could see Teseo's face tightened and darkened in an instant.

"How do you know this?"

"I overheard your friend, Maksym, speaking to someone on his cell phone on Deck 5 this afternoon. Sounds like a plot to take over the ship, maybe blow it up."

Teseo swore in Italian. "It just doesn't seem possible. I never thought of him as that kind of a person."

"He's got accomplices on board. Those Moroccans? The dancers that boarded in Casablanca? They brought a big, white crate onboard today. I saw it, Teseo, with my own eyes."

"Where is the box?"

"Fuck if I know. But Maksym sure does, and he's mad as hell about it. He was arguing with the person I think hired him to facilitate the takeover."

"Where is Maksym?" Jones asked the handsome officer.

"He's overdue, actually. Took an hour leave, hasn't come back yet. Captain's pissed, since we're pulling out."

"Any ideas?" Jones asked.

"I got one," said Mark. "I think I know exactly where he is."

He was thinking of the dark-haired, dangerous-looking woman in the cabin down the hall from theirs. Voluntary or involuntarily, she could have waylaid him. Or perhaps worse. Mark was filled with an urgent feeling that perhaps someone would start erasing trails before the caper began in earnest.

"I have to get back. I want to inform the captain."

"You probably should do that. Can he be trusted?"

"The guy is solid. He'll want to check with our home office, though. If it's going to be an incident in international waters, we have to inform them first, if we can."

"Then you do that." Mark said. "But Teseo, this is no drill. I think we for real have a threat to this ship and everyone on board. And I don't think we have much time. Kyle is speaking with Moshe right now, so he'll be in on it."

"Good. I'd trust him with my life." Teseo said. "I'll make sure I have a private conversation with the captain as soon as possible."

"We don't know who to trust, so probably a good plan, Tes." Mark was turning to leave when he remembered something.

"Your guys have any weapons?"

"Not official. Not allowed. But some of us pack anyhow."

"Roger that. We don't have much, either. But one thing I could use." Mark searched Teseo's face. The Italian officer's features started looking surreal as the bright sunset bathed him in rosy light.

"What?"

"I might need your rebreather. Can you get me your two extras?"

"Don't know how I can do that, Mark."

"I've got a stash on Lifeboat 26. It would sure be nice if you could leave anything for me there. Don't think there'd be anyone who would see you do it, know what I mean? Boats on that side aren't in front of a restaurant. Private deck off the backside of the galley."

"I know it. I'll do it. I'll stow anything I stash there out of sight, under the vests, or in the lockers."

"Thanks. I'll need them by tonight, tomorrow morning at the latest. I plan to be there for a few hours this evening." Mark hoped the bright orange sky didn't show the blush he felt on his cheeks. "You could also give them to Sophia."

"Sophia?"

"The Brazilian dance instructor?"

"Oh yeah, that one. That the one you were talking about?" Teseo's handsome face cracked a wide grin.

"Um hum. She knows right where Lifeboat 26 is. You give anything to her and she'll get it to me." Mark pulled a card out of his pocket. "And here's Kyle's cell, my cell," Mark handed Teseo a card with a small American flag on it that was otherwise completely blank except for the handwritten phone numbers.

Teseo slipped it into his vest pocket behind a small black spiral notebook.

"Kyle's is a sat phone courtesy of Uncle Sam. My service is spotty," Mark added.

"Will check back with him as soon as I talk to the captain. Thanks." Teseo and Mark shook, and then he shook Jones's hand. "Glad you boys are on board. Who would have thought?"

"I'm hoping they don't know what we do. But with their advantage of surprise gone, perhaps we can take care of this so no one else knows about it."

"That's the plan, then. Talk to you soon." Teseo ran to the gate, zipped his card against the metal sensor, and headed up the metal stairs to the Bridge. Mark hoped the captain was good under pressure.

CHAPTER 25

Maksym had gone to Helena's room and collapsed in her arms. He could tell she was startled at his needy behavior. She tried to talk to him. He was rough with her in return, masking insecurity and fear, finally finding one of her scarves and wrapping it around her mouth to shut her up. Her eyes sparkled as he ripped off her clothes, as he shredded her panties and took her. His need was so great he wasn't careful. She'd started by being gentle with him, drifting her fingers down his back and over his backside and he didn't want that.

"Niet," he said, getting right in face. Russian was the code for danger. Well, he was dangerous, all right. He scared her with his Russian. Trouble brewed in her brows. He held her two wrists together above her head with one large paw, hiking up her knees and thrusting himself inside her naked, pink body, pinning her to the bed, biting her neck and groaning guttural pleas in rhythm with his thrusting. He would have a hard time explaining why he felt this was going to be the last fuck of his life, but for some reason, that's how it seemed. It didn't matter whether she liked it or not.

He knew she loved the moment when her fear became pleasure, and she didn't disappoint him now. Subtle, but now she passed that threshold when she commanded *him* again, because his need was more urgent than hers. In those exchanges of gasping for breath and slapping skin, he had become the submissive and she the dom as he felt her body arch back, and saw her let herself fall into a delicious orgasm that sounded like childbirth. Maybe that's how it felt, too. The more he pumped her, the more he needed. He gave himself up to her and worshiped, filling her body. Every moan or rolling spasm became what he required, would have at all costs. She could literally kill him by withholding, he had given her so much power.

He flipped her over onto her stomach, pulling a pillow under her lower belly, splaying the cheeks of her flesh as his wet cock rooted up the cleft of her. He kissed her on one side, making a little bite that would draw blood. She arched back in a moan and then presented her peach to him, ripe with their combined juices.

He dove into her with his mouth, sucking her lips, running his canines on her delicate folds, lapping and feeding himself like he was starving. And he *was* starving for her. He hiked her hips higher, found another pillow and pushed it underneath her abdomen, raising her plump little ass on full display. He held her hair at the back of her neck and pulled, arching her backward like a bow.

He kicked his shoes off, but his shirt, his white pants were still on. The brass belt buckle with an anchor was slapping her ass as he rose up, positioned himself and rammed inside, pressing her down into the bed. He brought himself out, fully out, as she groaned. He let her feel the vacancy he'd created, then gave it back to her, pushing himself deep with a frenzy.

In and out he fucked her, riding her ass, pushing himself in to the right and then the left. He fucked like the more he did it, the bigger and harder he got, and he desperately wanted to be huge, wanted to explode and make her come.

She turned her head and looked at him out of one eye when he leaned over and French kissed her ear. He let her hear his cry of need, his complete despair, and his desire to mate, not to make love.

At last, while he once again pulled her head back by the roots of her hair, he felt her muscles milk him and pull him deeper still as he exploded, pausing to let her feel the force of him, the need of him. Her grunts of pleasure were music to his ears.

Mark heard the obvious signs of lovemaking on the other side of the cabin door. He thought the cabins on either side and across the hall would be able to hear, too. Jones' eyes widened and then he wrinkled his nose.

"Can't tell if they're fucking each other or killing each other," he whispered. "Day-am."

The loud bursts of ecstasy on the other side of the door subsided into silence. Mark heard the vibration of a text message on his cell.

Kyle: Teseo know anything about it?

He answered, "No. Telling the captain now."

Kyle: Good. You find Maksym?

He texted back: Oh yeah. He's in the room with her. Fuckin' animals.

Kyle: lol. Sweeeet. Don't get any ideas.

He answered: Oh I got ideas. Not sharing any of them with you.

Kyle: We're on our way down.

He texted his LPO back: Roger that. "I guess we get to babysit, sort of," he whispered to Jones.

"Um hum. Would be a whole lot more fun if we could watch, too."

"Don't push it."

Several people slid past them in the narrow hallway. Jones and Mark pretended they were waiting for someone from across the aisle. Mark made a point to look at his watch and frown every time someone came close.

At last Kyle and Moshe appeared. Fredo rounded the corner and started to say something off color, but was shushed by the crowd in the corridor. He stepped in line with the others. Moshe was right outside the door, so when Maksym opened it, he got a good view of the angry Israeli.

"What're you doing here?" Maksym said, then looked to see the other men in the hallway. His shirt was still not tucked in but his buttons were buttoned. His hair was a mess.

He came out and quickly closed the door to give Helena some privacy.

"Fellas," he said. He made a poor attempt to act like he'd been caught doing something naughty and needed a minor hand slapping.

Moshe was all business. "I'm afraid you'll have to come with me, Maksym."

"Or what?" Maksym grinned like it would save his bacon.

"Not funny, asshole," Mark chimed in and earned himself a glare from Kyle.

"We are two consenting adults, besides which, what concern is it of yours? The lady and I are in need of comfort. But I hold no claim to her…"

The door opened and Helena's eyes were daggers. She leaned forward to check out the hallway and then shouted a command.

"Inside, quickly."

All six of them proceeded. Kyle opened the door to the balcony outside, bringing in two three metal chairs and the table for them to sit on.

"This doesn't concern her," Maksym started to say. Helena cut him off.

"Oh, shut up and listen to what they have to say, Maksym."

She'd yelled at his back and he braced against the sting to his ego.

"Sit down," Moshe directed. "Next to her." He pointed to Helena, who was already sitting on the edge of the bed. Kyle and Cooper were on the leather bench seat. Fredo remained standing behind Moshe. Mark and Jones took their seats on the metal chairs from the balcony. Maksym sat, appearing in a daze.

"What is all this about?"

"The bomb," Moshe said.

"The bomb? What—"

Just then Maksym's cell phone rang.

"You will answer it, and you will allow us to listen." Mark was impressed by how commanding Moshe was.

"No. I cannot."

"Don't be a fool, Maksym. You have no choice but to cooperate," Helena spat.

Maksym turned on her, seething. He was going to say something unkind, but Moshe took the wind out of his sales just after the ringing phone went silent.

"Maksym, you're fucked," Moshe interrupted. "We know about your little plan, and now we're gonna tell your boss that we know about it. How valuable are you going to be if that happens? I think he'll feel some resentment towards you, don't you think? Your chips have just been taken away."

The Ukrainian was starting to look like a caged animal. A *dangerous* caged animal.

The phone began ringing again.

"Answer it. And do as we say," Moshe hissed.

"Da." Maksym flashed a look at Helena who shook her head.

"You fuckin asshole," she screamed and slammed him with a pillow. Maksym's grip on the phone faltered and it clattered to the ground.

He fell to all fours and scrambled to find it, putting it back to his ear. "My apologies Wolf. I am in a serious argument with my woman."

He pressed the speaker feature and the Team heard the clipped Italian accent on the other end of the line, full of restraint.

"Are you in a secure location, alone?"

"Helena is here, as you know. But yes, we're alone in the cabin." Maksym scanned his audience.

"You are both going to pay with your lives if this is not true."

"I have found some relief in her arms. The pressure is getting to me a bit, I admit."

"Time enough for fucking when this is over with. I know enough of Helena not to be concerned. She values her lifestyle, even if she doesn't value your lives." There was a pause and the man on the other end sighed as though it pained him to do so with patience. "So how did they find out about the bomb, Maksym? I hold you personally responsible for this."

Mark saw Maksym react quickly. "Sir, you told me there was no bomb."

He realized then that the captain's call to the main office must have tipped this man off. That meant he was connected with the home office. At least they now knew where the enemy was hiding. Or had been hiding.

"It's the delivery device, assuring us the plan will take place. They can't stop it now if they can't find it."

"Wolf, how can you be sure they found out about it? I've heard nothing."

"Because your captain relayed a suspicion expressed by some Americans on board. You know any such Americans?"

Maksym looked at the SEALs.

"There are several American couples I've met. Strictly tourists, I'd say."

Mark could see Maksym start to sweat. The officer closed his eyes and swallowed. "What is it you would have me do?"

"I want you to guard it with your life."

"Yes. But what if they contact me?"

"If they contact you, that means you are a dead man. If they know about you, then you are of no use to me. Make sure that they don't."

The man called Wolf hung up.

Maksym dropped his head into the palms of his hands, elbows braced on his knees.

"Where is it, Maksym?" Moshe demanded.

"It's safe. Locked in the engine room."

"That's the worst place for a bomb, and you know it, Moshe," Kyle snapped. "We gotta get it out of there."

"There's no way without alerting the crew. Someone will talk. At this point, I don't know who to trust," Maksym said.

"You can trust us," Kyle said.

"The chief engineer is my ally. We know there are others."

"When is this supposed to take place?"

"After the next stop, at Cape Verde. When we cross the Equator. The ship will be stopped. Ransom demands will be delivered to the company. The insurance company always pays. I don't even think there is a bomb, just something to make it look like the threat is real. I've seen it."

"Would one bomb, if it's big enough, sink this ship?" Moshe asked. He looked around to the faces of the SEALs.

"No. It would take several. It could disable it, but the ship is quite safe, and there are lifeboats to launch, plenty, not like on the Titanic," Maksym added. He buried his head in his hands again.

"Who stages the takeover, Maksym?" Kyle asked.

"There are supposed to be more coming on board in Cape Verde. We've reported engine trouble and a team of eight 'mechanics' are supposed to arrive in the morning when we dock. We've been given clearance to allow them and their tools on board."

"Sir," Mark spoke up. "We can't allow those men to board."

"I know it, Mark," Kyle said. "Moshe, you got anyone else you can call about this? We need some backup. We got nothing U.S.-connected nearby. You have any shipping companies that could be an ally in times of danger?"

"The Maersk lines, a Danish company, they might. But I wouldn't know how to reach them, or what ships are in the area. They're all over the world. Captain Phillips, do you remember him?"

"We remember. One of our guys was there," Kyle said.

That brought Maksym out of his misery. His tear-stained face looked up at Kyle with an almost hopeful expression. "You guys are SEALs?"

"Nah, man, we're UPS drivers," Kyle replied and winked at Mark.

Moshe and the Team regrouped in Mark's room. Armando joined them and was brought up to date.

"I don't like leaving Moshe on his own. I don't trust the guy," Kyle said.

"He's a dead man, and he knows it. His best bet is to align with us," Moshe said. "I'm going to go upstairs and start making calls to see if we can get some support from somewhere. I'm also going to notify the U.S. Authorities, not that they are likely to have any assets nearby. Closest would be the Mediterranean, and that's at least two to three days away."

"Maybe some air support," Tyler suggested. "What we did in Somalia."

"Not unless there's a real threat. We don't know for sure it's a bomb, or even if there is going to be a takeover. I don't think they'll commit on a hunch, sad to say," Moshe added.

They agreed to station Jones and Fredo near the cabins to guard the women. Everyone else was to be out and about, looking for signs of foul play, things that didn't make sense. Scouting out places to hide, to stage a firefight. Looking for anything they could use if they had to defend the ship from terror attacks every man knew was definitely going to happen.

Mark made a beeline for the Kasbah lounge. The sound of disco music wafted his way. A small combo was playing on a raised stage. The singer was a bit off-key and the volume needed to be turned way down, Mark thought. The screeching-fingernails-on-the-chalkboard singer stopped annoying him when he saw Sophia dancing with the Indian security guard.

Kumar's shiny satin shirt was undulating in moves Mark didn't know the guy possessed. His eyes were wide and alert with excitement, like a five-year-old in a chocolate factory, he gazed at his lovely partner, the soft and sensual Sophia. Mark's heart turned to putty as his libido kicked in. Though he liked the Indian and had spoken to him many times, he did not like the way the guy swung her around, sashayed up to her middle and held her tiny waist as he undulated his hips to their rhythm.

Mark could see she was actually enjoying herself, that is, until she spotted him in the corner. She faltered for a second, drawing the attention of Kumar, who raised his chin in polite greeting to him, as if to say, "Look at me, I'm dancing." Poor Kumar was oblivious. Mark actually felt for the man. His finest hour was happening just when all hell was about to break loose.

The set ended and the seated audience loved it. Couples who had watched from the edges of the dance floor, looking like garnish on a buffet table, clapped and cheered for them. Kumar held Sophia's hand and they took a deep bow.

Mark was there in an instant. "Sorry, dance party is over for Sophia," he said to the tall Indian, who looked puzzled and more than a little disappointed.

"Mark, please, don't." Sophie started to protest. But she glanced up and saw the look he gave her and closed her mouth. He led her off the dance floor and down to Deck 5.

CHAPTER 26

S he hoped the look in his eyes was urgency to be with her. She certainly felt that strongly about him too, but something else was present. Some kind of danger or unseen evil about to envelop them all. Mark had a message for her of some kind, and it was more than that he loved her. It was something stemming from deep inside his soul, from who he was as a man.

She felt like she was seven, that day when she and her dad had rushed to the hospital when her mother had taken ill suddenly. She trusted her daddy, but he was driving too fast, he wouldn't look at her with the reassurance she needed. He was scared for her mother, and because of that, she was scared. They ran to the Emergency Room, desperate to hear about her condition.

He only looked at her once he knew her mother was out of harm's way. He'd grabbed Sophia and wept into her chest. And now something awful was happening again. She could feel it. Just when her life with Mark should be starting, something had gone very wrong. She needed to be brave for whatever it was he was going to tell her. Whatever it was.

He had a vise-like grip on her fingers and it hurt, though she doubted he realized. He pushed through the door to outer Deck 5, their love boat number 26 very close by.

"Stop." She said as she pulled away her hand. "Tell me. Tell me what's going on, Mark."

"There isn't time, sweetheart." He pulled her into his chest, and that's when she heard the rumble of his stomach and the fast beating of his heart. The man was running on adrenaline. He was sweating, breathing heavily. "Please, just follow me right now, and I'll explain everything, baby."

He led her to the boat. She was surprised to see military-looking supplies stored there. Some large black nylon zippered sacks were tucked into the corner closest to the doorway, angled against the wall like they were sitting in a gun rack. She recognized some of the scuba equipment and ammunition boxes tucked under the orange life vests. Several white boxes with red crosses on them were stacked in the corner. She saw a wet suit and fins, several dry blankets and various other satchels.

It looked like Mark was planning a small war.

"What is all of this?" she asked.

"Come here, Sophia," he said as he sank to the floor below the level of the window, patting his thigh. She sat next to him, rather than on his lap.

"Tell me."

"The ship is going to be taken over by terrorists, who apparently have planted a bomb on board. We are assembling equipment...we are making plans..." He looked down at his hands, which were shaking.

She took his hands in hers and held them, kissing the palms. She searched his eyes and...yes, she did see fear there. Not for himself so much, but she knew he feared for her life.

"Mark, could it be possible this is just all a—"

"No. There has been a well-executed plan done in stages. We don't even know the identities of everyone involved, but we have confirmed there is probably a bomb on board. We don't think it is big enough to scuttle the ship, but it could cause damage or loss of life. What we cannot do is allow the ship and passengers to become the property of a warlord."

"I thought the pirates were on the other side of Africa."

"So did we. But this location makes sense, if you think about it. We have no naval presence here, yet we are a huge ship, with tons of passengers and crew, run by an American company. It's a huge, soft target."

"I don't understand. Why? There isn't much cargo that can be of value."

"Life. The ship contains 3,400 souls. The most precious of cargoes."

"Who is doing this?" She couldn't believe something so diabolical could be happening when, just thirty minutes ago, all she had to worry about was giving the wrong impression to Kumar, who was emboldened with each turn and dip of her body, each little glance and smile she gave him as part of their performance.

"Teseo and Moshe are to be trusted, but no one else, other than our Team guys, and of course Sanouk and the girls. Trust no one else, understood?"

"So what is all this?" She gestured at the piles of equipment.

"Teseo has been bringing things to this boat as a precaution, in case his quarters are taken over. We've asked for everything he can spare us, and they're stashing it here. It was the only place I thought safe enough to—"

The moment their eyes met the connection was made and the reality of the danger took a back seat to the love between them.

"I'm going to protect you, Sophia. Don't worry. I'm going to keep you safe," he said as he brushed his fingers against her cheek and then planted a sweet kiss on her lips. "I would die if anything happened to you. I can't—"

She'd closed the distance between them again and wouldn't allow him to finish, as if saying it would make it come to pass.

"Love me, Mark. Do you at least have time for that? I need to feel your arms around me, your hands on my body."

"Baby, I'm here. We haven't much time, but don't worry, we have enough. We'll have time. I just need to check on a few more things—"

"No. Now. I want you inside me now." She knew somehow it would all work out, but she needed the warm courage of this man, needed to be enveloped in his love.

He brought her down against the life vests, which were lumpy on her back, but she didn't care. He smoothed over her breasts and down to the juncture between her thighs, rubbing on her sex from outside of her dress. His fingers slipped under her hem and he slid up the inside of her thigh, to find and then explore her hot core encased in black panties. As he slid a finger underneath the elastic she closed her eyes and arched into his hand, a moan bursting from her chest when his finger found a home deep inside her. Stretching her arms above her head, she tugged at the canvas beneath her head. Her knees were bent, heels digging through the pile of jackets to scrape against the plastic floor of the little boat.

Opening her eyes, she saw Mark's clear blue eyes blazing down on her, brimming with desire for her. She'd not ever seen a man need her so much, had never seen a man she wanted to please so much.

"Ti amo con tutto il cuore, Marko. Tutto il mio cuore," she found herself whispering to him, as he climbed over her body, slipped off her panties and positioned himself at her opening. "I love you with my whole heart, Marko, my beautiful Marko."

He watched her face as his hands came up to hold her head, holding her steady against his hips as he slid his cock deep. He stopped, letting her feel the ardent strength of him. It was more than sex. It was way more than sex.

He dipped his chin and kissed the top of her breasts, kissed up along the side of her neck as she arched to receive him, licked and kissed just under her ear.

He stumbled with his Italian, but he whispered, "Amo tutti voi, Sophia, con tutto di me." *I love all of you Sophia, with all of me.*

She realized how hard he'd practiced to make that short phrase perfect. "Mi amore." She whispered back as he kissed her, plunging his tongue next to hers and sucking.

She lost herself in the luxurious feeling of this hard-muscled warrior who loved as hard as he played his deadly game. Her thighs rode his hips as he rocked them both into a rhythm that left her feeling timeless, floating and limitless. Every place he touched transformed her flesh into little jolts of energy. His kisses and wet tongue invaded her psyche, begged for love, for completion, for satisfaction. He was as relentless as he was deep. He was soft and hard. His body owned hers inside and out.

With another series of short strokes he spent inside her, just as she began to feel the fireworks erupt behind her eyelids, triggering her rolling orgasm, making her fall into the pleasure of his arms and the fullness of that space between her legs that had been so empty without him.

He arched and pressed himself, every last drop of him spilling inside her. With a gasp he fell to her chest, and they simply held each other, fully spent. After resting for a few seconds, he lifted his head and kissed his way up her neck to her ear again and whispered, "Marry me, Sophia. Let me take you home with me. I want you safe, living with me forever, Sophia. Marry me, please marry me."

She needed to see his eyes to deliver her response. With her palms cupping his cheeks, she smiled. "Nothing would make me happier, my Marko."

She could tell he'd prepared himself for disappointment, so his obvious delight she thrilled her.

"I promise to get better with the Italian," he whispered, as if it was important.

"I like your Italian, because it's the way you say it. Only you say it that way. And I love it."

"I like it when we speak Italian or English, or—" he peeled down the top of her dress to tease her nipple with his teeth, making her jump. "And when we don't speak at all." He sucked at her nipple and then followed it with a knowing smile. Did he know that every time he kissed her there it made her little peach quiver? Did he know that the place under her ear he liked to kiss was so delicately, urgently sensitive he could make love to her anywhere, anyhow if he just touched her there?

On any other night, they might have fallen asleep with happy dreams, but not tonight. She felt him stiffen as reality caught hold of him and, after several deep sighs, he sat up, bringing her with him, holding her to his chest with both arms wrapped around her. He settled one hand at the base of her spine as he rubbed the back of her neck, fingers massaging her scalp.

"I can't stay, but I think you'd be safer here."

She leaned back to examine his face. "What?"

"I'd feel better if you stayed here until it's all over."

"How realistic is that, Mark? I can't just abandon my job. I work for the cruise line. I'm supposed to protect the passengers in an emergency. You're actually asking I abandon my responsibilities?"

Mark nodded. "You're right, of course, just be careful. You are the only one, other than some of the ship's officers, who know about this place. If Teseo gives you things to bring here, please do it carefully, and watch your back."

She squeezed into his chest again, wishing it were not time to go, and hoping it wouldn't be the last time they were together.

"You be safe, too. You don't have to do anything heroic on my behalf. I'll be fine. We have procedures we follow. I'm sure the captain has contacted Miami and plans are in place."

She saw the faint smile on his face, indicating there was something up with that comment, but she let it go.

They heard the metal door to Deck 5 open and a discussion as two people who walked by. Mark and Sophia remained hidden beneath the window until the footsteps passed.

As they were getting dressed in the moonlight that bathed the interior of the boat in a surreal silvery light, they heard the faint whir of something mechanical.

Mark looked up as if he could see through the many layers of the ship.

"What is it?" she asked him.

"Helicopter."

Her blood froze.

CHAPTER 27

Mark heard the automatic gunfire before he could get halfway down the hallway to his cabin. He'd texted Kyle about the equipment in the boat, and contacted Fredo, who was standing guard over their women. He stopped briefly to see if he could hear anything at Helena's door, but could not.

Jones opened the door to their suite before he got his hand on the key card.

"Kyle's on his way," Mark informed him.

They heard screaming and more gunfire through the opened doors of their balcony. Sanouk sleepily walked into the room in his pajamas.

"Get your clothes on, dude. There's a firefight outside and we need you to stay with the women," Mark told him.

"You know what the plan is?" Jones asked Mark.

"Kyle's call, but some have to stay behind, some have to go underground. We got a couple of rebreathers, some ammo and gear in Lifeboat 26. Remember that one. On Deck 5, outside the chapel. You can make it to the kitchen from the end of the hallway. From there, you're on your own."

"Got my sidearm. Wish I had my H&K."

"You and me both."

"Moshe?"

"Haven't heard."

Just then they heard an announcement over the loudspeaker. The distinctive Italian accent of the captain crackled. They opened the door to their cabin to better hear the message, since the speakers were loudest in the common areas.

In Italian first, the captain made a brief announcement. "La nostra nave è stata comandeered da forze esterne che stanno chiedendo per la collaborazione."

"The ship has been commandeered by outside forces that have asked for your cooperation," Jones translated as Cooper and Fredo burst into the hallway, fully dressed.

"Where the fuck is Kyle?" Coop asked.

"Right here," Kyle said behind them, breathing hard. "We aren't going to have much time."

"Moshe get information off?"

"Ship's internet has been shut down. His call to the Maersk lines was interrupted. I had to get back here."

"Is he okay?"

"He was taken prisoner by two masked men in black. I escaped by hiding in the secret compartment he'd designed and had built at his own expense." Kyle and Mark shared a look. "Moshe knows he'd be one of the first they executed, if they want to make a statement. The man saved my life. I owe him."

"Understood," said Cooper.

Mark nodded. Yes, he'd help Kyle in that mercy, or death mission. His Team leader had a wife and child, and he would need help from someone who didn't. And they wouldn't be able to spare more than two others.

"So no one knows about this takeover?" Jones asked.

"The signal was sent," Kyle answered.

A distress signal had been broadcast, notifying all listeners within a five hundred mile radius. Problem was, Mark knew, it couldn't discriminate about who received the signal.

"But I got in the calls with my sat," Kyle added.

The scratchy voice of the captain came over the loud speaker again, this time in English.

"Ladies and Gentlemen," he began, as he had begun all his other happier announcements on board. "Our ship has been commandeered by persons unknown who are asking for your cooperation. I have been assured that, if everyone cooperates, there will be no danger. There will be no injury or loss of life."

That last statement had a chilling effect on the group. Several people in nightgowns and pajamas opened the doors to their cabins and stepped out into the hallway. Groups of family members and friends began to form.

"We've gotta move." Kyle said. "Say your goodbyes, quick. Jones and Fredo, you stay here with the women. If they start executing people, they'll start with the white boys first.

Sanouk peered out from the darkened room wearing loose pants and gi-type top that wrapped around his waist and tied at the side. Underneath, nestled in the folds of light gray fabric, Mark could tell he had secreted a curved, bladed knife. Mark had no doubt he fully knew how to use it, too.

"I'll be here to help defend, Kyle," the boy said.

"Fuckin' A. Now that's what I'm talkin' about," Fredo said.

"Mark, Armando and I are going to find Moshe. Tyler and Rory, you're on mission to go with Coop to the engine room and find the bomb. Nick and Grady, go see if you can find Teseo on the bridge. I'll text you, so keep your cells on. Everyone charged up?"

Nods all around.

"We have a small cache of weapons on Lifeboat 26, gents," added Mark. "But don't leave me stranded without any equipment, and—whatever you do— don't lead them there." You see Sophia, you need to get a message or something delivered there, she's in on it and ready to help. But be careful."

"Everyone have some sort of sidearm? Anyone short?"

The group shook their heads.

"Back in thirty secs," Kyle said and disappeared into his cabin. One by one the men slipped in and then back out of their rooms after a private farewell.

Armando and Mark waited for Kyle in the hall. Armani was checking one of the magazines he'd pulled out of the lower pocket or his cargo pants. He knew Armani's Sig was holstered at the small of his back, right where Mark carried his.

"Amazing they didn't spot these in our luggage," he said to Armando.

"I had mine disassembled and tucked all over the place. I don't think they knew what the fuck they were looking at."

"Great minds…" Mark was going to continue, but Kyle appeared at the doorway and quietly closed it behind him.

"We go," was all the guy had to say.

The men from SEAL Team 3 ran in two directions. Mark followed Kyle, with Armando bringing up the rear. They threaded through passengers who were confused and more than a little panicked. It was going to be bedlam soon.

"You really get through to SOCOM?" Mark asked Kyle's back.

"Left a message for Commander Ramsey and Timmons."

"Shit," Armando said behind him.

"They can track the phone," Kyle added quickly. "I had the tracking device installed last year. They'll know it was me, just as if I sent up a red flare, though. They'll figure it out."

"Hope it's in time," Mark whispered.

Kyle stopped and faced Mark. "You stop that shit, man. We're all going to make it out alive. All of us. No one gets left behind."

"I'm all aboard, Lanny. And if someone has to take the hit, it's gonna be me and not you. I'm clear on that," Mark retorted.

"Nah, not unless I get there first, man," Armando said behind him.

Kyle's phone began to ping. Mark recognized the unique ringtone of their Chief, Timmons.

"Bad timing, Chief," Kyle said into the phone as he watched the hallway.

"What's this thing about terrorists…"

"Look, I'm real sorry, but I'm waiting for a return call from SOCOM, unless you got a chopper or some reinforcements, I'm not being conversational."

Mark could hear Timmons yell at the insult. "You fuckin' prick. You think I'm just being conversational?"

"Get to the point, sir. We're outnumbered. You might retire in a couple, but we might wind up dead." Kyle delivered it with his blue-eyed steely stare right into the pit of Mark's stomach.

They all heard the crash as Timmons did the nasty on the frog statue the team had bought and replaced.

Kyle shook his head and had to chuckle. Mark had to admit it was a light moment, and they were needing a bit of that right now. "I see you got Flipper again. His replacement isn't going to like spending the rest of his days next to your wife's dolls."

"I don't want another one. Get your butts to a safe location and get yourselves home. I understand they're working on something. Just wanted to check for...for..."

"We're all good so far. A lot better than Flipper. No one injured or killed. Working to keep it that way. I gotta go, Chief. Will be in touch."

"You fuckin' do that, Kyle. You better get yourselves safely home."

"Roger that." Kyle hung up. "Okay, *now* we go balls to the wall," he said to Mark and Armando. No more distractions."

Kyle whipped around and continued running. Mark had to work to keep up with him. He wondered when the terrorists would get to the crew decks. He wondered if they would mess with the women or only go after the men. He stopped himself and corrected his thought pattern.

Looking for options. There are always options. Improvise. It was what they trained for every workup.

Way too soon to start thinking about casualties.

Rapid gun bursts were making staccato appearances on most levels, most of them seeming to come from the upper decks. The security officer's quarters were at zero deck at the backside of the medical bay. Mark was glad they weren't carrying anything but sidearms. No duty bags to draw attention. Not that the extra firepower wouldn't have been nice.

A tray had been knocked to the floor and broken dishes and silverware scattered about. They could hear heavy boots coming around the corner, so the three SEALs deflected toward the medical officer's station. On the way they noticed the cargo doors wide open, the night sea breeze refreshing the stale air of the zero deck. Laced in the salty sea smell was diesel engine fuel. The SEALs could see several smaller ships bobbing alongside, their lights flickering like stars. They were about to be boarded.

Luckily the doors to the medical office were unlocked, so they ducked inside the reception area, keeping the lights out, and hid behind the counter. They saw a trio of combat troops in dark camo run past the glass window of the sick bay door, headed toward the open cargo bay or the elevators beyond. A crowd of confused crew in their nightclothes converged. Multiple languages were being shouted angrily.

Mark remembered studying the footprint of the zero deck when he considered searching for Sophia before they'd begun their trysts in the lifeboat.

He scampered to one of the treatment rooms and pulled a lower cabinet off the rear wall. Listening to be sure he hadn't generated any attention on the other side, he kicked the wall once, his boot coming out the other side. With another two kicks and the help of Kyle and Armando to pull back the flimsy wall, they managed to make a hole large enough to crawl through. Armando was the last one through, and he pulled the cabinet behind him to cover up their passageway.

Inside Moshe's office they found the desk and drawers had been tossed. Kyle quietly closed the private door and heard a satisfying click as the built-in security kicked in. Broken pictures of the Israeli's wife and family lay at the floor. Mark noted the door had been ripped off the safe, rendering it useless.

"They get anything?" Mark asked.

"Nah, I got his Jericho and three clips earlier, thank God," Kyle said as he crouched near the door and peered out the tiny glass window slit above the key lock on the reinforced door.

"Armani, see if you can find some master passkeys. Moshe always had a handful of them somewhere in his office."

"Roger that." Armando and Mark searched through the mess on his desk, and then rummaged through the contents of the spilled drawers.

"Got 'me." Armando said as he held up a fistful of plastic key cards for Mark and Kyle to see.

"Think they were looking for weapons, but they'll figure it out sooner or later, after they get tired breaking down their twentieth door," Kyle said. "They'll be back for sure.

Just then they heard the unmistakable sound of the engines grinding to a complete stop. Lights flickered in the hallway as the power was rerouted.

"Shit. They've stopped the ship. Now what the fuck?"

They didn't have to wait long. A blast hit the side of the ship, knocking them to the floor and sending a couple of metal file cabinets crashing down on them.

"That can't be our bomb," said Mark.

"Sounded more like percussive flash bombs intended to scare anyone who thought they should stay put in their cabins. My guess is they're boarding us big time," Armando said.

As soon as he'd said it, shouts and single pistol shots were heard as the crew was rounded up and herded down the hallway. Women screamed and occasionally something was said in Arabic.

But then all of them heard the unmistakable command of a Russian officer. Someone tried to open the office door, then kicked it so hard Mark thought the hinges might burst. The butt of a rifle broke the glass window and a hand reached through to grab the lever on the inside of the compartment. Broken glass scraped against someone's arm and the trio heard swearing in Russian when the scrape caused more than surface injury. Wrapping his arm and hand in a rag, the man tried again to reach his hand through the jagged opening. His fingers could barely grip the handle as he pulled and frantically moved it back and forth without luck. Mark was grateful the door had that extra security feature.

The three of them breathed a sigh of relief, although only temporary as sounds emerged from their passageway on the other side, in the medical clinic, as bottles and glass cabinets were smashed.

The SEALs had nowhere to hide when at last all sounds from both sides of the corridors stopped. Muffled bursts of gunfire from far away and the gurgling of diesel engines from the flotilla outside the open hatches of the cargo bay gave them the impression it was raining bullets and destruction on everyone in the intruders' path. It was a full-on, well-planned assault on a defenseless ship, and they were getting up to speed fast. Mark's heart was in his throat, thinking about the women, hoping Sophia and the others, especially the ailing Libby, were safe, or left relatively alone.

The captain's voice began to crackle again over the intercom system.

"Ladies and gentlemen, we are asking that all the women and children come to Deck Nine immediately."

"That's the cafeteria level and outside on deck by the pool, on top of the ship. They want all the women on the top? It's freezing up there," Mark said.

"They're bait," Armando whispered sadly.

Kyle felt the buzz of his sat phone.

"Lansdowne," he whispered.

"This Special Operator Kyle Lansdowne?"

"Yessir."

"Hold on for Commander Vinson, sir," the voice on the other end of the phone spoke.

Kyle put his hand over the mouthpiece and whispered, "Do we know a Commander Vinson?"

Mark shook his head. Armando shrugged, "Nada."

The phone crackled to life. "I'm Commander Vinson of the joint task force at SOCOM substation in Miami working with the U.S. Coast Guard."

"Yes, sir."

"I understand you are running an operation on a commercial cruise liner and are in the process of being compromised, is my assumption correct, sir?"

"Hijacked would be more like it. That is correct, Commander. At approximately zero one hundred hours we got invasion units landing by boat, taking over the bridge and forcing the captain to request cooperation from the passengers. Then roughly thirty minutes ago we got a full hull breech, someone opened the cargo doors, and we believe many enemy insurgents came aboard, sir."

"How many men is your security force, son?"

"Security force?"

"We understand a Navy SEAL Platoon was dispatched to accompany a high level target on that cruise ship. How many men in your force, exactly?"

"Commander, there's no fuckin high level target here. We're on a fuckin' cruise ship. On vacation with our wives."

"Excuse me, would you repeat that?" The crackling of the phone was loud. Mark hoped the noise wouldn't give their position away. Mark took several of the security pass cards Armando handed him, sticking them into his vest pocket.

"We're on vacation. This wasn't a SEAL operation at all. We've just found ourselves in the middle of this shit, Commander."

They heard talking on the other end of the line. "This is not a U.S. Naval Special Forces operation, then, son, is that what you're saying?"

"Well, no. Hey, I called my Commander in Coronado, how did it get to you in Miami? And where are the SOCs?"

"We monitor all calls coming from international waters, and intercepted. After we heard the content of your call, thought we should do more than just listen. Have already placed a call into SOCOM."

Thank God someone got through.

"Fuckin' A. When am I going to get some backup?" Kyle asked.

"Believe it's in the works, son."

"Look, I'm in the fuckin' medical office of a cruise ship off the fuckin' coast of Africa. We're dead in the water. There's a bomb on board and they're taking hostages."

Both Armando and Mark's phones began to vibrate. Something was going on.

"Coop." they said in unison and showed their phones to each other.

"Look, I've got one of my guys down looking for the bomb right now. You better get some frogmen here, and we're in sore need of firepower. All we have is our sidearm."

"Roger that." Kyle gave him Commander Ramsey's personal numbers, the ones he had left messages for.

"Tell Commander Ramsey they're probably going to use deadly force with the hostages, and ARE threatening to blow up this boat, sir. We have thirty-four hundred souls on board, sir, nearly all of them civilians. Innocents."

The long pause was painful.

"I gotta take Coop's call," Armando said as he hoisted his cell to his ear. "Coop, I'm here," he whispered.

"What kinds of precautions does the cruise ship have? Is there an emergency plan?" the Commander asked Kyle.

Mark couldn't believe his ears.

"I'm not aware that the cruise ship has the ability to do anything but wait for some ransom demands," Kyle informed him. "The head security officer has been taken at gunpoint by masked men. I'd say he's in grave danger, sir."

"Son, you've definitely got our attention, but I'm going to be honest. It will take an hour or two to assemble a team unless we get some kind of miracle."

"That's exactly what we need, Commander. A fuckin' miracle."

"Roger that. Stand by." The phone went dead.

Kyle sat back. "Un-fuckin-believable."

Armando was getting information from Cooper. "Holy fuckin' Christ. Snakes?" Armando asked.

Kyle ripped the phone from Armando's hands.

"Report, Coop."

"We got a problem, Kyle," Coop said.

"Okay. Lay it out for me."

"We got a bomb. We got engines shut down, but appear to not be compromised, but we got a dead chief engineer and we got snakes loose."

"Excuse me?"

"When we got here they'd just finished shutting everything down, sending the crew upstairs somewhere, and murdering the engineer, who'd tried to be a hero. When they left, we found the bomb, uncrated. Seems as though someone had the bright idea to load the package with cobras and one of the commandos got bit in the leg and died within minutes. There are about twenty snakes, as best I can see, crawling all over the engine room floor. We're up on the catwalk."

"Holy fuckin' hell. So I guess you aren't going to have a good look at that bomb, then."

Cooper cleared his throat. "Does anybody know, do cobras climb trees? 'Cause I think I see one havin' that sort of an idea."

CHAPTER 28

Sophia had been forced to go upstairs with the other women of the crew and staff. She found Christy, Gina, Devon, Mia, Jasmine and a very ill looking Libby, who had brought a blanket with her and was lying on one of the bench seats in the Deck 9 dining area. Christy had gotten a glass of hot water and was trying to help Libby sip a bit of it.

She approached them. "Anything I can get for her?"

"She shouldn't be here. She should be in bed, in a warm cabin," Christy said.

"At least you got a spot inside. Some aren't so lucky," she pointed to the glass sliding doors which were sliding back and forth as people were lined up several deep, attempting to file into the dining area from the outside. A guard at the doorway blocked their entrance. He waved an automatic in their faces and several in the front screamed and fell, but were helped back up by the passengers behind them. A cold wind swiftly cut through the room every time the door swung open.

Sophia thought most of the commandos, and there appeared to be about ten of them on the deck, were Russian. She'd heard one speaking Arabic, but several spoke a Russian-like dialect she'd heard only a couple of times before.

She'd passed the Moroccan dancers, headed downstairs with a large contingent of elderly men. Their skinny bodies seemed out of place with the tall, muscular black-camo warriors surrounding them. They kept to themselves, whispering, with eyes darting back and forth. That's when she realized they'd been pawns in a very dangerous game, perhaps more deadly than they realized.

She wondered how the SEAL Team men were faring, since she'd not seen one of them. Sanouk had been allowed to accompany Libby, since she was too weak to walk on her own and needed someone to carry her.

Sanouk walked up to her and whispered in her ear. "She is very sick, mum. I am afraid for her."

"Me too, Sanouk. Let me see if I can get her something to chew on."

"No, mum. She can't keep anything down. Just seems to make her sicker. My mother would brew her some chrysanthemum tea, which would be good for her stomach."

"Well, I see they have warm water. Let me see if I can get some herbal—"

A heavy arm grabbed Sophia by the waist and pulled her back and away from the other women. She struggled a bit before she saw Maksym's face, which looked confused and hostile. He was unaccompanied.

"You will come with me and get one other who is strong." His grip on her arm hurt, reminding her of Roberto.

"Where are you taking us?"

"I'm allowed to keep a special eye out for troublemakers. I may have need of your services."

At first Sophia squinted at the insult she thought had been leveled at her. But a new plan began to form. Perhaps this officer, whom Mark had told her about, was beginning to sprout a conscience.

She whirled around and surveyed the group of SEAL women before her. "I need a volunteer." She didn't have time to evaluate the group properly. Mia stepped forward but was soon pushed aside by Gina. "I'm your gal." The two of them exchanged a look that informed Sophia that the other woman had some martial arts training and probably weaponry.

"I'm a cop," she whispered.

"Maksym, we are ready," Sophia said as she whirled around and found Maksym in an argument with a Russian nearly his size. The Russian had forced an armful of orange jumpsuits into Maksym's arms and left. She'd heard the guttural Russian and multiple times the word, Amerikanskiy, which indicated to her they were being singled out for some reason.

Maksym walked over to her with his arms full of jumpsuits.

"I'm afraid you must all put these on. It is ordered by the commander."

This would make it impossible not to identify them as some kind of high-value asset. Sophia wondered what plan they were being forced to play.

"No way I'm letting Libby put one of those jumpsuits on," Christy said sternly. She huffed as she jammed her legs into the oversized opening of a filthy one-piece jumpsuit. It was clearly made for a man twice her size, with legs nearly a foot too long, despite Christy's height. She rolled her cuffs up, as did several of the others.

Sophia put on hers, which smelled of oil and days old sweat. Surveying the room, she saw that several other women were being asked to put on the orange jumpsuits, and Sophia realized they must have also been Americans.

Maksym came up behind her and whispered, "Take it off, and get your friend to remove hers, too. Come with me."

Sophia and Gina did as instructed, waving fondly to the group before they followed the tall Ukrainian officer, who no longer wore anything that identified he was a member of the officer's crew. His jeans, black knit top and black leather jacket made him look like a wealthy tourist. Holding the folded jumpsuits they had previously worn, he led them towards the center of the ship to a men's restroom, closed the door behind them and locked it.

Sophia saw Gina go on instant alert. Sophia had known Maksym only for a year, but she didn't feel the same distrust she saw in Gina's eyes and stance.

"We have little time." He threw the jumpsuits into the trash bin under the sink. "Your friends have been chosen for execution. Public execution."

Gina's eyes widened.

"I cannot save all of you, but you two can pass for Italian, and you are Italian from now on, understood?"

They nodded back at him.

But Sophia could barely breathe. Her chest was heaving as she attempted to get air, yet she suffocated, her eyes stinging in pure pain. "You should not have let us go with you. We cannot abandon them."

"As I said, I cannot save all of you."

Sophia's eyes filled with tears. Gina was right there, putting her arm around her waist, and smoothing her hair behind her ear. "Come on, Sophia. You can do this. We'll figure out a way."

Maksym was staring at himself in the mirror. Closing his eyes, he allowed his forehead to drop to the glass surface, leaving a smudge from the sweat buildup there.

"For the record, I did not know all this would happen. This wasn't what I'd planned."

"This was your plan?" Sophia shot back at him. "You planned this?"

"No. This was never the plan." He turned and searched their faces.

Was he daring to ask for absolution?

Sophia hated him for his health, hated him for his greed, his good looks, the fact that he was alive and people her man loved were being targeted to extract a price for God knew what reason, hated his convoluted efforts to try to minimize his role in the terrible chain of events unfolding faster than any of them could have imagined. She hated her lack of power to do anything to stop it.

What would her father have done? Would he have stood for this? She knew the answer almost before than the question had come to her. She took a deep breath, willing the tears back behind her eyes, willing her nerves of steel, her birthright, the only thing left of him she still had.

"Maksym. What can we do to stop this?"

Now it was Maksym's turn to buck up. He seemed to take courage from her face. But then his eyes fell as he shrugged his shoulders and began to sob.

Sophia slapped him. "Maksym. Maksym, stop it! Stop it right *now*. What can we do?"

"Nothing. We're all going to die."

Sophia looked across the vanity to Gina's reflection. She saw the kind of resolve she needed in a sister, a team member. Something close to the connection Mark had with his band of brothers. It wasn't nearly as wide or as deep, but the look they shared was every bit as strong, forged by the understanding and agreement that the innocent should be protected and that in some way they'd fight this evil even if it was the last thing they'd do.

Looking directly into Gina's eyes, she snapped at Maksym, "Then, if we're all going to die, it's a matter of how well we die."

Unlike her slap, her words jolted Maksym out of his despair.

"You going to die a coward, an evil man...or a good man, Maksym?"

Gina's face was glowing in full approval. Maksym righted himself and brushed back the lock of hair that had fallen over his forehead, rubbing off the tear tracks staining his smooth cheeks with the back of his palms. He seemed to take strength from her.

"I am no coward. Not today, I am not."

"Good," Gina said briskly, "because the next order of business is to get our hands on some weapons. Maksym, how can you help us do that?" she continued.

He stared at the ceiling as he considered their options.

"We'll have to take them off someone. There are no caches of guns on the ship anywhere."

"Three against one. I like those odds, taken one at a time. I say we do it," Gina whispered, hardly able to contain the excitement she obviously felt. Sophia took strength from it.

"We'll lure them. You do the rest," Sophia commanded.

Opening the bathroom door a crack, she saw a lone commando with his back to her. Checking her line of sight in both directions, she whispered to the man in Russian. "Please, sir. My friend, my friend is bleeding." She pointed to the doorway to the men's room. As the soldier passed, she checked for observers, and, seeing none, gave him a kick in the butt, which sent him flying into the cramped space, the door closed, and she heard the sounds of a scuffle and a muted cry.

"Another," came the whisper from Maksym.

She motioned for a black clad soldier to come from nearly thirty feet away. She raised her finger to her lips and gave him a warm smile but continued telling him to keep it quiet. He tried to ignore her at first, but when she continued, he leaned into a colleague and both of them came forward.

Shit.

"Vy govorite po-russki?" *Do you speak Russian?*

"Da."

"Your colleague is screwing my little sister. She is only sixteen. Please help me." As they turned into the doorway, attempting to open it, she added the kill shot as she looked around her to verify they were not being watched. "I was just flirting, but he picked the wrong sister. Help me, please."

The door opened and she slammed her body into the two of them, causing them all to fall forward into the restroom. She barely was able to get the door closed before the scuffle began. Gina kicked the first one in the nuts as he attempted to right himself by holding on to the vanity surface. His compact semi-automatic fell to the floor as Maksym reached over and twisted the man's neck with a resounding crack.

Sophia had hitched herself up on the other man's hips from behind and was gouging at his eye sockets with her fingers. Gina delivered another blow to the man's groin, and then stepped aside to drag the body of the first soldier to the stall with the first one they'd gotten. Maksym removed a utility blade from the man's belt and gutted the last man from his navel to just under his breastbone with a force and speed Sophia had never seen before.

The man's pained grunting of stopped and he fell forward, dead.

Maksym was covered in blood, which glistened wet all over his black knit shirt. His jeans were also soaked, and as red as his hands.

Gina tossed a uniform from one of the men she'd disrobed and Maksym carefully put it on without getting any of the pooled blood on it. He wiped his shoes and rinsed his hands and face in the sink.

Sophia whispered to Gina, "Quick, I need something to sop up the blood. It's about to pooling leak out door." Gina threw her a shirt and the blood migration was halted temporarily.

Maksym actually looked like one of the Russians.

"Can I?" Gina asked as she slipped on one of the gunmen's shirts over her own. "Makes it more plausible I have a gun, perhaps?"

"Go with it," Maksym said. "You'll be the prisoner, Sophia, and Gina, you will be my accomplice."

Gina had been admiring her new weapon. The other one Maksym stashed uncomfortably in his belt at his back and covered it up with his shirt. "I can't give you one, Sophia, if you are going to be my prisoner."

"Understood," she said.

"I think we're as ready as we're going to be," he said. "We have a place we can meet your SEALs?"

"Not sure. Let's go to Deck 5 if we can."

"We travel the outside, avoid the interior stairways and the elevators," Maksym whispered. "We have to start by going up from the outside, then down a corridor to the outside stairs."

As they left the Deck 9 dining area, Sophia saw Libby and the other women being escorted to the back of the ship surrounded by a contingent of armed guards. Their hands were secured in zip ties. Other women and children were silent as they were led in the opposite direction. Some older women crossed themselves. Christy stood tall, the wife of the Team leader, and always would be, Sophia thought. Gina was behind her, and she heard her swear softly.

Sophia hoped to God they were able to connect with Mark and the others in time to save her life, as well as the lives of the other women. Sadly, Sanouk brought up the rear, carrying the blanketed body of Libby Cooper, who had been spared wearing an orange jumpsuit, but not a certain death, and who must have been terrified about losing her unborn child. It was just so fuckin' wrong.

Sophia said a little prayer as they turned to face whatever was lying beyond the glass doors.

CHAPTER 29

Wolf sat atop his Sikorsky S-434 helicopter and maneuvered down to the deck. Everything was going according to plan. He was pleased that he had not lost one of his men. Although he was going to have to make Maksym and the Moroccans suffer for their mistakes, he'd planned for those eventualities.

He was pleased the bomb had been discovered. Azziz's cobra had been brilliant. He liked the skinny Moroccan freedom fighter, even though the man could not manage one linear thought, thanks to his overwhelming religious fervor.

Makes you weak, his Russian handler had told him when he'd first been sent to the Middle East. He'd been told to never fear the Muslim threat because their fervor clouded their judgment. Made them completely predictable, in an otherwise unpredictable and dangerous world.

Like ten-year-olds with Uzis, Boris had said on more than one occasion.

Well, so far he'd outsmarted them all. The Russians, due to their harsh stance on dissidents and "subgroups," had given him a cadre of willing and well-trained mercenaries, distrusted in their own country due to their religious affiliation. He also had the Ukrainians, who were only too eager to do a private mission for wealth and the possibility of a new, anonymous life in the West. And you had the Moroccans, willing to die for their cause. It was all too perfect.

And if the mission didn't work out, he'd achieved what no other had done, brought a big American cruise ship to its knees, and probably sacrificed some

American women, which would certainly get everyone's attention. If he didn't get the payoff this time, next time he'd get double, so in a way it didn't matter. He could not lose.

And he'd planned it so he wouldn't have to share that fat bank account with anyone. The bomb would go off in less than two hours and, as long as he wasn't on the ship, the mission was a success. All he'd have to do in the future is threaten a takeover and they'd deposit any sum of money he asked.

When he got his funds he was going to buy himself a small country and the loyalty of its people. He had many prospects, but there would be time enough for that later, after the coffers were ripe and bursting with gold.

The $1 million helicopter set down exactly in the middle of the helipad's painted circle. Wolf stepped out onto Deck 10, which was lit by a string of lights that went from bow to stern.

His overcoat was buttoned to the neck. Even off the coast of Africa, the dark night air was chilly, even though the ship's engines had stopped was and the ship was merely drifting. Seeing stars this far out to sea was always a special treat for him, almost making him think of the supernatural powers some of his recruits thought he possessed. The knowing he had caused this giant ship to stop, had put so much fear into so many people, was extremely satisfying. He would have to confess he was actually giddy with pleasure.

One of his armed guards let him pass and opened the gate and stairway to the bridge.

Captain D'Ambrosini looked like a nervous wreck. He'd been held at gunpoint and was sitting in one of the two helmsman's chairs at the con. His eyes didn't focus on Wolf at first, but then, recognition flooded his face. D'Ambrosini shouted, "It is you!" and pointed, as if someone would step forward to arrest him.

"Now, Captain, please relax," he said in Italian. He knew a couple of the mercenaries understood everything he said, but he wasn't worried.

Though he was the captain, D'Ambrosini did not steer the ship. The helmsman usually stood at the wheel, leaving the captain free to supervise and move about the bridge, even attend dinners and parties. But today the helmsman sat idly by and watched the parade of individuals coming and going.

The Wolf gave his next instruction and waited for the import of his words to sink in. "You will now send the emergency distress signal."

The radio room, located behind the bridge, was given the go-ahead. The chief radio officer came onto the bridge himself with his headsets on. "Sir? Am I to send any word, a message in addition to the distress signal?"

"Let them contact you. I'm sure they will." Wolf told the radio operator.

Barely two minutes went by when the buzzing in the radio room began. The captain's cell phone chirped, as did the first officer's.

"Do not answer just yet," Wolf said. "Let them wait exactly five minutes." He checked his own sat phone.

One hour and forty-two to go.

"Where are your other officers, Captain?" he asked D'Ambrosini.

"I have no idea. Normally they would have checked in with me. I can only assume they've been detained," the captain said in Italian.

"Where is Maksym?"

The captain shot a knowing look at Wolf. It had been at Wolf's instructions the junior officer was hired.

"Not spoken to him since earlier this evening, since before we left port."

Wolf looked out at the distant lights of the African shore, barely visible. "Time enough for that. Time enough."

Wolf dialed a number and received an update. "And the women, they are dressed in orange?"

The captain and helmsman exchanged worried glances.

"The lights and video cameras are installed?"

Wolf noticed the captain was trying to send a text message from his cell phone.

"Give me that," he demanded. The captain handed over his cell phone sheepishly. The screen read T Dominichello.

"So you dare lie to me, and attempt communication with Teseo. Where is he?" Wolf demanded, raising his voice.

"Somewhere on board. I know not where. Truly."

"Then you will tell him to come to the bridge or your helmsman will lose his life." He handed the captain back his phone.

The young Italian helmsman moved off the stool and stood with his back to the map desk. All of twenty-six, he'd been employed by the cruise line for barely two years, Wolf recalled.

The captain dialed Teseo's number. Wolf grabbed the phone from his hands before he could warn Teseo.

"Yes Captain?" Teseo answered.

"Your presence is requested on the bridge, Teseo. If you are not here in five minutes, your helmsman will be shot through the head. Do I make myself perfectly clear?"

"Si, si. This is—Lombardi?"

"Never mind who this is. I am in command of this ship now, and you will come to the bridge at once or your man here will have his brains spread all over the equipment. Don't test me on this."

"Si. I will be there." Teseo hung up.

Wolf inhaled and savored the moment. "Now we call the company and let them know what troubles await them this morning."

Kyle took the call from Teseo, and then notified Nick and Grady that the time to take back the bridge was now, and promising that his troupe be up there as soon as possible. Moshe was being held downstairs in the jail, with just one guard. The three SEALs were hidden in a cabin that had been evacuated in a hurry earlier, and the door left open. It made good temporary cover for now.

Mark began to try to reason with Kyle. "You need to get back up there. Everything hinges on that bridge takeover, Kyle. Leave me here to take care of business," Mark said to his LPO. "Take Armani, here, and go."

Kyle hesitated for a second, and then agreed. "You get him out and get your butt upstairs."

"I plan on it."

Kyle and Armando quietly made their way down the deserted corridor to the crew stairwell and disappeared.

Mark could see the Israeli sitting on the padded bench, his cell phone chirping on the counter at the duty desk in front of him. The guard was making insulting comments to him.

"Your girlfriend says she needs to fuck, you little Israeli prick. She misses you, so she's gonna go find a Russian to get the job done."

He could see the panic on Moshe's face. He looked literally green.

Mark got ready to dart across the hall when he heard heavy footsteps. Two new guards spoke Russian to their colleague and dragged him to the hallway tearing off down the corridor after Kyle and Armando. As an afterthought, the first guard turned back and fired a warning shot, which ricocheted off the bars, earning him yells from his colleagues. He grabbed Moshe's phone and threw it against the wall, where it shattered. He pointed at Moshe. "Next time, your head." Then he turned around and stormed out.

Mark was stunned. As he waited for them to leave, he texted Kyle to give him the heads-up on the men coming their way.

He ran into the hold and Moshe bolted upright, a look of relief plastered across his face.

"Where are the keys?"

"No keys. Requires a pass card."

"Which I have right here," Mark said and pulled one out of his vest pocket.

"Right now, American or not, I could kiss you, Marky Mark," said Moshe.

"Kiss me after I get you out. What do I do with it?" He was looking at the door and couldn't find a place for it to be scanned.

"On the wall. There is a monitor on the wall. You swipe it like a credit card after you punch in the number two, and then the code, are you ready?"

"Yes."

"696969."

Mark looked at him. Grinning. "That's an interesting choice of numbers."

"Do it, damn you! I'll explain later," Moshe yelled.

After the cell was opened, they checked the corridor and took off to the stairs. Up two floors they heard the spray of automatic gunfire. Mark gave Moshe his extra sidearm, hung back, angling, and when he got a shot, caught one of the men in the back just at the base of his skull. He fell into the stairwell.

They were sprayed with rounds for their trouble.

"Can't stop, it's all going down now," Mark said.

All of a sudden another spray of automatic gunfire erupted and two more commandos fell down into the stairwell.

What Mark heard next was music to his ears.

"Mark!"

Sophia!

"On our way."

They took two and three stairs at a time, made the three-floor distance in under a minute. He grabbed Sophia, who was bloody but looking pretty damned good, holding her in his arms.

Maksym barked at them, "We need to get to the bridge. Gina is with Armando and headed up there now. Kyle has gone down to the engine room. No time for that." Maksym handed Moshe the extra automatic. Mark tried to give Sophia his Sig, but she scowled at him.

They exited Deck 6 and took the outside stairway to Deck 10 so they could see what was going on in the big arena one deck below. They opened the door and stopped in their tracks.

Christy, Mia and Jasmine sat in the center of the pool area, their restrained hands in front of them, wearing orange jumpsuits. The deck had been lit up for a celebration. The large screen monitor, which normally played Italian hip-hop and pop music showed the faces of the three women. A video camera was set on a tripod, manned by one of the Moroccans. Moshe swore under his breath in a language Mark didn't understand.

He wondered if Armando had seen this, and then noticed a flicker of movement to his right, spotting Armando and Gina as they peered around the corner. The bridge would have to wait. Armando must have figured the ladies didn't have much time and stopped to lend a hand. Teseo was probably being held inside, along with the captain, at gunpoint.

The rest of the SEAL ladies were in a second group of chairs tucked underneath the balcony, in the shadows. Among them was Libby, wrapped in a blanket, and Sanouk, holding her tight to his chest. Fredo and Jones were trussed up like turkeys, obviously being saved for the main course.

In an instant, Armando had his semi-automatic trained on a Moroccan gunman who raised a pistol to Christy's chest some thirty feet away.

Armando let the round fly, and the gunman's head exploded like a watermelon. Several soldiers guarding the rest of the prisoners made the mistake of leaving their cover, racing out into the open and attempting to return fire. They got sprayed with rounds from Maksym, Moshe and Mark's automatics. They then trained their guns on several others, popped off some rounds. Moshe hit the videographer, sending the camera and tripod flying to the side. Maksym and Moshe headed through the double wooden doors to check for more combatants inside.

For a few seconds, everyone waited. Christy and Mia were kicking a combatant who was on the floor, and his weapon skidded along the surface of the pool deck until it landed at Devon's feet. With both hands still secured, she picked it up and took a firing stance, looking like Nick or someone had been very smart and trained his woman.

Silence.

"I count ten down," Mark said. "I have no idea if that's enough." He turned to Sophia, "You stay here and watch with Armando," he said to her. "Stay in the shadows. I'm going up to the bridge to give Teseo and the captain a hand, if it's not too late."

Sophia nodded. Mark leaned over and gave her a long kiss. "You did really great, Sophia. You're holding up like a champ. Like you were made for this."

"Hardly. I'm a dancer, remember?"

"Oh, I remember, all right." He winked at her, and then checked the single ramp of stairs leading to the bridge. He thought it was odd no one had showed up from the bridge itself.

Armando cut Fredo and Jones loose, which gave him two more sets of hands to free everyone else.

Mark layered one more kiss and pulled away from her.

Just then, the door to the bridge opened and a tall man in an overcoat walked outside with the captain, his arm around the captain's throat, and a pistol to his temple.

Mark cursed that they didn't have an accurate, high-powered rifle. The shot was definitely doable. Shots were being fired from multiple smaller boats that formed a dangerous flotilla around them. He could tell that if they didn't get the situation under control fast they'd be boarded and everyone murdered, not to mention what would happen if the bomb went off.

Lights and rounds were going in all directions until he heard the welcome crack of a SEAL sniper's long gun. The man who had terrorized the captain dropped, having taken a round at the top of his head that exited at his feet. The captain fell to his knees first, and then scurried to safety as the terrorist leader slumped in a pile of flesh and blood. Teseo appeared at the doorway next and gave him the all-clear sign, the thumb's up and a big cheesy grin.

Mark looked up toward the night sky and saw one of their own. A Navy Seahawk that had come out of Heaven itself. He'd never seen anything so wonderful in his whole life. Then he realized that was what the boats had been firing at.

That meant there was a vessel out there in the dark that they could call friend.

He looked out over the now-calm deck and then got a text.

The bomb.

Of course, there was still a fuckin bomb to defuse.

Kyle's next text nearly broke his heart.

Stay with the women, offload them if you can. In case I don't make it, tell Christy I love her.

CHAPTER 30

Bedlam had taken over the ship. The remaining commandos were cornered and beaten to within an inch of their lives. Grandmothers teamed up and tossed unconscious terrorists over the railings. The terrorists were overpowered without a prayer of a way to get loose. One by one they were brought down by ordinary citizens who fought back to reclaim their ship.

Injured people lay all over the halls. People began to gather in the ballroom, broke into the bar, and started passing out bottles and glasses. Everyone stayed away from the windows, keenly aware there were enemy boats floating all around them. Some of the boats had retreated to the distance, chased by fishing boats from Cape Verde.

Mark hadn't seen so much blood in his life, or more people banged since the terrorist attack on the World Trade Center. The passengers were emboldened, stubborn, and having the time of their lives. Home videos were made using cell phones, as other passengers held up weapons and posed with unconscious or severely wounded terrorists.

Sophia ran to him, and he set down his automatic, pulling her tight against him and clutching her hair, while she hugged him so tight he thought maybe she'd squeeze the life out of him. Just then someone turned on the disco, of all things.

"Christ," he whispered. "They're looking for their fuckin' dance instructor."

"My dance card's full, I'm afraid."

"Roger that. Boy, is it full."

His cell chirped. Kyle.

No more snakes on a ship. We do have a fuckin' bomb to unload. Deck 5, boat 26.

"Holy shit, Sophia, they haven't been able to defuse the bomb. We're going to have to offload it. You stay with everyone else, okay?"

"What if—"

"Gotta go, baby. Either way we'll see each other very soon, sweetheart. Won't be long now."

Holding back tears, he jammed his sidearm into his pants, grabbed the automatic from the floor, and ran like hell. He didn't dare look back at her.

He flew down the stairs, one whole landing at a time, until he got to Deck 5. Kyle, Cooper, Tyler and Rory were gingerly carrying the white crate from the lower decks escalator. They crabwise moved down the deck to the front of Lifeboat 26.

Kyle barked orders. "Cooper, figure out how to lower this thing. Mark and Ty, free the overhead arm."

Mark looked up at the large rocker arm type contraption that held the little red vessel in place. Large bolts had been drilled into metal straps, which secured the arm in place for rough seas. Inside a utility box they found wrenches, and both he and Tyler began to crank the big lug nuts as, one by one, they removed ten of them and felt the arm holding the rescue vehicle free up.

Kyle kicked in the plastic door to the ship he and Tyler's went back to help them carefully set the bomb across two of the seats. Mark heard the whirr of something mechanical inside. The outside of the box was stained with pinkish spots. After they lowered the device a piece of a black snake carcass fell to the plastic floor of the boat and Mark jumped back instinctively.

The boat jiggled as Cooper began working the controls attached to a heavy metal beam between decks.

"We gotta clear the area where she's going to hit the water. Can someone spray some cover?" Kyle asked.

Immediately Tyler and Rory started firing over the railing at ships still hovering nearby, and they quickly dispersed.

Cooper jumped inside the cabin and turned on the power to the little craft. Headlights came on, and low-watt overhead lights flashed on.

"Thing's got a starter button. You only got one chance to make it work. It has to be in water or you'll scrape the hull and dump upside down. So who wants to be captain today? I'm, gonna need a volunteer."

Mark knew it was his turn to step up. "I'm going, Kyle. You stay here."

"No, I need two men. You wanna come? I'm up for it."

Tyler stepped up. "Sir, you let me help Mark. You got a family and I'm single. My turn, sir."

"No heroics. Get the boat in the water, get her untethered and get her the hell away from here."

"Roger that."

Mark ran over and got out the double sets of scuba gear Teseo had left behind, shed his pants and put on the skins and tanks. Tyler joined him, and soon both frogmen were encased in the rubberized gear.

Mark stood at the controls, hands on the small metal steering wheel, just tall enough to see out of the small Plexiglas window in front.

"Let 'er rip," he said. Everyone evacuated, Tyler stood right beside him.

Kyle was the last one to exit the boat. "Thanks, man. You get out there but not too far. We don't know how much time's left, since Teseo never was able to get the guy to tell him, but it's soon, so don't fuck with it, get it out there and then take your dive, okay?"

"Roger that," Mark answered. "Now you go tell Christy yourself you love her, 'kay?"

"And I'll be there, right next to your girl, partner."

Kyle turned to go. Mark said to his back, "Not too close. Just watch your fuckin' hands, you prick."

The hatch door was secured and Mark felt the boat swing out over the dark ocean. A faint pink glow on the horizon didn't help much, but it gave him a sense of how high he was. Too high.

The winches groaned and the boat took forever to lower to the water. As soon as they heard the slosh of the ocean on their underside, both men climbed out the hatch and unhooked the cables, sending them back to the hull, where they clanged. Mark assumed the controls inside, pressed the red starter button and the diesel engine sprang to life. They lurched over the choppy water, and then landed in a great big belly flop and splash that blew water into the cabin and all over them.

The sucker had no maneuverability, and he felt like he was driving a pedal car down a forty-five degree angle dodging parked cars, but soon he got the hang of it and let it out full, bucking and fighting the five-foot waves crashing around them. Some of those waves almost made them feel like they had sent them back to the mother ship, but soon Mark could see the lights of the cabins grow smaller and smaller, until they were the size of a postage stamp.

"Depending on what's in here—"

"You gotta go farther," Tyler said. "Coop says we gotta get at least two miles out."

"See if you can find something to rig up that'll keep it going. I say we jump ASAP. In five minutes, that should take it out about almost seven miles."

They strapped the wheel in place for a trajectory that would take the craft further off the African coast. Then they strapped the gas pedal to an oar they lashed to the seats behind. They had run out of rope and webbed tie-downs to secure it fully flat out, but Tyler found a roll of duct tape.

"Duct tape is the bomb," Tyler grinned.

Winding the tape around the pedal and then looping it back against the lashing, they secured the pedal in full-out position.

Each man quickly slipped on his tanks, sat on the outside of the boat in the night, with the lighted ship in the distance. They activated their emergency beacon devices, slipped on their fins, covered their faces and fell backward into the water as the little boat powered out to the open sea.

The water was freezing, and Mark knew they only had a few minutes before they became a recovery mission instead of a rescue. But he turned to watch the little boat speed off toward the east, appreciating the fact that they had successfully kept the passengers safe.

"I expected to be dead right about now," Tyler shouted over the water.

"Stick with me, kid. I just knew they'd make it," Mark announced.

"Now if I can just get on board for that midnight buffet, I'd say it would be a perfect day in paradise, wouldn't you?"

"That would be nice, but if I make it back, food is gonna be the last thing on my list."

Suddenly they heard the distinct sounds of a helicopter overhead.

"Isn't that just about the greatest sound in the world?" Tyler yelled.

"Makes me come every time I hear one, especially if I'm in the middle of the ocean off the fuckin' coast of Africa," Mark yelled back.

They both saw the bucket illuminated in early predawn light, and a friendly on board.

"You're secret's safe with me, Marky Mark. But you know they have pills for that sort of thing."

"What sort of thing?" Mark said as a strong arm grabbed him around his upper torso, strapping a hoist on him with a satisfying click.

"Premature ejaculation."

"Fuck you." Mark tried to kick Tyler in the head before he was lifted to the chopper. "You fuckin' tell anybody that and I'll toss you off the ship myself."

Mark watched as Tyler laughed uncontrollably while being helped into a crab net underneath and also pulled to safety.

Some of the gaiety of life began to seep in and thaw Mark's psyche then. Maybe, just maybe everything would turn out the way it was supposed to in those books.

In which case, he'd like to make that happen with the rest of his life, with Sophia at his side.

CHAPTER 31

Tyler was still yelling insults as they swung through the night sky. Mark was hauled inside the Seahawk and strapped into a jump seat. Tyler was strapped in next to him. A medic asked them a series of questions they both could answer "no" to.

They were rewarded with whoops and hollers from the crew, high fives and thumbs up all around. Mark actually began to feel the beginnings of a smile forming, something he hadn't been sure he'd ever feel again during the past twelve hours.

Both SEALs then became distracted by the little headlights below, illuminating choppy seas and heading in a straight line west. A couple of the flotilla of boats were chasing the emergency craft, closing in on it with superior outboard power.

No accounting for stupid.

The glow in the horizon grew rosier, but remained a thin line, a mere suggestion of what the morning would soon look like. The night sky was still pitch black, populated with a generous dusting of stars.

Mark felt his breathing slow down as he returned to a calm state, watching the intensifying rose sky, the black and frothy turquoise blue of the illuminated ocean. Sounds of the chopper were drowned out when a pair of noise-cancelling headphones were placed on his ears. He could hear Tyler breathing next to him as the Team guy craned his neck to watch the scene below.

One of the flotilla that had caught up to the fleeing lifeboat threw grappling hooks that didn't take hold.

"Something inherently wrong with that picture," Mark said into the microphone, referring to the efforts to board the emergency boat.

In the middle of the second attempt a large yellow-orange fireball consumed the emergency vehicle, rising in a fiery plume, enveloping the fishing boat and the one close behind it. Without the aid of the boat's headlights, the dark sky quickly consumed the blaze. Within seconds, the explosion was reduced to fuel burning on the ocean's surface.

The helicopter angled perpendicular to the site so Tyler and Mark could clearly see the destruction below, with the help of the chopper's powerful searchlight. Bits of wood and plastic and metal were still raining on the fiery cauldron. The ocean underneath was seething in anger.

"Like I was saying," Mark repeated.

"That's a picture I'd like to have," Tyler said.

Two other boats in pursuit but a good distance away abruptly turned tail and sped off in the opposite direction.

"Impressive. Like it when that happens," Tyler added.

"Too bad Rory isn't here to see it." Mark was referring to fellow Teammate Rory Kennedy, who had quite the reputation as a troubled teen for burning down his foster parents' garages, and who had grown up to become the Team's explosives expert.

The chopper banked heavily and headed toward the cruise ship.

A small welcoming crowd had gathered on Deck 10. Cameras flashed all over the ship as the luxury liner took on the look of a spring break orgy for the over-fifty crowd. The small chopper the Wolf had arrived in guaranteed the Seahawk wouldn't be able to squeeze in for a landing. Mark and Tyler were given helmets and airlifted in a crab basket to the deck below amidst cheers and well-wishers who clearly wanted to give a hero's welcome to the pair.

They removed the harnesses, helmets and other gear they'd borrowed, stowed it back in the basket and gave a thumbs up to the helicopter crew just before the Seahawk flew off into the night leaving the sounds of a satisfying thump thump of rotors in their wake.

Under the sparkling string of white party lights, the crowd attempted to hoist Mark and Tyler on their shoulders, but Mark insisted they keep their hands to themselves. He was wet and cold, and desperately wanted to shed his wetsuit and damp emergency blanket for a warm shower and some recreational time with Sophia. Everything else was a distance second in terms of need.

He was surprised to feel the vibration of his phone from inside his suit. Tyler's phone was jumping to life as well.

"I guess these cases really do work," he said to Tyler as he activated the phone by opening the case and touching a passcode to the screen. They'd been sold what were supposed to be one hundred percent waterproof cases on base in Coronado, but hadn't believed the hype.

"Hey there, Lanny," Mark said to his Team leader.

"So you guys good? Any injuries?"

"Other than an adrenaline rush that is *awesome*, I'm more than good."

"We got things mopped up. Captain's inspecting the engine room for any signs of sabotage, so we're lookin' to get the engines fired up. You ready for some beers?"

"Sorry, Kyle. My needs are of a different sort."

"Roger that. Well I guess Sanouk and Jones better find another place to go for the next twenty-four. She's back with the women in our cabins. Libby's frail, but Coop's with her, and I think she's going to be okay."

"Nice."

"Well, I got some more stuff to do here, but I'll see you some time tomorrow, unless something else comes up."

"All the bad guys gone?"

"Not gone, but either captured or killed. Seems the passengers here have exacted a penance they'll not soon forget, those that survived."

"The Moroccans?"

"Only one we can't account for is Azziz, but a couple of Germans told me they'd tossed him overboard, so I'm not worried. Armando, Gina and Jones are trying to confiscate the guns so we don't have any more innocent victims."

"Anyone seriously hurt or killed?" Mark asked.

"You know what? Amazingly, no. Can you fuckin' believe that? And we even got one bad guy dead from snake bite."

"News headlines for tomorrow."

"So we'll see you when you crawl out tomorrow late, hear?"

"Roger that. And sir, thank you. Thank you for everything."

"Yeah, it was one helluva caper, wasn't it? Best fuckin' vacation of my entire life," Kyle said and hung up.

Tyler had been allowing his body to be touched, hugged and kissed by all the lovelies who could squeeze their way through the crowd to reach him. He'd talked with Rory, and a couple of the wives who wanted to thank him. He'd told them they were headed back to the cabins.

Mark broke out in a loping run. Barefoot and cold, he scarcely noticed his condition, but as he got closer to the carpeted and much warmer indoor grand staircase, and then down the hallway towards the group gathered outside their bank of cabin doors he turned white-hot and urgent to get to a private rendezvous with Sophia. He hoped to God she was there with the rest of them.

Before he could make his way to the end of the hall, the door to Helena's cabin opened and Maksym blocked his way.

At first Mark had an "oh shit" moment, but then saw the shame and remorse on the man's face and noticed he had a hand extended for a shake.

"Not now, Maksym. I'm not up for a little chat." He slipped by the officer, who could have easily detained him, but who called after him instead.

"She saved my life. Your Sophia saved my life."

That stopped Mark. He turned and faced the officer, who had removed the cami top he'd borrowed from one of the commandoes and replaced it with a wool sweater over the pants he'd kept.

Mark took three long strides to cut the distance between them.

"Not sure those ladies would be alive today if it weren't for your Sophia," Maksym whispered, tearing up. "I'm so deeply sorry for what I have done, and I intend to pay for it."

Mark couldn't find it in him to forgive the man, but he knew Maksym had protected her, and that deserved something.

"Thanks, man," he said as he slapped Maksym's arm. "Later?"

"Absolutely. She's waiting for you. You deserve each other."

Maksym abruptly retreated to his cabin and closed the door.

"Mark!" He heard Sophia's voice over the buzzing at the end of the hall. She came running full tilt and slammed into him, wrapping her arms around him, hiking her legs up and around his waist. He held her while she sobbed in his arms.

"Baby, baby, it's all good. We're okay now, right?"

She was babbling things he couldn't understand in Italian, rambling on and on, and he could hear several words he did understand, like *amore* several times, her little body shaking with every syllable, with every inhale and exhale. He tried to unpeel her arms to give her a proper kiss, but eventually gave up.

"Baby, I'm not going anywhere. I'm right here," he said into the side of her face. "No one's going anywhere without you, sweetheart. Trust me."

"Oh God, I thought I'd lost you," she said between sobs.

"It's all good. Not to worry, baby. I've got you." He let her decide when she'd had enough of squeezing the life out of him. It was almost hard to breathe she hung on so tight.

Finally, exhaustion began to kick in and he leaned her back against the wall, his muscles unable to hold her up any longer. She dropped her legs but kept her arms about his neck, tipped her tear-stained face back and searched his eyes.

God, she was beautiful. All the warmth of her dark hair and chocolate brown eyes soothed his soul. At last they kissed, but she burst into tears again as soon as their lips touched.

He put his palms under her chin and pressed his forehead to hers. "Sweetheart, we're good. We're all good, safe. But please, honey, I need a shower and a bed, in that order. And I want you naked and strong beside me for the next twenty-four hours. Can you do that, baby?"

She smiled up at him. "I knew that day would bring me to this. I knew it the first time you kissed me."

"I did too." He slid one hand under her ear, back into the hair at the nape of her neck and squeezed, pulling her face urgently to his. His tongue penetrated her deep as he drank in the sweaty scent of her worry, her love, and her desire for him. The taste of her mouth ignited his insides, his chest needing to feel her naked breasts against him, his thighs rubbing against hers as he nailed her to the wall with his package between them, at the full and ready, stuck in the on position. "I'd like you to talk some dirty Italian to me now. Can we do that, please?"

Her eyes danced as she threw her head back against the wall and laughed. He kissed her under her chin, under her ear, that little place she loved in the hollow he found there. He kissed over her cheek, pressing his lips to both her watering eyes, feeling her come alive sexually against him. Her little moan and inhale when he found her gaping mouth again.

"Marko, vamos a ser amantes para siempre. Quiero follarte cinco veces por la noche para el resto de mi vida," she whispered.

Mark understood part of it. "Only cinco veces?" He smiled and she returned the smile. "If I learn too much Italian, we'll have to find another language," he whispered in return.

"Oh, but Italian is still the language of love, Marko. And I'll never tire of speaking it to you, whispering it to you. There are many, many words you have not yet heard, mi amore."

She unwrapped her arms from his neck and took his hand, leading him through the swell of well-wishers. Fredo and Mia were standing arms, around each other, as they spoke to the crowd. Mia was drying tears from her eyes and Fredo kissed the top of her head several times. Christy came out of Libby and Cooper's room and gave Mark a big hug.

"Thank you, Mark. Thanks to you for keeping him safe."

Mark shook his head. "I'll tell you one thing, next time Kyle suggests we all go on vacation together, I'm staying home. His idea of fun, while awesome, is going to make me an old man."

"That's my Kyle," she said in return. "Go. I'll try to get everyone to give you some peace and quiet.

"Wasn't looking for anything quiet," he looked at Sophia who beamed up at him, "but I could sure use a shower."

Inside their cabin he peeled her clothes off slowly, too slowly. His body was screaming at him, asking for the nourishment only her sex could give him. He kissed her belly button just before he slid her pants down to her ankles. Picking her up, he pressed her back onto the bed and removed her shoes and then slid her pants and panties off her dainty toes. Sophia had already removed her top and bra.

The wet suit was beginning to chafe and his cock was painfully demanding release from the form-fitting suit. He unzipped the front, peeling it off his arms and down over his hips as she lay back, her breasts covered with her arms folded across her chest, and watched him.

"Marko. Su hermoso cuerpo hace cosas hormigueo a la mía."

"You too, baby," he whispered back as he threw the wetsuit into the corner, shucked his briefs and dove onto the bed, covering her.

He wanted to take his time, but he knew he just wouldn't be able to this time. His fingers found her wet channel, already ripe and ready for him.

"Maybe I should learn Hungarian or Russian or some other language, so you can learn what it feels like to guess what I'm saying to you," he said to her ear. His fingers sifted through her hair as he pulled her to him. He nibbled over her lips, "but I understand this language best of all."

The kiss went deep and urgent, both of them sucking, needing more and giving all they could. He wanted to kiss down her front and make her come in his mouth, but he just couldn't wait that long. After a few long strokes with his forefinger to the tender, hot folds between her thighs, he smoothed his palm behind her butt cheek placing her knee over his shoulder and pressed his cock at her opening. She was vibrating, almost coming undone already, which was good, because he sure was. He wasn't even sure he'd make it to deep inside her, but he did, and his urgent thrusts coated him in her juices. His arm moved underneath her, as he pulled her shoulder, moving her torso down against him, onto his shaft. His hips angled slightly as he slapped against the backs of her thighs.

Her breasts were bouncing as he rode her, his strokes moving faster and faster. He bent and sucked her nipples, one at a time. Her body rocked to his thrusting, as she rolled forward and onto her side and he fucked her at an angle, adjusting to take her deeper. The more he thrust, the harder her muscles squeezed him.

"Fly with me, Sophia. Make me fly, baby."

"My Marko," she said between sighs. He could tell she was losing herself, winding out of control. "I—"

He put his hand over her mouth. His seed began to spill as he held her, slipping one knee under her butt. He held her strong back as she arched toward the sea, her perfect breasts and the deep red nipples presenting themselves to the ceiling, and then to his hungry mouth. Her fingers got lost in the tangle of her long hair as he kissed her from nipple to under her breasts, in the folds there that smelled of her arousal, and then back up under her chin, her temple. His thumbs moved over her cheek, one grazing her lower lip before he claimed them again.

She gasped, beginning to undulate and squeeze him inside her, moving her body gently back and forth to his thrusts, and then slightly to the side, and then all of a sudden she was molten. She threw her head back as he lifted her other knee over his shoulder, and held himself impossibly deep as he lurched inside her hot, vibrating sex and filled her. Her moans he claimed with his lips. She bit the top of his shoulder as she held him, squeezed him against her breasts while he rooted up inside her.

In the soft unfolding of their bodies, as he kissed away the sweat and heaviness of her breathing, as he felt her muscles quiet, the peace was delicious. Her eyes were on fire, filled with tears.

He began to say the words he'd practiced, the two little words he'd practiced all the way back in the chopper, thought about while he was swimming to what he hoped was a chance at a new day, what he heard as he saw the fireball below him and knew they'd all be safe.

"Marry me, Sophia. Make me the happiest man alive."

Her delicate fingers touched his cheek, tracing over his lower lip.

"Si, Marko. With my whole heart. I am already yours, completely."

The End

OTHER BOOKS IN THE
SEAL BROTHERHOOD SERIES:

PREQUEL TO BOOK 1

Available on Audible

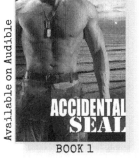

BOOK 1

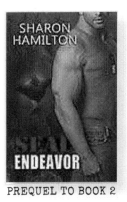

PREQUEL TO BOOK 2

Available on Audible

BOOK 2

Available on Audible

BOOK 3

Available on Audible

BOOK 4

BOOK 5
AUDIBLE VERSION
COMING SOON!

OTHER BOOKS BY SHARON HAMILTON:

The Guardians Series

(Guardian Angels, Dark Angels)

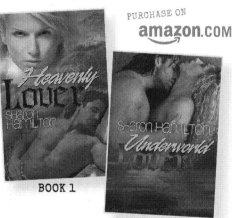

BOOK 1

BOOK 2

The Golden Vampires of Tuscany Series:

Available on Audible

BOOK 2

BOOK 1

Made in the USA
Charleston, SC
21 May 2015